LOST ONE STANDING

A CADE DIXON THRILLER

HECTOR HILL

The most sublime act is to set another before you.
— William Blake

You first.
— Cade Dixon

CHAPTER ONE

Rarely when a seventeen-year-old kid seriously considers leaping out a top-floor window is it for the right reason, but you might agree with me on this one. See, unlike the image you probably have of said seventeen-year-old swan-diving to his death on the pavement below, I wasn't jumping to take my life. I was jumping to save it. And if I was trying to save it, that means there musta been someone trying to take it. Fifteen someones, as a matter of fact. Three of whom were seconds away from succeeding if I didn't do something very stupid, very soon.

As I sprinted toward the stained-glass window, my brain was stuck on one question: had the gunmen chased me up three flights, or was it four? On any normal day, I'd say, "Eh, what difference does a floor make?" But on most days I hadn't just been chased across the campus square, through the mailroom, out the back, and up into the St. Frederick Academy history department building. And certainly most days I wasn't being shot at. On a day like today where I could hear the footsteps clamoring up the stairwell after me, yeah, that potential extra floor was an issue. In fact, it was the difference between smashing through a floor-to-ceiling glass window and hitting the concrete below at a velocity of 38.5 feet per second or 47.2 feet per second. I could thank *Fournier's Mathematical Principles*, required reading for Physics 3—a class I wasn't really taking—for that suddenly pertinent nugget of info.

If you were interested, I could have also told you that by jumping from that additional ten feet, the calcaneus bone would be the first to shatter on impact, likely followed by the talus and navicular an instant before my fibula splintered as it pressed up on the patella, all this thanks to Anatomy and Physiology, another class I wasn't taking. But that's another story. Well, no, actually, it is this story; it's just that the fact a seventeen-year-old kid stuck on the scholarship/probation carousel has been surreptitiously attending extra classes in order to then sell papers to trust fund kids is not relevant the way, say, deciding whether to propel oneself out a third (or possibly fourth) story window is.

The good news is, regardless of the 8.7-feet-per-second difference in velocity and the extra bones I was about to break, I had little choice. Because in seconds, all three of them would burst into this empty classroom and start, nay, continue shooting.

I used to roll my eyes whenever I'd hear people who, after all sorts of crappy things had happened to them, still said, "I wouldn't have changed a thing" or, "It made me into who I am today." As I sprinted around the desks and toward the window, I doubled-down on my metaphorical eye roll: people who say those things are either liars or are fooling themselves. After everything that had happened today, I would have changed a lot of things. Among them: I'd have told my mother to call in sick so I didn't have to see her with a gun to her head. I'd have preferred not to have had to choke out a stranger. And I would have done something, anything, to keep Kira out of it all.

On a dead run, I closed my eyes and hurled myself through the sheet of glass. The instant the glass shattered, four distinct thoughts scrolled across my mind:

— Here I was jumping out a window in order to save my life

2

when not two years ago I'd have probably welcomed a similar opportunity to end it.

— A quote from Samuel Johnson, courtesy of 18th Century Poets (this time, a class I was actually enrolled in): "When a man knows he is to be hanged in a fortnight, it concentrates his mind wonderfully."

— Actually, the quote was the third thing, if we want to get picky. It popped into my mind in response to this prior realization: a very sudden, yet absolute certainty that it was in fact the fourth-floor window I had just leapt from.

— And the last wasn't so much a thought as it was a word: *Shit*.

Earlier in the Day

Like every other time someone found themselves leaping through a fourth-story window, there is a backstory. A whole "where, what, when, and who" that needs touching upon.

I guess the "who" was the bored-looking seventeen-year-old kid in the passenger seat of the 2002 Toyota Camry. They say the Camry is the least distinguishable car on the road today. I'd believe that. Unless of course your Camry was in a private school parking lot with a 2018 Lexus LC in front of it and an accessorized Range Rover Sport HSE in the rearview. Never mind the three Beemers, two Mercedes, and a coterie of black SUVs that made up the rest of the cars in the row. Which brings us to the where: St. Frederick Academy, a prep school deep in the heart of New England. Heavy on the gray stone buildings, pre–Civil War statues, and immaculately manicured lawns. Take away the line of over-priced luxury cars and the teenagers face-diving into their various phones and tablets, and you'd be hard-pressed to know if you were in 1819, 1919, or 2019.

But 2019 it was. St. Frederick Academy's parking lot was where we were. The observant would notice how dusty some of the luxury cars were. You'd never guess the reason, though. These cars had sat there since the first day of the semester, un-driven because these particular kids didn't have their licenses yet, but they had parents who didn't want their precious little ones to feel left out.

Did that sound like jealousy? It wasn't meant to be. I couldn't be happier to not be one of the rich kids. This may sound like rationalization, but having been around these guys for the last three years, one of the craziest things I've discovered is that there is a near reverse correlation between happiness and wealth. Don't get me wrong, poor sucks. My mother was miserable for years (although there was a particular man who was at the root of most of that), but once she started working here for Headmaster Harkin, there was some happiness. She didn't make much, but it was enough. And what I've seen is that the further you get in either direction away from *enough*, that's where you find problems. You see it with drugs: the poorest guys I knew from my old school and the richest ones I knew here did the most. The rich ones just had easier access to the good kinds. Bored, lazy kids who have been shipped off to prep school since they were eight have another thing in common: an inclination to do the least amount of work necessary. On the plus side, they also have plenty of disposable cash. Which was where I came in. The scholarship that got me in here was great, sure, and the work study job in the mailroom put a few bucks in my pocket, but it was the bottomless supply of rich slackers that paid the alimony.

I should probably clarify: not *my* alimony. My dad's.

"Who needs Am Lit? I've got a Thoreau and a Willa Cather. B-plus, A-minus range."

"How much?"

I looked up from Weav's laptop. It was Harper. Decent guy.

Way too smart to need me to write papers for him. But as I had quickly realized, when it came to smart, rich, and motivated, generally most everyone here had two but rarely all three. Which made someone like Harper perfect for me: Lazy enough to be a customer. Rich enough to be a repeat customer. And smart enough that I could actually write something interesting for him to turn in without raising suspicions in his teachers.

"Forty. Seventy if you want some bullet points." That was something I had come up with this semester: talking points for seminar discussion. A nice entrepreneurial touch if I do say so myself.

Because I lived off campus, I needed a place to do business, and Weav was happy to let me use his dorm room. There was me, Weav, Harper, Reece, and three other of my regular customers. Weav was one of those sons of a son of a St. Frederick alum. But one of the good ones. I knew him even before I got the scholarship here. Back when I used to sit in the library waiting for my mother to get off work, he was the only guy who ever came up and said hi.

"Give me Willa Cather," Harper said. "But just the paper. McMaster knows something's fishy whenever I raise my hand to say something."

I took Harper's flash drive and uploaded a paper on the belief of justified fate vs. self-determination in *My Antonia*. As I did so, the door opened and Sean walked in with Preston, the new guy.

"Yo, lock the door this time," Weav said as he pulled out his wallet. "I'll take Thoreau."

Even though Weav loaned me his laptop to write papers and let me make my sales in his room, he always paid me for his assignments. Whenever I insisted he take them for free, he said, "Third generation, bro." Which was his shorthand for what he said the first time I had tried to comp him: "You know that saying 'the first generation makes the cash, the second one grows it, and the third generation blows it,' well my goal is to blow it.

They all did shitty things with the money or in making it. I figure me just wasting it is an improvement over any of them."

As I took the other orders, Weav pulled out his baggy and papers from their hiding spot in the closet. Weav was old school. No cotton-candy-flavored vaping for him; he smoked his weed the old-fashioned way. As he prepped it, he began explaining his third-generation theory to Preston, apropos of nothing. The guy had only transferred in a few weeks ago but had already become a regular customer, although, I don't think Preston even turned mine in. He was smart enough and motivated enough to do his own and probably only bought them to fit in with a guy like Sean. Most of these guys fell over themselves trying to fit in with Sean. Maybe it was because of his dad. Maybe it was his faux alpha-dog act. Preston was a guy who had apparently moved from school to school and learned the importance of ID-ing the alpha dog and aligning with him. Only three weeks here, and he'd been Sean's pet ever since.

". . . See, if I were to do a flat zero with my life," Weav continued as he lit the joint, "I'd still be ahead of my dad or granddad."

"How's that?" asked Preston.

Weav inhaled, held for a few seconds, and then blew it into the wet towel he kept to muffle the smoke smell. "Doing nothing with my life is a plus on the ledger compared to building stuff for the military so they can bomb the crap better out of someone. No matter how much coin they've made, me smoking weed and living off a trust fund will be a drastic improvement." Weav offered the roller to the rest of us. No takers. Which isn't as surprising as you might think. No one here was against drugs per se; it was just that out of these seven guys, I'd bet five were already on Adderall, Xanax, or some other drug of parental choice.

I handed Preston his flash drive. "That's fifty."

"Can I Venmo? I don't have cash."

"You can forget Venmo," Sean said laughing. "Cade doesn't

even have a phone." He said this last bit with a verbal ellipsis after "phone," which I knew was his chump brain churning away as it searched that empty cavern for some smartass remark. "Gotta pay cash or food stamps."

There it was. One more townie crack. Always his go-to with me. *Food stamps. Welfare. Section Eight. Haha.* Did I want to crack back at him? Sure. But it was a losing cause, as I learned two semesters ago that time with him and Kira. Besides, the only one I'd be hurting was my mother. Screw up this paper-writing gig, and there goes the alimony payment. I had spent enough time mooching off her all these years, so it had been nice to finally be able to put some back in. Not that she knew. She would never take it if she thought it was coming from me. Making the deposits look like my father was actually paying his child support was a win-win for all of us.

Ignoring Sean's existence was always the safest thing to do. And I had. Mostly. A couple weeks ago, though, I had been sorting the mail and listening to Reece, Sean, and a couple others through the mailbox slots. I had stayed silent through most of their humble-bragging, but when Reece said, "It was their own fault. They'd have gone bankrupt anyway," I blurted it out before I could censor myself: "Yeah, their fault for trusting your dad."

Reece had peered through the glass windows of the mailboxes and snapped, "I wasn't talking to you."

I could of course have left it there, but instead I went to the service window and said, "Well, I'm talking to you." Leaving it there would've been smart too. "You really believe your *daddy* wasn't to blame?"

"Hey, the nature of a private equity takeover is that some don't turn out as you want. But that's on the company itself. There's no takeover if they aren't in deep trouble to begin with."

"The *nature of.* Okay," I had laughed. "Your dad's company leveraged them to the point they'd never dig their way out. I wish I could borrow $700 million to buy a tech company and not put up dick of my own." There weren't many benefits that came with schlepping mail around campus, but unlimited access to *The Wall Street Journal*, *The Economist*, and every other publication to which the professors subscribed was one.

"He's the one willing to take the risk."

"What risk? It's all on the company he's taking over. Your dad's company raked in tens of millions in fees during the whole process with Burke Tech. Then they sell it to another company . . . *that they own*. More fees and paydays for your dad and the rest. And when they inevitably had to declare bankruptcy, shocker, your dad's company was the first to get its money out."

"You win some, you lose some," Sean had smirked.

"By win, you mean, the times they stay in business by gutting the company of half their employees for 'efficiency's' sake?"

"So, what's he supposed to do, keep everyone on, worthless or not?" Sean had said. "I'd love to see how your little socialist plan would turn out."

"Just because someone doesn't want to be an asshole, doesn't make them a socialist. But, hey, by all means, follow in Daddy's footsteps. I'm sure it's a perfect little life for you."

"So's this one for you," Sean mocked.

"For now."

"Oh yeah? What're you going to do with your life?"

"I'm doing it."

"Looks exciting," Sean said.

"I'd rather think about what I *am* doing with my life. Not what I am *going to* do with it."

"That's the rationalization of someone with a crappy-looking future."

Well, it went something like that. And there was more, but none of it got any better. Since then, we'd had an icier relationship than ever. Not that I cared.

"Your parents give you a credit card?" I said to Preston.

"Yeah."

"Go put in five dollars in gas and get fifty cash back. Your parents'll never look. They never do. Or if they did, they'd just think you're buying beer."

"Just don't stiff him," Sean said. "You might end up with a mysteriously broken hand."

Sean's other go-to: my stupid probation. When he didn't go the townie slight, it was the thing with my father. Hilarious.

Sean handed me fifty.

"Yours is eighty," I said.

"That's bullshit. It's the same class."

"But you're getting a B."

"What'd he get?"

"An A."

Weav laughed, knowing where this was headed.

"Writing his is easier," I said. "You know how much harder it is to write knowing I can't get higher than a B-minus without giving you away?"

"Fuck you."

Getting a laugh from the room at the expense of an asshole with a thin skin like Sean was always satisfying. But like I said before about the whole "I wouldn't have done anything differently" canard, it's all bullshit. Had I known what he would do to get back at me, you better believe I would have kept my big dumb mouth shut instead.

CHAPTER TWO

"Whoa, whoa, slowwww down," Reilly told Landry as they unloaded the crate from the electrical truck parked outside Carrington Auditorium. Reilly knew that if there's one way to give yourself away when you're pretending to be a local utility worker—instead of two guys about to sneak a case of explosives into a gymnasium—it's eagerness. Laziness, on the other hand, was never suspicious.

It was these little things that drove Reilly nuts. *Doesn't anyone else notice these simple nuances that make a job so much easier?* He felt like he spent 50 percent of his day telling these idiots what to do and the other half mediating stupid rifts like he was a human resources manager at some corporation. The only thing that got him through it was the thought that unlike the Verizon HR guy, Reilly could shoot the two whiners right between the eyes if he got fed up enough.

As he and Landry rolled the crate through the auditorium's entryway and past the glass case of old trophies and faded banners, he was almost offended at how easy it was to do this. A few fake uniforms and a couple vendor trucks, and you could do just about anything unquestioned. *I mean, don't people watch TV? Cop shows? CSI?* For a while he used to overthink it. Now?

He realized nobody paid attention to shit these days. Maybe it was all the smartphones. Maybe it's the self-absorption. Whatever it was, it had never been easier to infiltrate a target.

Inside the theater itself, Reilly could see a group of students rehearsing up on stage. *Midday on a Tuesday. Playacting. What a life*, he thought, shaking his head. When he was fifteen, he was already out of school and three jobs in. Not these little Bardolphs and Scroops up there prancing around, projecting their "art thous" and "wheretofores." He had to smile at the thought of these kids acting out *Henry V* just moments before what was to come.

"But when the blast of war blows in our ears, then imitate the action of the tiger."

Reilly knew it was probably vanity, his quoting Shakespeare to this meathead Landry who would never know it was from *Henry V*, but so what? Sometimes you are better than others. The fact was, he, Reilly, a high school dropout, could hear two lines of dialogue passing the theater door and know immediately it was Henry, aka Prince Hal after he'd stepped up his game like Reilly himself had. *Who else can do that?* he was thinking as they reached the stairwell doorway leading to the basement.

"You didn't say anything about stairs," Landry groaned.

"How exactly do you think one gets to a 'basement'?" It's always the biggest guys who complain the most about the physical parts of the job. Reilly would bet a thousand bucks Landry racked three hours a day in a gym and spent half his cut on steroids, yet this muscle-bound lunkhead wouldn't carry 150 pounds down a flight of stairs.

"There must be an elevator around here somewhere," Landry said.

Reilly took a deep breath. *Don't externalize*, he thought to himself. Isn't that what his therapist was always telling him? *See it from their viewpoint. They may be in the wrong, but that's not how they see it.*

Okay, Reilly thought, *maybe it is partially my fault; after all I did tell him to act like a normal government worker. He's nailing that.* "Fine. I'll get one end of it."

"You take the top on the way down; it hurts my back to bend over."

Fuck his viewpoint. I should shoot this asshole here and now. In the old days he would have, too. But that would just be externalizing. Not to mention self-sabotaging . . . all the wasted time cleaning up, then being one guy short, etc., etc. The new Reilly took the high road and said, "Sure thing. Wouldn't want you pulling a muscle." Then again, new Reilly also knew Landry would be blown into a bloody bouillabaisse along with the rest of his crew and the hostages by the time the day was out. Maybe his therapist was right: focusing on the positives in life really *can* make all the difference.

CHAPTER THREE

I don't know how things work in the real world, but based on the two work study jobs I'd had, I was beginning to wonder if most adults actually do dick in the work place. Not that I was complaining. Slinging envelopes in a windowless basement mailroom took twenty minutes, and my drops another twenty. After that, I had three hours and twenty minutes broken up between classes to do as I pleased. I used to try to find some tasks to do around the mailroom, but that ended when my boss got wind of it.

"I'm not against initiative, per se," Garvey had told me at the time. "I *am* against busy work, though. A job is a job is a job. Are we getting paid more if we do more than they ask? No. Do we do what they ask? Yes. Should they ask us to do more? Well, that's on them. And since no one has, I'm not about to turn over that rock."

With three hours and twenty minutes a day to kill, I needed to do something besides read leftover gossip magazines or listen to Garvey yapping into his Ham radio to a bunch of fellow recluses (it was invariably male voices I heard whenever I walked by Garvey on the radio. Not that I was surprised; I doubted the Ham radio scene was making a run at the Bumble crowd).

Garvey didn't care what it was I did, just so long as A) it wasn't more work, thus making him look bad and B) no one caught me not doing my job. If I had a phone, or any gadget for that matter, I'd probably just watch Netflix, but instead I started using that time to "take" more classes so as to sell more term papers. And I mean "take," because no one else knew or had okayed my attending these classes. Nothing would be more suspicious than a student sitting in on extra classes, so instead I just climbed into the ducts and attics above the classrooms and watched.

I had four orders for Advanced Econ, so after sorting the mail, I went up to the Carter Hall attic above Professor Blanchard's class. I'd already read the professor's own book and the rest of the syllabus, so did I really need to be here to knock off four papers on Ricardian Equivalence? No. Was there another reason I might sit, cramped, in an attic, my face pressed to the crack in the floorboard? Sure. But that one's a little embarrassing.

Before you judge, though, let me ask you: if you could stare at your crush unbeknownst to her, would you not?

Alright, "crush" sounds a little weird. Kira was just someone I found interesting. Mostly because of how *interested* she was. I mean, I found her interesting too, of course, but it's the being interested that really got me. She was an enthusiastic person, not in a fake, pretend-to-be-interested way. Even now, not realizing she was being observed, there she was listening intently, her eyes locked on the diagram on screen that Professor Blanchard was highlighting with his laser pointer. Even with something as boring as a graph displaying comparative advantage gains from trade, her curiosity was evident. You could see her visibly enjoying what she was looking at. I didn't know that was even possible (then again, I'm self-aware enough to know that someone watching me watch her right then would probably say the same thing).

Wanna know a couple other things about her? Speaks fluent

French. Loves any food that comes in mini serving sizes like those jellies you get in a diner, Trader Joe's samples, or tiny chocolates. Mini unless it's peanut butter. For that she gets big jars of all-natural peanut butter, but has to pour the oil off the top first. She wears a fur hoody even when it's about seventy out. Prefers Montreal bagels to New York ones (did you know there was such a thing? I didn't until the time we all stayed at her grandmother's). She can ride a unicycle. Seriously. That last one thanks to a couple weeks at Circus Smirkus camp. Which would lead you to another fact about her: she's not a nerd, per se, but maybe nerd adjacent.

You'd think by now I'd have gotten the balls up to do something about it, but for some reason I can't. I can rationalize all I want and tell myself, *Hey, what's the harm in telling someone you like them? Why be embarrassed? Even if they didn't like you, who would be upset to hear someone liked them?* But no matter how sensible that all sounded, there was no way I was ever going to do it. There's a lot you can learn reading every book you come across. One thing you can't? Learning how to say how you feel. To someone. Specifically, a girl. If there's a book for that out there, I haven't found it yet. Or, more likely, no one else ever needs it; I'm the only wuss out there unable to do something as humanly basic as tell someone I like them. I came close to that one time at the diner, but like always, I chickened out then too.

I've known her since before I was even a student here. I met her like I met Weav, back when I was waiting for my mother to finish work. Maybe I'm just self-centered, but I was always struck by how interested she seemed whenever we talked. Sure, it probably wasn't me, but she made you feel it was. I knew I wasn't the only one who felt that way. Not that I believed the stuff Sean used to say about the two of them. The guy said that about half the girls here. But still.

I could see him three rows back from Kira. Even now I'm sure he wasn't typing class notes in his laptop, but sending messages to someone. If I had to guess I'd say it was to Reece, right there next to him, smirking into his laptop, the two exchanging crude messages about the girls in the class. I can only imagine what those two and the others talked about in their little secret society that gathered out at the old Wentworth crypt for whatever blue bloods gather for when they start secret societies. I'd bet anything Sean and the others saw themselves as some sort of Dead Poets Society, but one that read Friedman and Adam Smith as opposed to Byron and Walt Whitman. A Dead Economists Society. A bunch of future financial drones, sneaking into a musty tunnel, drinking beer and play-acting.

I'd actually been out to the crypt once after overhearing Sean and Reece discussing it as they debated which freshman to nominate, Raj Mareeh or Beth Roberts. What used to be a secret society of entitled rich white legacy dudes was now a secret society of entitled multi-racial, gender-mixed rich kids. Only the bank account mattered. I guess it's progress: now anyone can be a rich prick.

Then again, I couldn't really work up too much of a lather over how creepy the two were, seeing as one could argue it wasn't really any creepier than secretly lying in bat guano and spider webs thick as shoelaces, staring at someone whose schedule I knew by heart, the girl with her arm raised, waiting to be called on. Given that my last thought had been on just how beautifully toned Kira's raised arm was, I'll concede the point.

Below me, Blanchard called on Reece instead of Kira. "When my father was negotiating the purchase of GXC Holdings," Reece said, "the Fed stepped in and . . ."

As I watched Kira, I was glad to see I wasn't the only one whose eyes rolled.

CHAPTER FOUR

If anyone was really paying attention they might have noticed that it seemed an odd coincidence that the Northern United Foods truck, the Harvest River Produce truck, and a Crowley Distributing soft drink van were all making their deliveries at the same time. And all on Tuesday. *But why would anyone?* thought Javier. As Reilly was always harping on them about, no one pays attention to the small things.

Javier and the other two drivers stationed their trucks in position and waited for the call from Reilly. He looked at the clock on the dashboard of the Crowley van. Fifty-eight minutes. Fifty-eight interminable minutes. *Fucking Reilly,* Javier thought as he stared at the clock; *the guy's so paranoid we're going to flake, he makes us get here an hour early.* Javier instinctively reached to his jacket pocket for a phone that wasn't there. Reilly again. Everyone had to leave theirs behind. *No tracing, I get it,* Javier said to himself, *but come on. An hour with nothing to do? It's worse than when I tried giving up smoking.*

It was a good thing Reilly paid so well. Or whoever it was that called Reilly's shots. Reilly always acted like it was his job and his only, but Javier was certain Reilly was *yes sirring, no sirring* someone too. Javier wasn't against taking orders from above. It did, however, bug the shit out of him to take orders from someone taking those same orders from someone else and passing them on as his own. He had a lieutenant like that in Kandahar. Acted like the entire war was his to decide. Reilly better hope this turned out better for him than it did for Lieutenant Baynard.

He looked at the clock again. 1:05.

Fucking Reilly.

CHAPTER FIVE

After Econ, I had planned to do what I did most lunch breaks: go to my spot and knock out a couple of the papers. Following Garvey's orders to stay out of sight, I had found a dusty unused storage space in the basement of the history building a while back. If anyone ever came across it, they'd think I was Unabomber 2.0, what with the stacks of syllabi books I'd found discarded by kids whose parents superfluously bought both the digital and hard copies. Not to mention the dozens of half-finished term papers that they'd probably take to be my manifesto in the making. And the hundreds of other books I'd found around campus—chance findings that led to an ever-changing list of favorite authors which at the moment landed on Watts, Vonnegut, Chekov, and Maugham. But what would probably stump them the most were the three homemade birthday cards taped to the wall.

My basement hideout was where I had planned to go at lunch, but I didn't. Instead I was standing in the psychology lab with an empty mailbag over my shoulder pretending to deliver nonexistent mail.

You know how it feels when you think you're the oddball? The one who stands out, and not in the good way, not in the way where you have your shit together? Everyone else seems to be the normal ones. There hasn't been a day on this campus that I haven't felt like the odd man out. Well, suddenly for one tiny moment I was the least weird one in the room. There was only one other person to beat, but when that person is standing with their back to you, barking into a mirror, you could probably feel safe in knowing you were trumped on the weirdness scale.

Kira hadn't seen me enter the psych lab, so I was able to watch as she barked. And we aren't talking in the figurative sense. Honest to goodness dog barks. Barks that alternated between angry growls and cartoonish, uninhibited "ruff ruffs" and however else she apparently thought a dog sounded.

"Woof woof," I said, causing her to whip around. Yet she didn't look the least bit embarrassed, thus knocking me back to being the weird one again—the one standing there gawking at a girl casually trying out different dog barks in a mirror.

"Hey, Cade. What're you doing here?"

"What am *I* doing?"

"Yeah."

I looked at her, waiting for her to explain what the eff she was barking at, but she seemed content to stand there leaving the unspoken question with an unspoken answer. As she waited for me to answer her question, she picked up the to-go coffee cup she had on the lab table. She pulled off the lid and took out a brownie and a cookie. You weren't allowed to take food out of the cafeteria, just tea or coffee, but Kira had found this loophole (rather, created it) and would usually smuggle out an afternoon snack.

She took a bite of the cookie and watched me as I said, "Uh . . ."

I know: not exactly a rousing start to a conversation with a girl I rarely got to stand in a room with alone. Not from a lack of trying—the psychology lab wasn't on my route, but knowing it was her favorite, I'd often dropped by in hopes of bumping into her. And here I'd found her. Alone. I'd been trying for weeks, and now I had finally hit the jackpot and found her here by herself. *Great. Now talk, asshole.*

"Mail," I continued (not that one more word beyond "uh" can really be considered *continuing*; it landed as more of a thud).

Two words in, and I was already pancaked on the conversational pavement, unable to come up with something to say that might reboot the conversation. You'd think something I'd read would have come out through osmosis ("He stepped down, trying not to look long at her, as if she were the sun, yet he saw her, like the sun, even without looking"), but instead, nothing. I swear to God, I always turned into an idiot with her.

"Oh, okay," Kira answered. Still she said nothing about the fact she had been barking like a lunatic a few seconds ago.

"You're not going to tell me why you were barking?"

"Practicing."

She pointed to her copy of *Perception vs. Deception* sitting on the lab table. I recognized it from the syllabus for Abnormal Psych. I'd read it, as a matter of fact. As a matter of another little fact, though, I wasn't actually in Abnormal Psych class. But I did sit above it every Tuesday and Thursday afternoon watching Professor Wright lecture. Was I writing papers to sell? Was I a Professor Wright groupie? Nope and nope, but it was my favorite class.

Basically because it was hers. She had told me once that she hoped to grow up to be a psychologist or therapist of some sort. Fix broken minds. Not only was it one of my favorite things about her, but I'd always had this fantasy of being her patient one day. I knew that sounded odd—which was why I'd definitely never admit it to her—but the thought of sitting across from her in some sterile office like the one they made me sit in with Dr. Phelan, it relaxed me. Sitting just the two of us and me telling her everything. Telling her about Christmas, 2017. And about all the other things that scared me. About watching my mother through the space in the floorboards of my bedroom when I was eight, maybe nine, staring at her as she silently cried.

The only time I'd ever seen someone cry over nothing. Even at the time I sensed it wasn't really over nothing, but there was no movie on or music or another person in the room, just her sitting alone on the couch, her whole body shaking as she cried and cried.

And if I got the chance, I'd also tell Kira about herself. That I knew. And that she didn't need to hide it.

"It's for an assignment. We need to do something totally crazy in front of random people and see how they react to abnormal behavior. Have you ever seen the video of that high school basketball team, where they're inbounding the ball, it's with seconds left, and one of the players got on all fours and started barking?"

I had, but I played dumb (a trick I'd seemingly mastered when around her).

"The other team all stops and stares, frozen at the curveball thrown at their brain, a crazy action that never should happen in that context. The teammates of the guy barking, though, knew it was coming and so when he started howling, his team passed the ball in, and they scored easily. They won while the other team just stood there mesmerized by the abnormal action. Don't tell anyone, but I'm going to do it next assembly. Wanna do it with me?"

Another thing I always liked about her: an absolute immunity to giving a crap what others thought about her. Me, though? Even getting to do something together with her wasn't enough for me to agree to make a complete ass of myself in front of everyone. "No, thanks. I'd never have the guts for that."

"You always seem like you don't really care how you come across. Sar; you don't." Another thing about her: for some reason she randomly abbreviated (or "abbreved," as she would probably call it). Like instead of "sorry" it was "sar." Coffee was "cof." Restaurant was "resto." Why? Who knows why; I'd never asked. I liked it, though.

"I don't?"

She shrugged.

Maybe she was somewhat right. I cared about making an ass of myself, but as far as caring about all the things these prep school dudes care about, I guess I didn't. "Caring implies their point of view is better than mine. Wow, did that just sound pretentious."

"A little," Kira said, then grinned. "Maybe the others are right sometimes."

"*These* guys? Maybe some, like Weav. Or, well, you. Most of these guys, though, all think a certain way because someone told them that. But where did *that* come from? Someone else. And that person didn't figure it out on their own either. They just got it from some other jagoff up the chain." If I didn't think I'd sound even more pretentious, I'd have told her the Oscar Wilde quote that stuck with me from one of the books in my stacks: "Most people are other people. Their thoughts are someone else's opinions, their lives a mimicry, their passions a quotation." Instead, I said, "It's all just a bunch of random shallow stuff that becomes 'truth' somehow."

"So what's your idea of 'the truth'?"

"I like to make up my own approach to life."

"That's a little cocky."

"I'm not saying mine's better. But it's mine. I like to read. I like to talk to you. I like to do MMA. When I don't anymore, I'll find other things to do. And not because someone told me to. If I like turkey, I'll order a turkey sandwich. Too many people like turkey but opt for roast beef. Okay, I admit that sounds stupid."

"You can't hit them all."

I really needed to stop talking. *She has to think I'm either the boringest guy she's met or the dumbest,* I thought. *Because I either never say anything, or when I do, I sound like the world's biggest idiot. What I want to do is shut up and ask her questions. I already know me. She's the one I want to find out about.*

"Yeah, that was pretty lame. I just mean, at least I don't fixate

on stupid things just because my parents did, like all these guys."
Stop . . . talking.

"I wouldn't expect that from someone with as nice a mother as yours."

"Doesn't mean much when the other half is a prick." *Seriously. Just stop.*

"Sar, I didn't, I . . ."

That was stupid of me. Here I was, finally getting something more than a fifteen-second, "How's-it-going-good-you-great-see-you-later" interaction with her, and I somehow had steered into this conversational iceberg. A crappy father only means the son is going to follow suit. Not exactly what I wanted her to focus on. "Don't be. I sound whiny; a father whacking a son isn't exactly something unique. There's a million hackneyed stories like mine. And I should be the last one to whine; mine's never doing it again."

"Maybe the fact something like that is hackneyed is the problem." Kira reflexively touched my forearm as she said this.

Did I feel a tad sheepish that this of all things had led to maybe the most intimate moment I'd ever had with her? Sure. Then again, I didn't feel too bad. If you're going to get your ass kicked regularly by your father, I figure you should at least get something out of it. Would she be this nice, though, if she knew the rest?

"Was that why you're on probation? I'd heard it was something you did to your father?"

I thought about it. I really did. Here it was; the opening I'd sort of always hoped for. As close as I'd probably ever get to that crazy fantasy of lying on the couch telling future therapist Kira. If I'd known what was about to go down in a few hours, I would have. Because in a few hours all that stuff with my father would seem infinitesimal.

Instead, I attempted to lighten the mood in that tried and true way: by crapping on someone else. With as haughty an air as I could muster, I imitated Reece, "Well, when *my* father was negotiating the terms of the GXC Holdings . . ."

She laughed. "Yeah, he loves to let you know how important his dad is."

"What about you. Who are you related to?"

"Oh, all of us here must be rich and connected?"

I raised an eyebrow.

"Head of Glenrock Financial," she said a little sheepishly.

"I won't hold it against you." I also knew she spent her summers working full-time even though she didn't have to. She wanted to be able to contribute some part of her tuition. It may have only been a symbolic amount given the insane cost of this place, but I didn't know another rich kid who did. And if they did, they'd never stop letting you know. I only found out by mistake.

As I watched her smile, I didn't say anything. I just wanted to sit in one of those rare moments when for whatever reason, whether it was the words or the look, whatever it was, it gave me that feeling I'd read about in *Zen in the Art of Archery* (yet another Kira favorite), a nothingness that you couldn't really describe, but a feeling better than any other.

It was weird, but I had this thought rocket, almost like a premonition, that I should remember everything about this moment. Like that song I'd been into recently, the Canadian guy singing about how he never appreciates the good things while they happen. Maybe it was my brain telling me I might as well soak in as much as I could so at least I could enjoy the nostalgic memories of this moment, since I'd never have the real thing with her. I wanted to explain this to her, but it sounded muddled in my head. I could only imagine how it would come out of my mouth. Maybe I should have just asked her to search for the song on her phone. Let "Sweet Things" speak for itself. Before I could say anything, in the outer office to the psych lab behind her, the corner of my eye caught something. Garvey. Talking to the department secretary. And like a barking dog in a basketball game, there was something out of place about Garvey here. Ominous even.

A quote from some book I'd read for a sociology class flittered through my brain. Malcolm Gladwell, I think . . . something about saying screw it to dwelling on things, that you're better off with a snap decision. And at that moment, I wanted to ask her out. And if I didn't do it in this blink of the eye, I had a feeling I never would.

"Want to get together sometime?"

"What do you want to do?"

"Nothing." It popped out before I really thought about what I was saying.

"Nothing?"

"Well, I mean, something, but . . ." I paused, trying to think of what I meant: not nothing, but just something without all the phones and tablets, the swiping and tapping, and all that stuff that had to be driving everyone crazy. "Maybe nothing would be nice for a change?"

She laughed.

"I'm sorry. I'm an idiot. That sounds stupid."

"No, I just thought it's funny, I was thinking earlier about this book from class that you reminded me of. It was about how all the great things in science have come from people pursuing things for no objective reason. Guys like Newton and Einstein weren't thinking about a job, house, picket fence, two cars. They were just curious for the sake of curiosity. They dicked around, thinking big pointless thoughts, and came up with ideas that eventually led to flying and space travel and all sorts of stuff."

"*Usefulness of Useless Knowledge*. Abraham Flexner."

"Yeah, how'd you know that?"

The way she was looking at me worried me. I hoped she wasn't piecing together the coincidence of me knowing yet another thing off of one of her syllabi.

"I'm the king of useless knowledge. Like knowing that."

Through the doorway behind Kira, I could see Garvey

walking toward the lab with the psychology department secretary.

I don't know if it was me knowing the name of the book or something else that just tripped in her brain, but Kira suddenly asked, "Wait, how'd you know 'bout the GXC thing? You're not in econ."

Garvey couldn't have timed his entrance any better, walking in with the secretary just at the moment I was fumbling to find an answer to how I might know about something from a class I'm not in. His timing was great, but the reason for it was not. "Cade, you gotta come with me. Dean Harkin needs to see you immediately."

I couldn't believe how crappy my luck was. Just when I had finally struck up the nerve to ask her out, there was Garvey dragging me out of there before I could get an answer. I didn't think of it at the time, but had I remembered the Taoist tale I had read in one of those Alan Watts books, I'd actually have been grateful for Garvey. The one about the farmer who is dismayed when the good fortune of finding a horse later leads to his son falling from the saddle and breaking his leg, but that in turn keeps the son from being conscripted into the army and having to go off to war. The point being, no one ever knows how any one incident will turn out in the long run. So, what seemed to me at first to be a negative outcome, inadvertently saved me from later being rounded up with the rest of them. Then again, just as in that Taoist tale, positive outcomes aren't always what they seem either. In fact, they may lead one directly into something much, much worse.

CHAPTER SIX

Of all Reilly's guys, Trotter figured he probably enjoyed this stuff the most. Pretty much all of them were ex-military or private security contractors, but most were just looking for the paydays. Paydays exponentially larger than the $55K plus benefits that he and Landry and Torres were making back in their unit. Sure, Reilly didn't offer any bennies, but twenty times your yearly wage makes up for no dental or 401K. Besides, Trotter had few delusions he'd make it to retirement age, let alone forty. His military bennies meant squat.

He could have stayed in the Marines, been a lifer, but the moments of true action were too few and far between for his liking. Seemed he spent his whole time *yes sirring* and *no sirring* and not enough time getting the juices flowing. This private stuff, though. You got the adrenaline kick and the shooting people part, but—though Trotter would never admit this to anyone—without the trained enemy shooting back part. The difference between some shit-show mission in Mosul and a hostage takeover like this was the difference between getting in the ring with Floyd Mayweather or throwing with some drunk frat boy in a bar fight. Be it Floyd or frat boy, you got an adrenaline rush and the chance to potentially crush someone's orbital socket. But only with the latter were you guaranteed not to end up the bloodied pulp.

As soon as he closed the cafeteria rooftop door behind him, Trotter peeled off his Northern United work shirt. He knew it was necessary to wear it as he had wheeled the dolly loaded with boxes of paper products into the cafeteria building and toward the storage room. But now that he was alone on the roof and opening the box labeled *compostable coffee cups*, there was no need anymore for deception. Maybe it was vanity, but Trotter never felt comfortable when they had to wear disguises. *A dolly jockey I am not,* he thought to himself as he pulled on the tight black jacket he had hidden in the box along with the antenna and other electronics gear.

He slipped the Sig Sauer P226 into the sewn-in holster slot and then pocketed a small radio transmitter and a thin black case the size of a smartphone. As he pressed a Bluetooth piece into his ear, he looked at his watch: 1:43 p.m.

Seventeen minutes. He could feel that familiar buzz percolating through him already.

When I saw my mother, I could tell immediately that she didn't know any more than I did why the headmaster wanted to see me. In fact, I probably had the better guess.

She was sitting at her desk in the outer room to Dean Harkin's office. Her desk was a pretty good representation of her personality. A computer screen, pad of paper, one pen, a lone picture frame, and a dish of mini Peppermint Patties, Dean Harkin's favorite. Minimalist and practical, just like her.

My mother had been working at St. Frederick for the last five years. Based on what I'd seen, she was attractive enough to be hit on regularly by the married teachers, but smart enough to decline. I didn't think she hated her job or loved it. More tolerated it. Tolerated eight hours pretending she enjoyed fielding calls from rich parents, or more often, assistants of rich parents, about their children's myriad of food allergies (read: preferences) or requests that the school no longer provide plastic straws or whatever other environmental cause they recently read about in the *Times* trending articles section. Never mind that one less visit on their private plane would do more for the planet than a lifetime of sippy straws.

She didn't mind Headmaster Harvin so much. A little needy, but, as she told me once, nothing that three or four decent courtesy laughs a day didn't cure. She'd learned to spread them out like snacks to a toddler. Me, I still hadn't worked out the whole courtesy laugh thing. Say something funny, I'll laugh. Don't, and I won't.

I remembered how happy she was when she got the job as his secretary, knowing it was a way in for her son. She always had such faith that I was going to be some Horatio Alger story, she the proud, working-class single (thankfully, she would tell you) mother with the precocious kid who earned a scholarship here at St. Frederick. Alas, no. The working class part, sure. Precocious, no. That's just the term they use for the poor kids that get in. If you're wealthy and here, then you're smart and educated. Poor? Then you must be some random biological lottery winner, with some quirk in the brain chemistry. But that wasn't me. The reason I aced the admission tests? I credited it to simply being a kid with nothing but alone time growing up. Time spent reading book after book after book while my mother worked her evening job at The Garden (Olive, not Madison). The proud part? Yeah. But that didn't mean she'd been happy with my recent life choices. And I had a feeling I was about to give her another one she didn't much care for.

"Morning, Ms. Dixon," I said to her as I entered. "How's the kid?"

Normally I'd get a crack back along the lines of "The boy's a bit of a smartass." Today I just got the look.

From where I was standing, I could only see the back of the

picture frame, but I knew it was the same one she'd had on that desk the entire time she'd had the job. She must have seen the trajectory of my eyes, because she looked down at the photo. I could see her shaking her head ever so slightly. It's amazing how much frustration you can convey with just a slight head movement.

"Tuck in your shirt. You're on the job."

"Yeah, schlepping mail. I don't think my sartorial choices matter all that much."

"You dress for the job you want, not the one you have."

"Board shorts and tattoos?"

"Funny. MMA is not a job. Besides, if I ever see you with a tattoo . . ."

I tucked in my shirt. "Maybe I already have one."

She eyeballed me a moment. She always told me she could still read me better than I thought. She grinned ever so slightly. "It better at least say 'Ma.'" Maybe she normally could read me, but the fact she was able to smile in that moment meant she couldn't always read me. If she could, she'd know I was about to let her down. Hard.

As Reilly dialed the number, he marveled at the spherical, night-black device he held in his hand. Aside from the number pad, there was nothing to indicate what the sphere might be. No obvious holes for a speaker or a mic. No plug-ins. Yet somehow, it was still a phone. Not only that, but one that—at least according to G—was un-tappable. *It had better be,* thought Reilly. More for the fact of what else it would mean if G was wrong. If the phone encrypter didn't work, then that might mean the same for the other tech. And that was the one that concerned him. That was the one that was going to make this whole thing work.

"How long?" the voice on the other end asked.

"Eight minutes," Reilly said, surveying the campus from the cafeteria roof.

"What're you calling me for then?"

"You said you wanted an update before we made the final go." Reilly used to think it was just the dumb meatheads working for him that didn't pay attention. After working for G on these last two jobs, he knew even the smartest, most successful of people are just as distracted.

"So update me."

"Everything's in place." Reilly knew G didn't really want a rundown on it; it was just micromanaging. And wanting acknowledgement that it was *his* plan. His mission. Not Reilly's. "We're ready for your call." As he said the word "your," Reilly added just a faint dusting of derision.

"Okay. Roll on it."

Roll on it. God, did G annoy Reilly. *Roll on it.* G always play-acting like he's a soldier too. "Yes sir," Reilly answered, the "sir" sufficiently dusted as well.

"And just know, if your guys hurt him, it's on you."

There's no reason I should have ever thought it wasn't going to come to this. You can keep a secret with yourself. Even that's not easy. With two people, maybe. Three, unlikely. And with each new person dialed in on the secret, the chances of it leaking grow exponentially.

Add to that someone with an ax to grind, and I should have known. Dr. Phelan would have said I was looking to get caught. Why else would I sell term papers to fifteen different guys, one of whom hated my guts? Was I looking to get kicked out of a place I never felt comfortable at? Maybe. Well, if I was indeed trying to self-sabotage, I really hit the jackpot when Sean turned in Weav's laptop to Harkin. Getting kicked out of school was something I had always figured would happen at some point, and who cared; I had no plans for college. Rather than racking up debt, I was going to travel, hitchhike, and read. Get random jobs along the way to pay for it. That would sure beat four more years sitting in old stone buildings being further indoctrinated into the system. But now, as Harkin had just made clear, I had broken not just the school policy meaning I would be getting kicked out, but my probation officer was going to be notified, and—stupidly on my part—I hadn't had the forethought to realize getting caught meant a violation of probation. Which meant the old charges would be returned. Which meant detention. And not the kind of detention that results in an extra hour after school.

Fucking Sean. I could see him turning me in, but with the laptop he was essentially willing to throw Weav in the trash as well. Harkin hadn't believed me when I told him I had stolen Weav's laptop unbeknownst to him. Even offered me semi-leniency if I admitted to who else was involved (I'd at least had the sense to always have the others attach their own title page afterwards, so that there were never any names stored on the laptop).

There was a moment when I considered it. Right as I passed my mother on the way out, when I saw the look on her face, for a split second I thought about turning around. I could go full rat on everyone, begging Harkin not to let the first domino fall and knock over the expulsion domino that would topple the revoked probation tile, then the juvenile detention one, which would flatten that last piece: my mother.

But I didn't. Harkin had given me until the end of the day to decide if I was going to fess up to who else was involved. If not, I was gone, and he would notify Brolin. Seemed pointless to head to the science building now and learn about gravitational waves or Archimedes's Principle or whatever else Mr. Cervane had in mind for today's Physics 3 class. Instead, I went to the history building. What I'd have really liked to have done was beat the world out of something or someone. But seeing as that's kinda what got me into this whole probation mess in first place, I did see the circular nature of it and the ill-advised-ness of such an outlet.

So I opted for the next best thing. Sure, a book's not as good as punching someone who deserves it in the face, but it did take my mind off it. Off of everything. It always had. Probably why I'd always liked books and MMA so much. The only two things I ever found that emptied my brain of everything else.

Over the years I had been through every building on this property, and I had found the basement of the history building to be the least used. There were boxes and boxes of storage that hadn't been touched in decades, and stacks of old desks gathering dust. On the far side there was a large closet, and in there was my Unabomber lair, hundreds of books in precarious-looking stacks or splayed out like tumbled over woodpiles.

I'd started hiding out in here even before I got in as a student. Back when my mother started working at St. Frederick. The only person that ever found me here was Miss Farley, a librarian who was in the basement looking for old history textbooks. But she had been happy to look the other way. Not because I'm a townie like her, but because I was a teenager that read an actual physical book. Miss Farley had told me it drove her crazy: books all around them and not a single kid ever had one in their hands. She'd sit in the library watching them on their tablets or laptops, knowing there was a roughly zero percent chance they were currently using that device for reading Proust or Joyce or even Dr. Seuss or anything other than crafting the perfect social media image.

I'd read everything in here at least once. Most of them multiple times. Textbooks I'd found around campus, borrowed novels from the library, discarded paperbacks, an eclectic mishmash that for me was like a numbing drug. Something that pushed back the anger (and, if I was honest, the fear behind it) running just below the surface.

And now, with it all coming down, I just wanted to put it off for a little while. Put off thinking about what I had done.

Let me clarify. I didn't feel guilty in any sense. Who gave a rat's ass if I made a few bucks helping a bunch of rich kids cheat the system? It'd happen one way or another. But two things did bother me. One, my mother being devastated. And staring at those three birthday cards on the wall, I thought about the other. It was going to happen anyway, but now it hit with a slap, a finality that I wouldn't have time to come to terms with. It had been in the back of my mind all semester, knowing the reality: senior year would end; Kira would be off to McGill, and I'd never see her again. But now the never seeing her again was going to start early. It would start today.

I picked randomly from the pile in the corner, the way an alcoholic might grab a can of beer from the fridge. Didn't matter which one. They all numbed.

The Nature Nurture Essays on Abnormality

A book from a past syllabus. I had to laugh. Nature-Nurture. I kinda wished I'd known about Nature-Nurture that day I finally took a shot at my father. I would have asked him which he thought was the reason his son was trying to shatter his father's nose. Was it Nature? Me being the offspring of the type of guy who could regularly take a swing at his fifty-pounds-lighter wife? Or was it Nurture? The fact that getting the shit beaten out of you once or twice a month just might turn one into the type of person who would try to kill your own father when you finally got the strength to do so?

CHAPTER SEVEN

Kira looked at her phone. Seeing it was already 1:50 p.m., she texted Sean she was going to be a few minutes late. When she hit send, the undeliverable symbol came up. She tried resending, but when the same happened, she now noticed the "No Service" notification in the top left corner. Odd. The psych lab wasn't usually a dead zone.

She grabbed her backpack off the lab table and headed to the student union, where she was supposed to meet Sean, Reece, Weav, and Becca twenty minutes ago to cram for the econ exam. Gun to her head, Kira couldn't decide if the reason she hadn't noticed she was twenty minutes late was that, try as she might, she couldn't get as interested in what people did as she was in why they did it. Hence, her lingering at the psych lab rather than cramming econ theories. Or was the reason a waning interest in her study partners? One in particular. Nothing wrong with Sean. They had always gotten along, and then they had gotten together a couple times. But while there was nothing really wrong about him, there was nothing really right either. *That's harsh,* she thought. *Would I want someone to judge me just because they weren't into the things I like?*

Whenever she found herself thinking negatively about someone, she tried to think of one positive trait. She settled on the fact he always aced economics, so he wasn't a bad study partner to have when you yourself couldn't stand the class. A class Kira would never be in if it were up to her. An impartial observer would say it was an elective; it *was* up to her. She'd agree, but it wasn't worth the fight with her dad. At least she'd been able to convince him to let her take one psych class for every econ (and the only reason he had agreed to that was that it showed she had a negotiator's instincts).

As Kira entered the student union, she saw Preston.

"Hey, Press, have you seen--"

He hustled right past her without a word. *That's odd,* she thought. He was a new guy and had always seemed to be pretty social. She was surprised to see him completely ignore her.

Kira went to the Kennedy room and saw the four others at the back corner table that Reece and Sean always occupied, like they were Sinatra and Martin at a reserved table at the Copa in one of those old movies she watched with her grandmother. There was a brief moment upon seeing the foursome that she thought: *I kinda wish Cade were in this class.*

Not the first time she'd thought something like this. She liked the others and all, and wasn't thinking about Cade in *that* way, per se, but she did think he was—*was what?*—weird, really. At least that's what most everyone thought. He was different, she had to admit. Maybe that was why she had that sudden wish he was here studying with them. He always had a unique view of things. Even if he was a little . . . well, yeah, weird.

For all the hassle, for all the complaining, for all the prep work, there is this, thought Reilly. *That moment when it all started.* His men fanning out, the jammer on the roof flicking on, the energy palpable. Anticipation. Reilly swore you could literally feel it, like a ripple in the air.

Everything else about these operations was a big *eh*. The prep was a pain in the ass. And the event itself was always a series of other people's screw-ups that he had to constantly manage. And afterwards, if he was being honest, it was always a little bit of a letdown. Even when it went well, it was great for what, two weeks? Probably not even that. Within a few days the malaise was always back. Even with this job, and the massive payday that was coming, he knew it'd be the same. What was he supposed to do, invest it in a bunch of index funds on eTrade and spend the rest of his life sitting on the proverbial beach, sipping umbrella drinks with a few bikinis next to him?

That first rush of anticipation, though, there's nothing like it. That sense of knowing that from here on out hundreds of lives were in his hands. And he could do with them as he pleased. *I'd love to ask my therapist why I need other people's lives in my hands to enjoy myself, but that's a touchy subject to broach. I'm guessing client/therapist privilege doesn't cover that one.*

The initial panic was always more fun to watch from above, so Reilly had taken a position next to the mushroom antenna Trotter had set up on the cafeteria roof. The jammer on the auditorium roof had taken out all phones and electronics across campus, and now, at exactly 2 p.m., the show began.

Reilly watched Hertz, Richards, and Carpenter hop out of the Harvest River Produce truck and fan out in military formation. The same should be happening out of the Northern United Foods and Crowley vehicles. Fourteen men locked, loaded, and about to scare the living shit out of an entire school. Even with 800 students and staff to wrangle, fourteen men was probably superfluous given such a soft target as a prep school. Not that he was planning to keep all 800 anyway.

The scene below him unfolded quickly. There were pretty much three responses to a guy in black wielding an AR-15 charging toward you:

There's the "run for your life" one, like the boy there sprinting across the green and into the library. Those were the ones Reilly knew his guys liked the most—it was like chasing wounded quarry through the woods—but they also took up the most time. Thankfully, the majority response was "utter bewilderment." Their brains couldn't fathom this thing happening in front of them. It's nothing the brain has ever prepared for, and so they shut down. These were about as difficult to rustle up as a pen of lobotomized bovine.

The third category always made Reilly laugh. The "blubberers." They looked like they'd melted as their knees buckled and they literally slumped to the ground, leaving them a blubbering lump of fear and tears—sometimes even piss—as they begged for someone, something, *anything* to help them.

He had to admit; his guys were good. They looked like old ranch hands, deftly corralling their charges toward the auditorium. Sure, a few made it out the front gate, but so far, none of the ones his men would have to chase down. As he watched the large group of students being led out of the student union, he spotted one that his men would have had to go after had that one made a run for the gates. Reilly thought to himself, *I kinda wish we'd gotten to chase that one down.* Reilly knew that would be counterproductive, but it would have been fun to hear G's reaction when they horse-collared that kid.

You could tell an efficient job by the dearth of gunshots. If you needed to shoot, you hadn't done something right. So far his guys hadn't triggered a single shot. Sure, once in a while a little resistance required a gun butt to the side of the head, but mostly there was little pushback. There rarely was. People are cattle. Easiest animal in the world to herd.

Over by the main gate, two of his men unloaded the massive roadside construction light units from the trucks. Another of his guys should right then be inside the campus radio station destroying the console. Jammed cell phone service, cut phone lines, no internet, all the digital now useless, but this added detail Reilly was proud of. Most radio stations had moved to digital, but Reilly had thought to consider that a campus radio station would, with its low range, still be analog. None of his men were going to realize all the details he had to consider that they didn't, but Reilly could at least take satisfaction in knowing it's the little things that set one apart.

He pressed the encrypted Bluetooth receiver into his ear and looked at his watch. 2:03. In less than seven minutes the campus should be wrapped and every remaining student, teacher, and staff member would have been crammed into the auditorium, every one of them struggling to work their mind around the fact this might be the last day they would ever see.

Reilly's estimate was slightly off—the campus wasn't completely buttoned up until 2:14, but wrangling 800 people from all corners of the campus into the old Victorian-era auditorium in fourteen minutes, still mighty impressive.

Before heading to the auditorium Reilly made a stop at the deans' offices, where Landry was waiting for him, the latter's gun pointed at Headmaster Harkin and Cade's mom, Liz.

"So," Reilly said jovially as he entered the outer waiting room where Liz's desk was, "how we doing today, Ron? Ready to give me a helping hand?"

"H-how do you know my name?" Harkin stuttered, his voice barely audible.

"So you're a fear guy."

"I don't . . . I . . . what?"

"You can always tell what motivates someone. You, it's fear. Don't take it as a criticism, Ron. Most people are exactly the same when put in the position you're facing. Your brain floods your nervous system with chemicals. Fight or flight, right? And you. All you want to do is run out that door. Every cell in your body is screaming, *Run. Find a way. A way to get out of this situation.* Well, Ron, it's your lucky day. I suppose not in the *good* way, but at least it's not going to be your *last* day. I just need one thing from you." He pointed his handgun toward the computer on Liz's desk. "Punch in the password for the student body personal records."

The Headmaster didn't move.

"Come on now, Ron, this is not a time to panic. A little fear is good, but I don't want you to go catatonic on me."

"I, I can't. I don't know where they are. She does." Harkin pointed to Liz.

Why is it, Reilly said to himself, *that it's never the leader who leads?* Deans. Chairmen. CEOs. They were always the first to fold. You never could anticipate who the strong ones would be, but the weak give themselves away immediately. "How chivalrous of you, Ron. Throwing Liz here under the bus." He turned to her. "Your turn, Liz; get me the records."

"No."

One single word out of her mouth and Reilly could already tell—flight was not in her DNA. "No? Oh, is that right?"

Landry nudged her with his gun, but Liz didn't budge.

"Give him what he wants!" Harkin squealed.

Reilly grabbed Liz by the hair at the back of her head and dragged her toward her desk.

"Ah, Ron, buddy, ya gotta relax in these situations. Thing is: she will."

Reilly shoved Liz into her seat in front of the computer. "Password." With one hand still on the back of her head, he aimed his handgun toward Harkin and said, "I will start with him and make my way through however many students it takes before you give me the information I need. So shall we just cut to the chase?"

~

Initially, I thought it was just a fire drill. I had heard the footsteps overhead and assumed the building was being cleared. I hadn't even bothered to leave the closet and look out the overhead basement window to check. The first time there had been a drill here I had been afraid some overzealous teacher would come through on a sweep of the building and find my hiding spot. I needn't have worried. Overzealous they are not. Since then, any drill I just stayed put. I probably would have stayed right there this time too, replaying that conversation with Kira in my head, if it wasn't for the silence that followed. There was something peculiar about it, like something was missing.

It took a moment, but it had finally hit me: the alarm. Rather, lack of an alarm. Any time they had done a drill in the past, it started with, duh, the alarm ringing. When I finally went over to the window, I couldn't make out much from below, so I climbed up on a box and looked out. Wanna know how to screech your brain to a complete halt? Wanna override in an instant the dynorphin neurotransmitter that's been flooding your system with mopey thoughts as you were replaying in your mind what might be the last time you ever see the girl you've been wanting to ask out for only, oh, three solid years? All ya gotta do is stand on a box and look out a basement window and watch a bunch of men pointing automatic rifles at your fellow students and—like the simple act of a branch falling on a power line, sinking an entire house into darkness—poof, there goeth all other thoughts. Quickly replaced by a sphincter-tightening *WTF!?*

My first thought had been, just go upstairs and figure out what was happening. There had to be a logical explanation for men running around with guns. My second thought was, if there was a logical explanation and there was nothing to worry about, then finding out what it was twenty minutes from now rather than this very second wouldn't matter. And if there *was* something to worry about, there's zero point in running toward it. So I waited to see if it would come to me.

Hearing the door to the basement stairwell open, I realized it had.

CHAPTER EIGHT

Now that they were finally in the mix of it, Javier was feeling much better. Nothing like making people literally piss themselves to wash away the ennui of prep work. Javier would probably say 98 percent of his job blew, but it was all worth it when it came to this.

They'd already penned everyone into the auditorium, but Reilly being Reilly, he made the crew do final sweeps for any stragglers. Javier didn't mind; actually he loved this part, that moment when you come up on some cowering saps hiding behind a door, fear coursing through them, that feeling he had of absolute power as they begged for their lives. Begged *him* for their lives. The rest of his day he was nothing more than an anonymous schlub to everyone he interacted with—a nothing— but in that moment, he was their everything. So far, though, he'd come up empty handed. Both the science lab and English building were empty. Ditto this one, the history building. Maybe it was just his unlucky day, but he also wondered if it was something else entirely, whether things had changed. It seemed people used to run more. Or at least hide. Now, they just gave up. Probably the parents' fault, Javier figured; turning today's kids into a bunch of wusses.

Having started his sweep of the top floor, Javier reached the ground level and paused. *Is it really worth the effort to check the basement too?* Probably not, but Javier knew Reilly would lose it if it turned out he'd missed someone.

He pushed open the door and took the stairs to the basement. He could already smell the dank, musty odor of old books and cardboard boxes. Reminded him of the library his mom used to dump him off at. It's funny, he hadn't thought about it in ages, but he loved libraries. Not for the books. He read, sure, but never one of the grimy finger-pawed books you'd find in a library. What he loved about libraries were the cubbies. His mother made him go to the library next to her job where she cleaned offices. He'd have to go after school and wait for her. He hadn't thought about it in years, but he now remembered how he would sit in one of the cubbies they had in the kids' section, and he would pretend it was his secret cabin. A room he didn't have to share with four other asshole brothers. Javier would sit in that cubby for hours pretending he was out in one of those square states he'd seen on the map, like Colorado or Wyoming, places he never thought he'd see. Guess what? Maybe when this thing was done, he'd take his cut and buy a house in Colo-fuck-ing-rado. Go hunting. Something his deadbeat brothers never could afford.

As he slowly zig-zagged his way through the stacks of storage containers and piled-up furniture, he heard something. Barely anything. The untrained ear wouldn't even notice it, but as a guy who had done hundreds of search and snatch missions back when he served, he knew it was the slight rustle of someone adjusting their position.

Javier unclipped the safety on his rifle and moved slowly toward the closet door on the far side of the basement.

~

The auditorium was crammed full by the time they dragged Kira in. Maybe "dragged" wasn't the right word, but she was no blub-berer or run-for-your-lifer. She was scared, sure; you'd have to be a psychopath not to be. Still, she knew the worst thing you could do psychologically was cave. Even if everything was telling you otherwise, you needed to resist. Even in the smallest of ways.

The only other person who seemed to give the slightest resis-tance was Preston. She had seen him yelling at one of the men who had stormed the student union. At the time she wondered how he could be so antagonistic. But now as he continued to struggle against the gunman pushing him into the room with the barrel of his gun, she was even more amazed. Impressed, even.

Kira watched as the gunmen brought the last remaining students and teachers into the auditorium. Every seat was filled, with the overflow sitting cross-legged up and down the aisles. As she and the others from her study group had been led over, she'd seen confusion on their faces more than fear. Looking at them all crammed into the rows around her, she noticed a change. Fear was now visible on the others' faces. Weav and Becca, in particular. Sean too, but his was mixed with . . . maybe not anger, but annoyance. As Kira scanned the rest of the room, she could almost visualize this energy rolling across the auditorium as what was happening started to settle in. And when one of the gunmen suddenly bashed Preston in the jaw with the butt end of a gun as Preston tried to push the gun down, the faces changed in unison. Confusion became panic.

"What the fuck?!" Sean yelped.

"They're going to kill . . ." The rest of Becca's sentence caught in her throat. It looked to Kira as though Becca's body had been overcome with shock. Almost like a complete physical lock-down. It wasn't just her voice that caught. It was everything.

"We gotta get outta here," Sean said.

"No, we got to shut the fuck up and put our heads down."

Weav is right, Kira thought; *don't do anything.* The gunmen had to be on edge too. You didn't want to give a nervous person extra provocation. That's when people did rash things.

Be calm . . . and breathe . . . Kira told herself over and over. *Just breathe. The worst thing you can do now is panic.*

Calm? How does one stay calm as . . . as . . . as what happens? *Terrorists?* It was all happening too fast. She could feel the panic rising in her throat, everything in her tightening. Everything except her head. That felt like it was floating off, leaving her in a hazy fog.

Caaaaaallllm, she told herself again. *This is nothing more than the mind exerting itself. It's psychological, not physiological. Nothing more than weaponized stage fright. This, I can do something about.* Be mindful, that's what they learned the other day in the meditation workshop Ms. Hopkins led right here on the stage of this very building. Mindful of your present state. Mindful of the physical sensations of the moment. Easy for Ms. Hopkins to say. She didn't have to be mindful of a bunch of armed men pointing automatic weapons in her direction.

My breathing sounded to me like a raging category-five hurricane. I knew it was only the result of the sensory overload hitting my brain, a traffic jam of anxiety and panic and cortisol smashing together in the sympathetic part of my autonomic nervous system, but knowing something doesn't mean you can do anything about it. Especially when there are footsteps coming slowly toward you, maybe ten feet from the stack of storage boxes you are hiding behind.

Callllllllm. Be mindful and control the breathing, Ms. Hopkins had said. *Stay in the present mind.* I sure as shit was in the present moment. But sometimes you'd prefer not to be.

Maybe this guy would turn and go back upstairs, but I doubted it. Unlike history teachers, guys like this were likely the overzealous type.

I heard the gunman continue slowly in my direction. I hadn't seen the guy, only heard him, so to be fair, he may not have been a "gunman," but seeing as I had about three seconds before this guy poked his head around these boxes, I figured it was probably prudent to assume he had one ready to stick in my face.

~

"Okay, turn off the jammer," Reilly said into his Bluetooth. He was standing on the auditorium stage looking out at an audience of panicked students and teachers. A handful of his guys were posted in the aisles like ushers, albeit brandishing rifles instead of Playbills, offering menacing glances in lieu of assistance.

This must be how actors feel, he thought, *a packed house hanging on their every word and movement.* He would bet 20 percent of these kids had been diagnosed with ADD. Adderall or not, 0 percent were currently having any issue with keeping anything less than a laser focus on him standing centerstage. His own men too. But their laser focus came not from fear but from the "go pills" they'd taken earlier, these even better than the official ones they'd gotten back when Reilly was in the Air Force running night missions. G had gotten them black–ops level stuff this time. Maybe it was the scholastic environment, but for some reason Reilly thought in SAT question form as he looked out at the hundreds of eyes glued to him: Adderall is to G's pills, as decaf coffee is to . . .

. . . a rail of pure Bolivian coke.

Even though Javier and Russell hadn't returned from the sweep, Reilly figured it was safe to begin. "Take out your phones and call whomever you need to," he said in his deepest baritone. "You have one minute starting now."

Nobody moved. A mass terror kept them from following the order.

"I said, call." Reilly nodded to Trotter. Trotter unloaded his clip into the ceiling above the crowd. Plaster, paint, and shards of wood rained down on the crowd as the rat-a-tat-tat of the M-4 filled the air.

When the rifle went silent, Reilly continued, "59, 58, 57 ..."

Frantically, nearly everyone in the auditorium pulled out a phone and dialed. The room was filled with the sounds of screaming and crying as they desperately begged for help into their devices. The kids who didn't have their phones on them pleaded with those next to them to use theirs. One person doing neither was Kira. Not because she didn't have a phone. Not because she was too scared to call. Because of Braydon.

When the minute was up, Reilly radioed his guy on the roof to turn the jammer back on. Even though all phone service was lost again, for some the crying and pleading into the phones continued for another minute. Those dozen or so who were still pleading to their blank screen, those, Reilly knew, those were the ones who would do anything to get out of this. When fear had overtaken all sense of reason, you owned that person.

CHAPTER NINE

Theoretically, a fist hitting the side of a human's head should feel the same whether on an MMA mat or in the basement of the history department. Whether the head in question is your welterweight opponent or a man holding a gun searching for you. You know what, though? It sure as fuck doesn't. Having the advantage of surprise (great, sure, but I'd have preferred his advantage, that of a gun and who knows what else) I had leapt from behind the boxes and landed a headshot. It had felt like my hand had travelled through his cheekbone and out the other side of his head. It felt effortless. And it reminded me of the book Kira lent me back when we first met. *Zen in the Art of Archery.* I read it but had dismissed it as something some teacher had added to the syllabus just because of the *Hunger Games* movies. Between that and *Brave*, there was a semester there where every girl in school had been obsessed with all things archery. But now I understood. My body doing something without any conscious control coming from the mind.

The same could be said of the underhook to the meat of the guy's neck, the overhand right to the temple and the double leg takedown that I took him to the floor with before he had a chance to retaliate. Knowing the guy had size and undoubtedly experience on me, I figured I needed to level as many hits as possible before the one advantage I had—surprise—was lost.

The second we hit the ground, I slipped my arm around his neck and crammed my forearm back up and into his throat, hoping to get him in a rear-naked chokehold before he realized what was happening. Pressing my forearm inward, I used my other arm to wrap his right arm backward. I jammed my knee up onto the arm, pinning it against his ribcage, and then pushed my own arm into the back of his neck, squeezing my two forearms together, with the neck in between.

I had never choked anyone out before. I'd gotten a lotta opponents in this exact hold, but they had always tapped out before getting any further. As the body started to go limp, I wondered, where is the line exactly? That sweet spot where you can be assured someone is out cold but not out forever? I was pretty keen on the former, but being responsible for the latter scared me almost as much as I feared for my own life.

If this were a movie, this would be when "Washington, D.C." appears on the bottom of the screen with the staccato sound of teletype over a sweeping view of the Capitol Building, the Washington Monument, and the White House. Maybe followed by a few folks striding purposefully into the Oval Office. Or a general entering the briefing room. Today, though, it's just the seventeenth fairway at Congressional Country Club. Senator Ben Hastings standing over a Titleist XL-3 with a 7-iron in his hand, 150 feet from the pin. A golf cart hurrying towards his foursome from the direction of the green.

Hastings didn't wait. He took a full cut at the ball and lofted it over the oncoming golf cart.

"Sir, there's been an incident," the man in the passenger seat said when they pulled up next to Hastings.

"Twenty bucks says a cop shot someone," Hastings said to his playing partner.

"I'll take 'train derailed,'" laughed the other man.

"There's been a school *event*."

"I knew I should have taken school shooting. It was too easy, though."

His aide held out a briefing report, but Hastings ignored it and started to get into his cart.

"Sir, I think you should look . . ."

"Put out a release, 'horrible tragedy . . . and in these times we must all stick together,' yada, yada, all the rest."

"Sir, you'll really want to take a look."

Hastings snatched the briefing from the aide's hand and started to scan.

It wasn't until he saw the words St. Frederick Academy that his face blanched.

As Preston set up his gear in the back corner of the stage, he was still fuming at Reilly. He didn't blame the guy, Trotter, for bashing his jaw with the rifle. Trotter had no idea he was one of them. Preston figured Reilly, though, would have told them all that they had someone on the inside, doing intel beforehand. But no, Reilly, being Reilly, had kept it to himself. Now Preston had . . . maybe not a fractured jaw, but he was definitely going to need major dental work when this was over. Preston knew he looked way younger than the twenty-eight years he was; that's why Reilly chose him to enroll and gather info on the place they'd never get from building plans or staff schedules; but once he started yelling at Trotter that he was one of them, he assumed the big dummy would figure it out.

Preston rubbed his jaw as he plugged one of his three laptops into the theater's AV console. The large screen at the back of the stage lit up with a four-sectioned video feed. One corner of the screen showed the scene outside the gate where squadrons of police cars unloaded. The other three quadrants alternately displayed more locales around campus, streaming from all the minicams Preston had set up over the last few days.

Reilly stood behind Preston and surveyed the scene outside the gates. "Alright, we got the local. Let's see how long it takes to get higher up the chain." He handed Preston a flash drive. "Pull up their pictures."

As Preston loaded the flash drive, Reilly toggled one of the remote cameras, focusing the feed on a Channel 3 Local News van pulling up. Reilly smiled. "It's a statement of the times that the news gets here before the Feds do. This is going to be catnip to them. Rich kids. Hostages. Terrorists."

Preston pointed to the newscaster climbing eagerly out of the van. "Look at him. He looks like a guy who just hit the lottery, can't even pretend he's not ecstatic that he's finally going to get to do national news."

"Story of the year, my friend, story of the year."

CHAPTER TEN

If there was ever someone who could simply hide out until all this—whatever *this* was—blew over, it was probably me. Whether it was from taking classes I wasn't in or just killing time, I knew every attic, air duct, and cubbyhole throughout St. Frederick. But I had to get out of this particular building first. And fast. They'd be looking for the guy I had just choked unconscious. At least, I thought unconscious. It might be worse; I hadn't waited around to check for a pulse, and now the prospect that I may have killed someone sent a chill through me.

There was one problem with hiding out, though. I could do it, but what about my mother?

If I had stopped to really think about it, I would have answered that question with another: *what exactly do I think I could ever do?* But I hadn't stopped to think about it, and instead of doing the sensible thing and finding a place to hole up, I had sprinted out of the basement and was now peering out the side-door window that faced the wide stretch of lawn, maybe two hundred feet standing between here and the Headmaster's office building. From my vantage point I couldn't see anyone, so I pushed the door open.

Stop.

My brain finally caught up to my body.

Stop.

I can see how people do stupid things when panic sets in. The last two minutes or so since I had jumped the guy were a whirl of chaos. And the panic coursing through me was about to send me barreling out this door into who knows what.

I leaned back against the door frame and closed my eyes. The sound in my ears was like a white noise machine hooked up to a 10,000-watt concert amp. *Stop,* I repeated to myself. *Let it settle.* I knew it was just a physiological reaction, my body literally increasing blood flow, muscle tension, heart rate—all animal reactions to a perceived threat. But it wasn't perceived. It was the real thing. Still, I had to get my brain back to running things and not merely animal reaction.

Okay, so what was going on out there? I generally viewed things through an Occam's Razor lens where the simplest solution is the most likely, but I couldn't imagine what was the most obvious scenario of whatever the fuck was happening right now.

I hadn't heard many gunshots, so it wasn't a death toll they were after. Hostages? Were they looking for someone? And how many were doing the looking?

I peered back through the window and watched for maybe five minutes. Twice, gunmen walked through this section of campus. Farther away, I could see two other men in black fatigues running some sort of wire along the length of the high stone wall that encircled the campus. Every twenty feet or so, they hitched a small metal device the shape of a hand grenade. I couldn't tell what they were, but it didn't take too much extrapolating to tell it wouldn't end well for anyone trying to scale the wall. In or out.

I figured it would take me eight to ten seconds to sprint across to the Headmaster's building. Staring down the barrel of that two-hundred-foot stretch of open lawn, I now wished I had thought to take one of the guns off the guy I choked out. I highly doubted I would be able to shoot someone, but, put in the right (rather, wrong) situation, who knows? It was irrelevant, though. I had taken the guy's rifle and handgun but only to hide them so he wouldn't find them if he woke up. In searching him for the second gun, I had also found a radio-looking device, three spare cartridges, and a thin black case, about the size of a smartphone.

Ten seconds. That's all I needed. The green was empty. The only person visible now was the guy on the roof of the cafeteria, and he wasn't even looking in my direction. His rifle was propped up on the roof's edge and targeted out toward the arriving cop cars. He had his gaze through the gunsight, but if I were to make a run for it across the green, then the movement in his peripheral vision might make him look my way. If I walked casually, though, I might make it. It reminded me of the psych study with the gorilla that Kira was telling us about on the trip up to New Hampshire. Supposedly, they had subjects focus on a video of two people throwing a ball back and forth. At some point in the video, a gorilla—well not a real one, but a guy in a gorilla suit—walks behind the pair throwing the ball. Should be obvious, sure, but in the instances where the subjects were told to count the number of tosses being made, they often never even noticed the gorilla. Another crazy quirk of the human brain— our minds going myopic when we focus on something.

Cool study, sure, but was I really going to risk casually walking out into the wide open space in the hopes this guy's focus wouldn't be jarred? Just because of some stupid study with a dude in an ape suit? Not a chance.

Not a chance . . . *if* I had a better option. But the only other option I had was to hide. And while that might be the Occam-y thing to do, I couldn't. Even though I knew it was stupid, I needed to try. Maybe they already took her. Maybe she escaped. Or maybe she was…I didn't even want to think about it. Either way, it didn't matter. Whether there's anything I could do or not, I needed to know my mother was safe.

I stepped out the door of the history building and walked at a casual pace, every part of my being screaming, "RUUUUUU-UUNNNNN!" To calm myself, I counted my steps. Figured it's about eighty of them to the Headmaster's office. I was at twenty-one when I realized something: the gorilla study might not be so ridiculous after all. Not because the guy hadn't noticed yet, rather for the fact that for twenty-one steps I was so focused on not giving in to the panic to run, that not once had I wondered whether the guy on the roof was at this moment turning his rifle in my direction and about to put a .30 caliber bullet through the side of my skull.

22 . . . 23 . . . 24 . . . 25 . . .

≈

Cue the "Washington, D.C." teletype again. This time: The Oval Office. The President, his advisors, and Senator Hastings were watching a cable TV "Breaking News" segment that, for a change, truly was.

" . . . if they are, Michael, we don't know yet," the reporter on screen said. "There have been no demands made. I've been told it appears there may be ten, even twenty armed men. At this point, the police seem to be assessing it as a hostage situation, not a terrorist one . . ."

"Fuck's the difference?" muttered Hastings.

" . . . Much of St. Frederick Academy's student body is made up of children of elite, wealthy parents." As the reporter contin-ued, a stock photo of the school appeared on screen. "So—and not to speculate here—we could very well be seeing a ransom scenario here."

"Not to speculate?" the President said, shaking his head. "Do they ever hear themselves?"

The Chief of Staff handed the President a briefing paper and said, "At this point we are in a holding pattern. We've got a few Feds on the ground there, but we don't want to turn out too big a presence in the event—"

"What are you talking about, Cal?" barked Hastings. "Send in everyone."

"Look, Ben, I realize this is a personal situation for you," the Chief of Staff said, "but you have to look at it from a macro standpoint."

"Fuck you and your macro standpoint." Then, turning toward the President, "Sir, you need to get every SWAT team in the Northeast on alert. I don't want some dumpy local cop trying to save my son."

"Look, Ben, they are taking care—"

"That isn't good enough. I need you taking care of it." Hastings leaned forward against the desk. "You *owe* me."

~

. . . 78, 79, 80. I now realized I had vastly underestimated. Eighty steps and yet the door to the Headmaster's office was still another thirty or forty away. An eternity at this pace.

Off to my right, but out of sight behind the building, I heard two voices getting closer. Run and risk the sniper noticing me, or keep walking and hope the voices didn't appear before I got in the door. I did a mental coin flip and, heads, I kept walking.

Fifteen feet from the door, the voices got louder. My stomach got queasier.

Ten. I watched the corner of the building around which the voices were closing in.

Five. I saw the shadow of two men poke around the corner. *Fuck it;* I sprinted to the door and slid in. I ran up the steps, hoping A) the sniper wasn't now calling over the radio to say he'd seen me go inside, B) the two men weren't racing for the door to follow me, and most pressing of all, C) there wasn't a gunman standing at the top of the stairs outside the Headmaster's office. If there was, I was about to run directly into him.

~

"All set," Preston said to Reilly.

"Put 'em up."

Preston tapped his keyboard a couple times and the footage of the cops and news crew disappeared. Taking its place up on the auditorium screen were ten photos. From the audience section came scattered gasps.

Reilly addressed the crowd of students and teachers. "You ten . . . up here now." Nobody moved. "Am I really going to have to have someone shoot up the ceiling again? Get up here now. Or one of these guys will be dragging you up here."

A girl in the third row stood and walked toward the stage. Slowly, others stood and joined her, Sean, Reece, and Weav among them. Nine students of varying ages, varying degrees of fear coursing through them, stood at the edge of the stage, matching headshots on the screen above.

"Yoohoo, where are you?" Reilly cooed in a sing-song voice. He looked at the nine kids and then up to the pictures. He had an almost savant-like ability to distill information; it took him a mere glance to narrow out who was missing. "Oh, Braaaaaayyy-donnnn . . . you missed your cue."

Reilly scanned the audience. It wouldn't take a savant to figure out who Braydon was. The cluster of audience members staring at the occupant of seat 32E would clue in even the slowest among his crew. Its occupant apparently had a pretty good excuse for not having responded to his request, though. The terrified ten-year-old boy's face had a purplish hue and, hard as he tried to inhale, he couldn't seem to catch his breath. Stress and asthma did not go well together. Rather, they went *too* well together. And for Braydon, the combo had supercharged his asthma attack. He may as well have been breathing under water.

~

At the top of the stairs I bolted to the right. Being a novice at the whole running-for-your-life thing, I didn't consider what I might be running directly into, but luckily, at least so far, I hadn't encountered anyone. I ducked to the floor and slowly made my way under the windows of Headmaster Harkin's waiting room, where my mother's desk was. I paused by the door and listened. Nothing. I peered around the corner. Empty.

I stood and entered the waiting room. The door leading to the Headmaster's office was closed. Which was strange. Harkin took the "open door policy" literally, and never closed his. My mother had told me once it was more out of loneliness than anything else. I snuck as quietly as I could and pressed an ear against the door. Again, no sound.

Was I worried about what might be waiting behind a closed door when there were a bunch of jacked-up men running around loaded with military-grade weaponry? Um, yes. Did I still push the door open? Yep. Although, as I eased the door open and peered around, I did think—and way too late—that I had zero idea what I was going to do if someone was there. If they had my mother at gunpoint? This might have been one of the dumbest ideas I'd ever had.

Luckily, no one was there, but I stopped again and took ten slow breaths the way Ms. Hopkins had taught us. I needed to calm my whole being. I was being stupid, not thinking right, and if I kept it up, I wasn't going to do my mother or me any good.

I stood in my mother's office, my ears on alert for the sound of anyone coming, but my eyes closed as I slowly breathed in through the nose and out through the mouth. As my brain started to finally slow, I could see the stupidity of my earlier rashness. Exhaling on number eight, I decided what I'd do. Seeing as they must have searched in here already, and have little reason to come back, I'd hide in Harkin's closet and wait this thing out until the cops or whoever did something. I took the next breath even slower, and the idea of hiding safely calmed my mind even more. It was on the tenth breath when it hit me. *Her picture frame.* It had been lying flat on its face. This must have registered in my subconscious when I came in looking for her. I opened my eyes and for a moment, I wondered if she had been so disappointed in me when I left earlier that she couldn't bear to have her son staring back at her, even the eight-year-old version, clutching that tiny chess trophy and grinning at the camera. The thought stopped me long enough that I noticed the rest. On the computer screen were some student photos. But that wasn't what caused me to freeze. What did was the blood smeared on the keyboard—from which the letters J and K were missing, presumably from when whoever's blood this was had their face slammed into the keys.

I had been scared earlier. From the moment I heard that guy enter the history building, to when I sneaked across the green, to when I walked into this office, all that time I could feel my heart on tilt, and a constant fear coursing through me. In a flash it was all gone, replaced by something even more visceral. Primal.

Seeing the blood on my mother's keyboard, I could extrapolate to one of these gunmen smashing her small face to the desk, busting her nose, her lips, maybe knocking loose a few teeth. I'd felt this way once before, and it was triggered by something depressingly similar. The sight of my mother's blood. And like that time when I stood behind her watching her spitting blood into the kitchen sink, I felt the same rage flooding through me again, making me focus. And as I had known that night when I went looking for my father, I knew it was a doomed cause. But I had to do something.

CHAPTER ELEVEN

Kira had had her eye on Braydon from the moment they brought him in. Poor guy was probably too scared to move, she thought. She had noticed him slumped in his seat earlier, but now with his face a disturbing purple shade, she knew it wasn't just fear, and she instinctively stood and made her way up the center aisle.

"*You.* Sit," Trotter said as Kira approached Braydon's row.

"Look at him. He needs help."

Trotter looked to Reilly up onstage. Reilly studied Kira a moment, then nodded, and Trotter lowered his gun.

Kira slipped in next to him. "Bray, it's okay. It's okay." She softly ran her hand over Braydon's arm, then patted his pants pockets. "Where is your inhaler?"

Braydon tried to speak between gasps but couldn't get out any words. He pointed toward the door.

"Your locker?"

Braydon nodded frantically.

Kira helped Braydon to his feet and started up the aisle. Trotter stuck the end of his rifle into her chest. "Sit."

"No."

"I said sit. No one goes anywhere."

"He's got acute asthma." Kira said this directly to Reilly, not Trotter. It was obvious to her who was calling the shots. "He needs his inhaler."

"Half of everyone in here is on Zoloft or Adderall or who knows what? I'm supposed to let every one of you get your meds?" Reilly grinned at her as he spoke.

Kira looked at the gunman standing over her. *How did this happen?* Not just the situation as a whole. Rather, how did she find herself here with Braydon? She hadn't meant to do anything. It was instinct to stand. She remembered what it was like being a ten-year-old kid here. Her parents had sent her to boarding school in second grade. Every single day those first couple years, she was scared. Of everything. It took a while, but she had grown from it and had promised herself she would never be scared of anything. Never scared of being alone. This was different, though. The fear had started to come back. But when she had seen Braydon, scared and panicked and in trouble, she hadn't hesitated. Now, she did. If this guy let her get the inhaler, what would he do once they had it? It occurred to her that it was the ten kids they were interested in. She didn't know why. It meant the others were expendable. And she was one of the others.

"He will die."

"Does it look like something I'm bothered by?"

Kira was no dummy. "He's one of the ones up there," she said, nodding toward the screen.

Reilly stared at her for a beat, then grinned again. "Take 'em," Reilly said to Trotter. "Both of them."

By the time they reached McKinley Hall, most of Braydon's weight was on Kira's shoulder. As Kira labored to get him up the entryway stairs, she said to Trotter, "You could help me move him, you know."

"Oh, I know." Trotter smirked. "You look like you got it under control. I'll get the door for you though." He opened the tall oak door to McKinley Hall and swept his hand in an exaggeratedly obsequious gesture.

Kira dragged Braydon down the hallway. "Bray, which one? Just point."

Braydon gestured toward the far end of the hallway. The lights were off and even though it was daytime, the hallway's lack of windows gave the place a look of twilight. Again she thought to herself: *How did this happen?* With each step she seemed to be getting herself drawn further into something she couldn't control. But still, she moved up the hallway.

At the locker, Braydon whispered the combination. Kira entered it, but when she yanked on the lock, it didn't open. "33-10-8?"

Braydon shook his head side to side. He tried to say something but couldn't get any words out.

"33?"

Braydon nodded yes.

"10?"

Yes again.

"8?"

He shook his head no and pointed to the ceiling.

"9? 10?"

Again Braydon shook his head. He jabbed his finger toward the ceiling multiple times.

"15? 20?"

Braydon's eyes closed.

"Braydon!" Kira shook him, but he had gone motionless. *33-10-What?* Kira realized she didn't have the time to try all the variations. It sounded like eight, but he had said higher. Maybe he had said 18. Kira spun 33-10-18 and yanked. The lock held firm. "Come on! Open!" She spun again as fast as she could, trying 33-10-28 this time. As she turned the dial right from 10 to 28, she thought, *If this isn't it . . .*

She stopped on 28 and pulled.

The lock didn't open.

Out of frustration more than hope, she yanked again, this time much harder. The corroded lock clicked open. Pulling the door open, she dug through the backpack hanging from the hook. *It's a good thing asthma is on the rise these days,* Kira thought. Otherwise she wouldn't have known how to assemble the gadget. But seeing as she had watched Fiona and a bunch of others do it hundreds of times, she knew to take the gun cartridge–looking thing, shake it, slip the cap off, and cram it into the plastic spacer. She then pressed it up against Braydon's face, covering his mouth and nose, and squeezed the top of the cartridge.

Kira couldn't tell whether Braydon actually inhaled anything. She squeezed off another round. "Breathe!" She shook Braydon and then pumped the cartridge again. This time she could feel Braydon's chest expand ever so slightly. "Come on, Bray . . ." Kira gave him another three pumps, hoping you couldn't give someone too much.

His eyes remained closed, but slowly Braydon's breathing returned, if not to normal, at least to a serviceable amount, and his face, though still discolored, began to lighten.

"Okay, let's go." Trotter lifted Braydon by the collar of his shirt and dragged him back the way they came.

"Hey! Easy!" Kira said, getting to her feet.

"He's out of it. He ain't feeling a thing." Trotter grinned.

As Trotter dragged Braydon up the hallway, his shirt collar tore and he thumped to the floor. Trotter leaned over to adjust his grip, Kira grabbed his arm. He swatted at Kira, slamming her up against the wall.

"You know," said Trotter as he picked up Kira by the neck and pressed her against the wall, "we may need him. But you? No one gives a shit." He squeezed his grip tighter, his fingertips burrowing between the tendons of her neck. Kira writhed in pain and tried to squirm free, but he had more than a hundred pounds on her. In the throes of sheer panic, an image shot across her vision. A fuzzy image of a body running toward her, behind this man who had his hand clasped around her neck. *It must be a near-death hallucination,* she thought as panic turned to hopelessness. *One last vision before everything goes black.*

But, odd, this vision had a chair leg in its hand. Even odder, this vision was swinging said chair leg toward the side of the man's head. And oddest of all, she thought as her eyes started to close, this vision looked a lot like Cade.

~

Outside the gates the police presence had grown from a couple local sheriffs to what now included an alphabet soup of agencies: FBI, NSA, USSS . . . ETC.

Two copters lowered to the ground, their blades blowing dust toward the large, sleek silver control trailer that had been brought in by the Homeland Security team.

So far the chain of command had changed hands three times. But none mattered once they saw Britt Pruitt step out of the second copter and cross to the control trailer. Jackson, the FBI man and latest in charge, thought, *Wow, Pruitt? She wouldn't be here without a call from high up. Way up. The top.* Kids in a hostage situation, he expected Homeland Security, sure, maybe even NSA, but Pruitt? You know you're up there when no one really knows your acronym.

Once inside the trailer, Pruitt, a thirty-five-year-old woman with the demeanor of someone who had just finished a two-hour Hatha yoga session, scanned the room. Her surface calm should not be mistaken for serenity, though. Beneath that calm was a ferocity hard earned from her Army days and all the stops since. She locked eyes with Jackson. "So?" Pruitt said, posing this open-ended two-letter question to him alone.

"Fifteen armed. At least. Possibly twenty. 828 hostages. Kids. Teachers. Staff. 828, that is, if no one took a sick day today." He tapped his finger on the video monitor displaying an overhead satellite shot of the grounds. "Gunmen here, here, and here. This building here, the auditorium? Most, if not all, hostages are being held there."

"Contact?"

"Not from them, but there was a sixty-second window of calls coming out before they jammed the signal again."

"You gather the numbers?"

"No."

"Get them. Every person that was called, I want to find out details. Anything that might have been said to give us a hint as to what is going on in there. Contact carrier servers."

"You heard her," Jackson said to the three guys staffing the large computer terminals below the video screen.

"So no cell service now. Have you sent in a line of communication?"

"Before we could, they sent this." Jackson held up a small radio.

"But no contact yet?"

"He said he was waiting for you."

CHAPTER TWELVE

Did I want to be punching someone in the throat right now? There were two answers to that. The simple one: *No fucking way.* The second, overriding one: *I don't have a choice.*

Well, theoretically, there was a choice to be made. Watch this dude choke Kira to death or jump a guy who A) was huge, B) had a gun, and C) probably had many other guns. I wouldn't even be facing this choice if I hadn't made another one only a few minutes ago. That was when I had peered out of the Head-master's building, trying to decide what to do next, and saw Kira and Braydon being brought into McKinley Hall for some reason. I had no idea why, but it couldn't be good.

McKinley Hall abuts the Headmaster's building, so it was easy to sneak over. Now, though, watching them in the reflection of the mirror at the end of the hallway, I froze. My back pressed against the wall, I again hesitated on my next move. It seemed insane to think I could try to rescue the two of them. *Rescue.* What was I thinking? I had gotten lucky with the guy in the basement . . . caught him off guard and was able to take him out. What were the odds of it happening again? 1 percent? This guy looked bigger and meaner. 0.0001 percent? But what's the other option? Run? Hide? Turn myself in and hope?

That was sounding like a much better option. At least until the guy grabbed Kira's neck in a vice grip. Did I run toward them because of some involuntary heroic gesture? Sure, let's go with that. And not the fact that it may have been spurred by a cold rationalization. It doesn't take much wisdom to know this about human nature: it's not the things we do that we regret; it's what we don't do that eats at us later. And I couldn't imagine going through the rest of my life knowing I hadn't tried something.

The *something* started well: a chair leg to the side of the guy's head. The punch to his neck fared well too. Two for two. The guy released his grip from Kira's neck, and I could see her drop to her knees, sucking in air. But after that, it started to go downhill.

You'd like to think a wooden chair leg to the head, paired with a wad of knuckles to the side of the neck, would be enough to drop—if not KO—someone, but all it did was daze him. Given his significant size advantage, I had been counting on a little more than dazed. I'd have even taken stunned. I swung again and hit him with two quick blows below the ear. This punch I had learned not from my mixed martial arts coach, but rather from Mr. Craig, a janitor who always stopped me on my mail route to expound on some non-sequitur. One time he was telling me about how he'd taken care of a bully when he was in high school. "Don't go for the face. Go for the ear. If you want to take the fight completely out of someone, one quick blow just below the ear sucks it all out of them." Probably great advice for taking on a cocky sixteen-year-old bully. This guy barely flinched. His back was still to me when I punched him, and without turning he swung one paw around and grabbed a handful of my hair. Pulling me forward, he slammed me to the floor. I tried to roll out, but he drove his knee into my chest and then rammed his forearm into my neck. Leaning his weight into it, he cut off my airway. If I were fighting at the studio, this was the point I would be tapping out. Actually, *way* past that point.

But tapping out wasn't an option. If I didn't do something in the next few seconds, my world would cease to exist. Kira had once told me about sense memory exercises in acting. You layer something from your past on the words in the play and a similar emotion comes out, or something like that. I tried thinking of the worst thing my father did. Tried to channel every bit of anger I ever had and thrust myself up at him, but the guy was too big. He just repositioned himself and squeezed harder.

And then, from somewhere deep in the recesses of my brain, I saw it. The move I needed. I didn't even know the name of it, but my instructor must have taught it to me at some point. I reached up and wrapped my hands around the crown of the man's head, then, pressing my forearms in on his jaw, I yanked hard right. The head leads the body, and his body rocked enough to the side that I was able to get a knee free and drive it up into his torso, toppling him over. As I rolled up and out, I slipped my right arm under his and bent it backward. The man's right arm rotated so far back that it looked like an optical illusion. His primal scream indicated it was anything but an illusion.

Not surprisingly, an arm torn from its shoulder socket took a little of the fight out of this dude. While still wrenching his one arm back, I used my other arm to slowly choke a man out for the second time today.

"Is he dead?" Kira said in a raspy voice as she got to her feet. The way she stared at the limp body now lying on the ground, she looked like she may have still been in shock.

"No." I was pretty confident I'd gotten a better idea of the sweet spot this time. "Just unconscious. We gotta get outta here." I nodded at Braydon. "Is he alright?"

Kira bent down. "I don't know. He's breathing. But not by much."

She checked on Braydon, and I reached inside the big guy's jacket looking for his gun. As I slid it out of the holster, I noticed another slim smartphone-shaped black case, just like the one the first guy had.

"Let's go. They're going to be wondering where you guys are." I tried to slip the gun into the back of my waistline like I'd seen in so many movies, but it wouldn't fit. *Crap, these things are thicker than you think.* It wasn't as easy as they made it look; I'd have to loosen my belt buckle if I wanted to get it in there.

"No." Kira propped Braydon up against the lockers. His eyes were closed and his face was a color I'd never seen.

"He's breathing. They'll find him. If we go now, I think I know where we can hide."

"These guys don't care about him. They'll let him die."

"We can't drag him out of here."

"I know. You go."

The thing to do would be grab her arm, pull her off, and say, *That's crazy; let's get out of here.* But knowing Kira, she would never leave him. Definitely a quality I've always loved about her, this sense of, I don't know what you call it, this sense of always doing the right thing. Although in this moment, I wished she were a bit more of a selfish dick.

Even in the craziness of it, I found myself editing what I wanted to say. I started to say, "No, *we* have to go. If any—" but then I stopped. Instead I just stood there wasting what little time we had. It's something that drove me nuts. Always editing what I say. Every conversation I had was a series of things I wanted to say, and then all the things I said instead. Especially, it seemed, with Kira. I'd never left a conversation with her without getting the feeling I misspoke. Or rather, didn't speak the thing I wanted to say. It's never about not knowing what to say. It's not having the balls to say it. Even now.

There was a loud bang from the other end of the building; it sounded like someone slamming open the front door of the building. If so, we had only seconds. Ten if they guessed the right hallway. If they didn't, then at best, thirty.

"They probably have no idea you're here," she said. "Even if I tried to run, they'd know to look for me. You can still go. Hide somewhere. You know this place better than anyone."

I wasn't great at reading people's facial expressions. I was always amazed when someone, like say my mother, could call me out on my mood based on a look. Maybe I was a sociopath with no empathy, so that's why I could never read anyone. But for a second I saw something in her look when she said I knew this place better than anyone. It was like she knew something about me. Like she was wordlessly saying *I know you better than you think.*

Then again, maybe it was wishful thinking. And, with the footsteps banging closer, kind of a stupid time for me to get mushy.

She was right. I could still run; she couldn't. And so I did.

As I ran into the lecture hall and toward the side door that led out onto the green, I thought about what it was this time that I hadn't said. It was this: *If anything ever happened to you . . .*

But this time, in my mind I even imagined a response. Kira looking up from her spot on the floor against the lockers, smiling ever so slightly, and saying, *If anything ever happened to you . . .*

It really made me think there may have been something wrong with me. This was not the kind of thing you were supposed to be thinking about as you ran for your life.

CHAPTER THIRTEEN

Liz pulled her shirt collar from where she had been pressing it against her bloated lip. She'd stopped the bleeding from when Reilly had slammed her face into the keyboard after she pretended to be unable to access the files, but she could still taste the salty sensation of the blood in her mouth and feel her right eye closing up as the area around her cheekbone swelled.

Even if somehow Cade is hiding, she thought, *what if someone realizes he is missing and says something?* She silently pleaded as though somehow he would hear her thoughts: *Come on, Cade; be smart and stay in one of your hiding spots.* He thought she didn't know about that, but there were a lot of things she knew that he didn't think she did. Like the fact she knew his mail route didn't really cover the Headmaster's office. Garvey had told her once that Cade took this stop from another kid. Having him come by to drop off her mail each morning was the best thing about her day. Hopefully right now he was tucked away in some attic, waiting this whole thing out. She couldn't imagine what she'd do if he was one of the nine kids these maniacs had at gunpoint up onstage.

Liz had been watching the men in black return now and again with another stray kid they had apparently rustled up, or, now, Kira and Braydon, who were being brought back in. The larger man was carrying Braydon over his shoulder, and she couldn't be sure if he was still alive. Each time the door had opened, she had expected to see Cade being brought in, but he hadn't shown yet. *On the one hand, that's good,* she figured; *maybe he got away. On the other, maybe they . . .*

She couldn't bring herself to finish that train of thought.

While the other eight kids on stage watched as Braydon was carried in and dumped on the stage with them, Sean had his eyes on Reilly. Sean knew this was the man he had to figure out. No one else mattered. This guy controlled the situation, and if Sean was going to get out, it was through him.

"What the fuck?" Weav whispered. He was seated shoulder to shoulder with Sean. "Is he dead?"

If anything, Sean was more pissed at Weav and Reece than he was at the men with the guns. Those two lost it from the start and had been blubbering on and off since they got pulled up on stage. Sean, on the other hand—at least after the initial shock— had been pretty fricking stoic if he was going to be honest with himself. "He's fine. They need him." Sean hadn't figured out yet why, but he was fairly certain they needed the ten of them that were on stage. And it occurred to him that, paradoxically, they were probably in the safest spot.

"For what?"

"Whatever they need us for." Sean had an inkling. He didn't know for sure, but as soon as he had looked at the other nine they had chosen, he realized a connection of sorts.

"No shit. But what's *that?* They're going to fucking kill us."

"If they wanted to just start killing some random people, they wouldn't have chosen us," Sean said, his eyes still on Reilly, who at the moment was stepping off the stage and walking slowly toward Kira. Sean still couldn't believe how stupid Kira had been offering to take Braydon; she was lucky they hadn't killed her. He had to laugh. *I guess all that social worker save-the-world yada yada she talked about sure as shit wasn't an act.*

"What are you talking about?"

Sean looked at Weav. *Fucking stoner.* "Really? You don't see the connection?" Sean turned his attention back to Reilly, who was standing over Kira.

"The security guard?" Reilly asked skeptically.

"Yeah," Kira replied.

"She said the guy jumped Trotter with a chair leg," Edwards, the one who brought her in, said. He was laughing. "Trotter said it was a baseball bat."

"What security guard?" Reilly asked.

Edwards shrugged. "We searched the building. There was no one there."

"A security guard," Reilly said dryly. "And then he just took off?"

"What, you think it was me?" Kira said. "Me who jumped your guy and choked him out? I wish."

"Preston, run the names again. The support staff." Then to Kira, "Name. What's his name?"

"Spencer. Dickie Spencer." Kira was ready. She said it without missing a beat. In fact, she even slowed her answer a split second, knowing that too eager a response would read suspicious. Once Cade had finally run off, Kira knew she'd have to give someone's name and she knew Mr. Spencer always took his mother to dialysis on Tuesdays.

"Get me a picture."

"Ahead of you, boss. Here." A picture of a security guard in his mid-thirties appeared on the auditorium screen. Kira was relieved to see they had pulled his application photo from ten years ago. From back when he still exercised and hadn't gotten into the cooking shows he was always talking about. From when it looked like it was at least feasible he might have snuck up on a guy like Trotter and taken him out.

"Edwards. Martinez. Josephs. Find him. Shoot him."

They never will, thought Kira. Never would Dickie Spencer have been happier to be at his mother's dialysis treatment. This didn't make Kira feel any better, though, seeing as the person they were going to find instead was Cade. Like Liz, she too had some silent advice for Cade, but hers went more like this: *Hide. Just hide, and don't do something stupid.*

She didn't have a lot of faith.

~

As I pressed myself up against the outer wall of McKinley Hall, hidden behind the ivy draped on the side of the building, I watched three men, guns pulled, run across the green toward the building . . . *this* building. Literally fifty feet away, in plain sight. Plain sight for me, that is. They, on the other hand, ran right by me without noticing I was hidden behind the lush ivy hanging off the side of the building.

When I had left Kira and Braydon, rather than run, I had counterintuitively stayed put and hid in plain sight. I'd always rolled my eyes at these ivy-covered buildings. Where else but some snobby prep school would you ever think to obscure your walls with plants and thus trap moisture, which only leads to rot? But now I was grateful for such an idiotic tradition. I could see out, see everything across the main campus green, and unless they thought to take a close look—and why would they? What kind of idiot wouldn't be running for his life?—they'd never spot me.

It was a good theory, but in practice it was beginning to freak me out. At least running felt like you were doing something. Standing dead still as a guy with a rifle walked by, not twenty feet from you, washed a tsunami of panic over you. It was like a case of claustrophobia wrapped in a suffocating bubble. My whole being wanted nothing more than to rip away the ivy and run. But running would have only made me more likely to be caught. Or shot. Staying put was still the safest bet.

But how long before they found me? How long before I freaked the fuck out?

~

"They sent it out by drone," Jackson said as Pruitt took the radio from him. She shook her head. *Who thinks this shit up?* That's the problem with technology. It used to be, pick up the phone, dial a number, hear the demands, and there you have it. Now a radio flown out by drone? These guys were always like little boys with toys.

"Yesssss . . ." Pruitt said into the satcom radio.

A couple beats. Nothing.

"Playing hard to get?" she asked.

"Agent Pruitt. Glad you could make it," Reilly's voice came over the radio. "Did he call you directly or did he have the president do it?"

Pruitt waited him out. She wanted to see what kind of mindset he had. Jumpy? Eager? Too casual?

"Sorry about the jammer," Reilly continued when she didn't answer. "But do feel free to keep your satcom going. You'll be needing a Wi-Fi connection soon enough."

She could tell he was calm. And not the faux, over-compensating kind, but the kind that came with having done this before. Which was impressive in itself. 90 percent of hostage takers were killed or taken. And the 10 percent that got away with it, she knew that almost none of them ever tried again.

"Shall we get all the particulars out of the way? Your fake name. How this is your last score. All the fun stuff."

"Reilly would be lovely."

The young tech next to her typed it into his system. Definitely not a real name, but her guy could maybe at least get something running the vocal patterns, Pruitt hoped.

"And sure. It's all beach drinks, sand, and women once this is over. All the usual things."

"So what's it going to take to get you into one of these lovely Suburbans we have out here? And drive you off into the Caribbean?"

"Maybe I don't plan on getting out of here."

"If I thought you were explosive vest and suicide pact types, we'd already have raided your ass. But, given what I've seen so far, this is a cash grab. So, what's your number?" Pruitt was doing some rough math in her head. The scope of this was pretty ambitious. Base minimum, they'd have to ask $50 mil. Probably a hundred. And the president had already authorized she could go full Sotheby's. This guy Reilly must've known it.

"Not my decision to make," Reilly said.

"Oh yeah? Who's in charge then? Put her on the radio." Pruitt always loved doing that last bit.

"I didn't say I wasn't in charge. I just said the amount isn't up to me. Here's what we are going to do. As a good faith gesture I'm going to send you out half of the hostages right now."

Good faith gesture, Pruitt scoffed to herself. The fact it's a logistical nightmare to hold eight hundred hostages was more like it. Bladders alone would drive him nuts. This guy had zero interest in good faith but realized, like she did, that you could just as effectively stave off a bum rush by the cops with twenty well-chosen hostages (read: rich, young, or best of all, both) as eight hundred. She had found that, paradoxically, the larger the hostage group, the more desensitized the authorities became. Humans needed to put a face on things. And if that face was a cute, scared young kid, all the more effective.

"I am going to give you ten sets of names. Once they all arrive, I will start releasing even more hostages. But if these twenty parents are not all standing beside you by 7:30 tonight, I will begin eliminating a student every fifteen minutes after."

"If you hadn't noticed, you chose the middle of nowhere for this little gathering. 7:30 is going to be tight."

"You got here from Arlington in less than an hour. I'm sure they have the assets to make it happen. Pity the kid whose mommy and daddy went to St. Kitts for the week, though. That'll make a lot of fifteen minutes."

"Give me the names. And let's keep it civil in the meantime."

"Done. The bidding will start at precisely 7:30."

The radio light blinked off.

Jackson looked at her. "Bidding?"

CHAPTER FOURTEEN

By 7 p.m. the place was a hive of activity. The construction lighting units set up by Reilly's guys lit up the HSA trailer and surrounding staging area. Overhead, the thwap-thwap of rotor blades echoed. The first four hundred hostages had already been released and shuttled away, and now for the past couple hours, private copters and high-end SUVs had been arriving at a steady pace, each occupied by a different set of parents. Or in the case of the Hastings, each in their own copter. The latest copter hovered above, its two landing skids reaching softly for the ground. A couple in their mid-forties climbed out and were led across the parking lot and into the makeshift command center. Now that Braydon's parents had arrived, seventeen of the twenty parents had made it in time. The majority of them were nervously fidgeting with their phones or huddled up in small groups whispering as they awaited news of their children.

The makeup of the seventeen parents ran the gamut. The gamut from Incredibly Rich to Obscenely Rich. Hedge funders, CEOs, old money, new money, middle-aged money. These were the one percenters that the other one percenters looked up to with the type of disdain and envy the ninety-nine percenters had for them. A good number of the parents already knew one another from traveling similar circles or serving on boards together. Three of them, Bill Weaver, Chris Taylor, and Senator Hastings, had buttonholed Pruitt and Jackson. Each of them was used to being the alpha dog in any room in which they found themselves, and they saw no reason to believe differently now.

Pruitt had been trying to explain the situation, but hadn't gotten very far seeing as the three men continually interrupted her with an ultimatum, accusation, or pontification.

"Your children are—"

"No. No, I need to speak with them now," Taylor demanded.

"That can't happen, sir," Pruitt said flatly.

"You call Ken and he will authorize it," Hastings said.

Ken. Listen to this chump, Pruitt laughed to herself. *Did he really just try to first name me the president?* "The president has given me authority on scene. I need you—"

"No, *I* need. I need you to let me communicate with these men."

"We will do everything we can to get every kid and teacher out of there unharm—"

"You better," Hastings snapped.

"Ben, you're not helping things," Weaver said.

"Neither is she," Hastings blurted out like a five-year-old on the losing end of an argument.

If I were this guy's kid, Pruitt wanted to say, *I'd probably rather be in there with a gun to me than have to spend two minutes with this prick.* "We will handle this, sir."

"The Lawrences are ten minutes out," one of the techs said.

Pruitt looked at the clock. 7:08. *Okay, they'll make it. That makes nineteen.* She looked at the woman standing by herself. "Any word from your husband, Mrs. Collier?"

Mrs. Collier, her face white, shook her head, no.

Pruitt nodded, thinking, *Someone picked the wrong night to go off the grid with his mistress.*

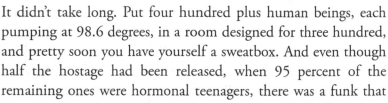

It didn't take long. Put four hundred plus human beings, each pumping at 98.6 degrees, in a room designed for three hundred, and pretty soon you have yourself a sweatbox. And even though half the hostage had been released, when 95 percent of the remaining ones were hormonal teenagers, there was a funk that no amount of Axe body spray was ever going to conceal.

The kids and teachers still looked scared, but now—five hours in—subdued. Not the ten kids on stage, though. Having been singled out, their fear had not subdued in the least, save for Sean. They were a mix of kids who on face had no evident relationship. Five girls. Five boys. You had a couple lower-school kids, the ten-year-olds, eleven-year-olds. You had some older students like Weav, Reece, and Sean. And there was Braydon, eyes closed, head slumped in his chair, his skin still a purplish hue. His slowly rising and falling chest indicated he was still breathing, but beyond that things didn't look great.

When Kira had returned, she had taken a spot on the carpeted floor at the front of the middle aisle with a group of third and fourth graders. Since then, she had been doing everything she could to keep the young kids as relaxed as possible and their minds off what might be about to happen.

If Kira was being honest, she would have admitted it was herself she was trying to keep relaxed. *Where is he?* She had been watching Reilly this entire time and knew his men were still looking for the missing "security guard," which was good in a sense; it meant Cade must still be safe. But for how long? She looked over at Ms. Dixon, and the thousand-yard stare on her face was one of the saddest things Kira had ever seen. She wanted to go over to her and tell her. Tell Ms. Dixon she had seen him. He was alive. But she couldn't without drawing suspicion. So instead, she had to sit on the knowledge and watch this poor mother slumped in her chair, likely praying that her son had found his way off the property. Kira hoped Ms. Dixon hadn't come to the same conclusion that she had: even if he could, he wouldn't. He was a momma's boy, Kira knew. She didn't mean that in a bad way; in fact it was one of the things she liked most about him—he sorta had that indifferent attitude he put on, but when it came to his mother, you could just tell he would do anything he could for that woman. She first realized it that weekend they had all stayed up at her grandmother's in Hanover. Sean, Allison, Weav, and Becca all had fake IDs and went out after the Sam Roberts show. She and Cade sat in a diner and talked random stuff for what must have been three, four hours. You could fake anything for five minutes. Four hours sitting across a table at a twenty-four-hour diner was like a lie detector. Eventually the real you was coming out. It didn't hurt either that it was also the first time he had tried coffee. It had made her laugh that night, how fast he was talking, all wired out on five cups of diner coffee as they made a list together of all the places around the globe they each wanted to visit one day. Thinking of that sheet of paper with the Blue Wagon Diner insignia that she kept folded up in her backpack, and the things he'd hinted at about his father, she suddenly felt one of those waves of sadness that rolled over you now and again. More frequently than she'd probably admit.

For all she knew, he was already dead.

There was no reason she would have ever thought to do so, but if she were to look above her, about thirty feet back and to the right, and if it wasn't almost directly into the overhead light, Kira could have had her answer.

She would have seen part of an eyebrow and a right eye peering through the crack next to the framing around one of the light fixtures hanging above the auditorium. And if she could have seen the rest of Cade's face, she would have also noticed the relief wash over it as he scanned the crowd, finally spotting his mother. Safe. Maybe only for now, but safe.

CHAPTER FIFTEEN

7:29:14

7:29:15

Less than a minute to go and Pruitt was one parent short, still not having heard from Mr. Collier. *How in today's world can someone go off the reservation for four hours?* Pruitt wondered, somewhat enviously. When was the last time she had been able to turn her phone off and disappear? 2008?

Now the question was . . . *Is it a bluff or is this Reilly guy really going to start offing people every fifteen minutes?*

7:29:33

7:29:34

She stared at the blank screen above, waiting for Reilly to come on. Her gut was telling her this guy didn't bluff.

That's it. Pruitt looked around the room. "Frost. Outside. Now!"

7:29:45

As Pruitt rushed out the door with a confused Officer Frost, the rest of the team and the nineteen parents watched the clock tick toward 7:30.

At precisely 7:30, a wide shot of the crowded, terrified auditorium appeared on the command trailer's video screen. A few of the parents audibly gasped.

As the screen shifted to a closeup of Reilly, Pruitt reentered the command center without Frost.

"So . . . the moment of truth, as they say, has arrived. Well, the *first* one at least." The camera on Reilly panned out to show a cowering, lip-quivering, if-he-lives-through-this-he-will-never-live-it-down, tear-drenched fifteen-year-old boy with Reilly's gun pressed to his temple. "Show them to me."

"Take the gun off the boy's head and I will," Pruitt said sharply.

"You first," Reilly said in a sing-song voice.

Based on years of experience, Pruitt knew by looking at Reilly, the way he held the gun to the kid's head, his tone, the body posture, all of it removed any question she had that he might have been bluffing. This man would happily shoot a teenager, maybe multiple teenagers, until Mr. Collier arrived.

Behind her, Pruitt heard the door to the command center open and footsteps crossing the room. *Well, here goes.*

"Okay." She nodded to the tech next to her. He held up a camera and turned it toward the group of parents. There was a beat as Reilly counted them.

If it was me on the other end, she wondered, *would I think to ask? It would seem obvious to, but I don't think I would. I would already be thinking about the next step. I might not even think to confirm the twenty people I was looking at were indeed the twenty parents, and not nineteen parents and one Officer Frost dressed in a borrowed suit from one of the TV reporters.* She assumed Reilly would have known some of the faces in here, but to know all twenty by first glance was a stretch. There were just enough recognizable faces in this crowd, like that senator and a few other business types that even she had watched before on CNBC or seen in the *Times* that would distract from her bluff.

That said, if he did recognize the switch, she was screwed. They were all screwed. Because no one knew where Collier was and every fifteen minutes was going to come fast and often until they found him.

"Okay . . . we can begin," Reilly said. On the screen he pushed the kid away and holstered his handgun. "I'd like you all to say hi to some of my new friends." The shot on the screen panned out further to reveal the ten kids sitting on stage. Or rather, nine kids sitting and one still too zonked out to do more than slump in his seat.

Pruitt watched the initial wave of panic sweep through the trailer. She wanted to see who was going to need to be babysat through this whole ordeal. There was the woman who leapt to her feet and instinctively, albeit highly ineffectually, lunged toward the screen and the image of the unconscious boy. And the convulsing young father, who was probably in his late thirties but looked like he was barely out of grad school. *Shit, if he's crying now, wait till things really get hairy.* She was kinda impressed with Frost. He had gotten right into it, the haunted look of a grieving parent on his face, the figurative hand-wringing. Not too shabby for a Corporal. Maybe his, "No, not Kaylah!" wail was a touch over the top, but given the mad chaos in the room upon seeing all their children next to two rifle-toting thugs, she doubted Reilly picked up on his lack of thespian nuance.

"Everyone is fine. You needn't worry. Well, yes, you need worry, but not if you follow everything I say. In that case, you will be fine. Your children will be fine. As will the others," he said, sweeping his hand over the crowded room behind him. "Not that you're nearly as interested in them, I gather. I don't blame you. They are nothing more than pixels on a screen when compared to the actual DNA of your very own darlings sitting right here with me." Reilly slowly ran his hand along Braydon's head, smoothing out the stray hairs.

Hastings, who had been glowering at the screen in silence, barked, "What's your name?"

. "Ah, Senator. Good to hear from you. Name's Reilly. Now, does that make you feel more in control?"

"If you so much as touch my son, I will have you hunted down and—"

"Yes, yes, I know. Hunted down and dragged off to some black site or some such and torn into pieces or waterboarded, etcetera, etcetera. Noted. Now, may I continue?" He paused. "Thank you. So . . . here's what we're going to do. A little capitalist experiment. I have the product. You have the demand. The question is, how much are you willing to pay for my product?" As Reilly spoke, he circled slowly around the group of ten children so the parents could see each one of their terrified faces up close. "I have just sent over off-shore routing numbers which you each will begin to transfer funds to. The amounts you put in are completely up to you. Think of it as a Kickstarter campaign. And like any good crowd-sourcing project, you can expect to receive a gift in return. For the higher bids, something like, oh I don't know, your child's life? But, just like the crappy coffee mug you might get for a $20 donation to your niece's film school project, bid too low and your gift will be your child's head. Get the picture? You have one hour to transfer your funds. Tell your tech guy to put the counter I just sent over up on the screen."

A moment later ten columns appeared on the screen in the command center, each column at $0.00.

"How do we know we gave you enough?" Taylor, ever the hedge funder, asked.

"You'll have to figure that out yourself, Chris. But here's one thing to help you decide. There are ten of you," he said, placing a hand on Sean's shoulder as he spoke. "As long as you aren't the lowest bidder, well then, you gave enough. Simple as that. And in an hour we'll know which will walk out no worse for wear." He moved his hand slowly to the next kid and softly dragged his hand along the cheek of the frightened ten-year-old girl. "But, whichever of the ten of you gives the least, your child will . . .

spoiler alert . . ."—he put his finger to her head and mimicked a shooting motion—" . . . get a bullet in the head."

Well this is a first, thought Pruitt.

"Why would you do this to my daughter?" Ms. Collier wailed.

"Because you all were lucky enough to be the 1 percent. The 1 percent of the 1 percent. You ten families are the ten wealthiest of the student body here. Now, one of you gets to see what it feels like to be at the bottom. One family is going to be the bottom 10 percent. And you will see what it feels like to suffer for being "poor." This is a chance for the 99 percent to have its revenge and . . ." Reilly stopped. "Nah, I'm just fucking with you." He laughed. "I don't care about that. I just had an inkling I could get way more by pitting the rich versus the rich and letting them fight it out all the way to market equilibrium. Right, Chris?" Reilly let this all settle in a moment and then said, "Do you realize how much you can get for a roomful of rich kids? Me neither. So, let's find out together."

A few of the parents in the crowd were already frantically making phone calls.

"You have one hour."

"I don't know if we can liquidate within an hour," Bill Weaver said.

"I'm sure you can pull the necessary strings. And if not" — he shrugged and put his hands on Weav's shoulders—"well, someone has to be the poorest. That's life."

~

Brilliant. I had to give it to the guy. Pretty brilliant idea. Completely nuts, sure, but brilliant. I had been watching this Reilly guy give his spiel as he circled Sean and Weav and the others on stage below me. Even if all ten families banded together to keep the price low, there was no way prospect theory wouldn't set in (or maybe it was loss aversion that Professor

Elliot was talking about in Economic Theory. Not that those ten were much concerned with which economic concept was in play here). Even though the outcome would be the same whether they all ponied up $2 million or $2 billion, there was no way to avoid a bidding war. It was human nature that lower probability is always over-weighted and higher, under-weighted . . . and that's even before factoring in that the price of being last in this case was a gigantic disaster.

This guy may have been a little theatrical, but it worked. I had been watching him from above the auditorium as he had given his demands to the camera, and from there he looked like a shark slowly circling his prey, debating which one of the ten he would pick off.

I wanted to feel a little more relieved, knowing in all likelihood, my mother was immaterial to them; there was no money to be gotten from her. Based on the mortgage and credit card debt, the dude would end up in the negative. Still, I couldn't help but feel there was something about him that suggested that if things went bad, he couldn't care less if he took out everyone to save himself.

In retrospect, it was probably insane to have snuck over here and up into the attic, but it had been pretty easy. No one expects to see someone running toward the hurricane. Once I had timed the gunmen's rounds, I slipped out from the ivy and over here. I could see everything from the gap in the edging of the light fixture, but from this spot, I couldn't hear once the guy below stopped performing for the camera and had joined his men convening at the back side of the stage where . . .

Was that *Preston* happily tapping away at a laptop? Funny thing was I wasn't really surprised. Not that it wasn't crazy to see him there, more just that *everything* seemed crazy right about now, so nothing seemed out of the ordinary. This was just one more blip in the firehose of insanity that was blasting me in the face.

As I considered what to do next, I watched my mother.

From the look on her face, I was guessing she thought I was dead. I looked over at Kira. She, on the other hand, knew I wasn't, but she was also smart enough to know that she couldn't tell anyone, not even my mother. It was horrible, though. To have to watch the one person who has done everything for you, to watch them suffer. Even from that distance, I could see the weight of the situation crushing her. Literally slumping my mother in her seat, her body quivering.

I counted five armed guys in there, plus Preston and the one giving orders, who called himself Reilly. Add that to the five other men I had counted when I was watching from behind the ivy before. And the two gunmen I had choked out.

There's a sentence I never thought I'd say: "And the two gunmen I had choked out." This was not how my day was supposed to go. Econ, Abnormal Psych, Physics, write a couple papers, read the Edith Piaf biography I saw on Kira's desk, and then a little sparring at the gym after school: *that* was how today was supposed to go.

Fourteen guys. Maybe a couple more somewhere else around the grounds. What exactly did I think I could do besides hide up here and watch? *Nothing.* I was helpless. All I could do was watch my mother and Kira and hope these guys were only after money and not something a whole lot worse.

I had a sudden thought. The first upbeat one since this whole thing began: *Thankfully, Kira's parents aren't rich enough to make the cut.* I knew they had money, but I was glad to see it wasn't enough to pit her against the ten kids on stage.

The door on the far side of the auditorium opened and the guy from the basement walked in. He still looked slightly woozy. Good. Prick deserved it. That said, as I watched him climb the steps to the stage, I realized how relieved I was that he was alive. I didn't think I could handle being responsible for taking someone's life. Unfortunately, I doubted these guys would feel that way about me or any of the other people in this room they had to off.

He and Reilly spoke, but from this distance I couldn't make out what they said. Earlier, when Reilly had been speaking to the parents, the place had been completely silent as the entire room strained to listen to his demands, but now the chatter in the room blocked out whatever the two were saying. As the guy spoke, I could see Reilly's gaze move across the auditorium, his face taut.

It was a little late, but I now realized I should have tied him up so he wouldn't be able to come back and describe what I looked like. Not that I was thinking about much of anything back then other than getting as far from that basement as fast as possible. Didn't even think about what was happening or might happen. Didn't think about the worst case. The fact this guy could tie me to my mother and use her. Threaten her. Shoot her.

And a best case? I was bone dry out of those.

I crouched below a collar tie and edged along the rafters on the right side of the attic. Walking softly so as not to be heard below, I made my way over to the stage end of the auditorium to get closer to the two men.

Above the stage, there was an opening for the electrical wires running from the stage lights. I lay on the floor and peered through the gap. Below me, Reilly and Javier—as I heard him call the basement guy—stood over Preston, who had set up his laptops stage right.

Wow, I really am a bit of stalker, I thought, realizing the reason this stage direction term ran through my head was from watching her rehearse Hedda Gabler last semester. Watching her from more or less the same spot I was in now.

" . . . I can't tell you. I mean . . ."

"I don't care," Reilly snapped, cutting off Javier. "Find that guard."

"You got a picture?" Javier asked Preston.

Reilly glared at him.

"What? I didn't get a great look," Javier said defensively. "He sucker-punched me."

I could see the Reilly guy's glare turn more to disbelief than anything. Dumb's one thing; I mean, I was guessing you didn't get into a career like Javier's if you spent a lot of time in a classroom. The hiring pool for these gigs was probably a tad shallow. But the dude seemed stunningly un-self-aware too. Did he not realize just how stupid he sounded blaming getting his ass kicked on being "sucker-punched"? Someone slamming you in the head was not a sucker punch when you were hunting them with a gun.

"You need a picture?" Reilly asked.

"Yeah, I said I didn't get a good . . ."

"A picture of the lone person running free around here? Everyone is in here. Everyone out there is in black fatigues except one lone security guard. I think you'll figure it out."

Javier grunted, "Okay. I'll grab Carston and go look for him."

"No, I want Carston staying downstairs. Until we find this guy, I want someone by the bomb at all times. No chances."

Wait, what? *Bomb?* One thing that I had wondered after the ransom call to the parents was, how did these guys plan to escape once they got their money? Presumably, they would be asking for a copter or something to get themselves out. Probably take some hostages with them until they knew they were safe. But what if that was only a cover? What if they went with a distraction instead? What more of a distraction than a bomb exploding underneath a roomful of kids? Or maybe I was only overthinking it. The threat of a bomb could just be a way to keep the police from rushing in. That reasoning made me feel better for all of three seconds before I realized: If that were the case, why hadn't this guy Reilly mentioned to the cops that he had a bomb? If you didn't plan on using it, *that's* when you mentioned it. If you kept it secret, the opposite was probably true.

Someone had to let the cops know. For the first time in my life, I actually wished I had a cell phone. Not that I'd know whom to call. *Uh, 911, can you connect me to the SWAT team camped outside St. Frederick Prep? There's this little thing about a bomb . . .*

A cell phone would be a moot point anyway; they must have knocked out cell service. Not to mention land lines and any Wi-Fi connections. Ironically, I bitched all the time about everyone being so constantly wired in, but now, the one time I wanted it, needed it, the entire digital world had been cut off.

The entire *digital* world. Maybe not analog, though. In today's world, who would have thought of that? I had to get to Garvey's office. It was only 500 yards, but once again, I was going to have to expose myself. *Is it really worth it?* I could have been wrong about the bomb. And who was I to be the one to try and do something? This wasn't my responsibility. What I should do was say screw this, hide out, and let somebody else sneak across campus, through the gunsights of a bunch of thugs, and radio to the cops about a bomb from Garvey's Ham radio set. Except, there wasn't somebody else.

I be it.

CHAPTER SIXTEEN

Back in the command center it was chaos. People barking into cell phones. Couples arguing. And Mrs. Collier, screaming into the phone at the real Mr. Collier, not the one in the reporter's suit sitting next to her.

Up on the screen was the running tally of bank transfers. Pruitt found it interesting that you often heard numbers tossed around about billionaire this or Hamptons mansions and eight different homes that, but she never realized that when it came to the actual dollars these people had, it wasn't much. Nearly every penny was tied up into something. So to get it, and transfer it, you needed to sell things: properties, stocks, companies. And it's not as quick a process as you'd think. You'd assume, okay, this person was worth $800 million, just click a button like she would on her TDBank checking account and whoosh, you transferred it to another account. But no.

Mind you, the numbers scrolling on the screen were still mind-boggling to her, but it was a piecemeal process: three million here . . . four and change there. She also had an unsettling feeling that there might be some sandbagging going on by a few of them. A crazy thing to consider when it was your kid in there, but she guessed some of them, say, the hedge funders who were practiced at divorcing themselves from the particular commodity or derivative at hand, had no problem playing close to the vest. The same way they could short a struggling chain store even as it decimated the lives of the thousands soon to be laid off, they could slow-play their bid so as to not jump out ahead of the pack and overpay to be in the top nine.

Thirty minutes in, and the entire total had reached $353 million. The top "bid" thus far was Senator Hastings at $53,543,000. Made you wonder what they were paying senators these days, thought Pruitt. Rather, *who* was doing the paying.

The Collier woman had obviously gotten her point across, because suddenly the Collier column jumped out of the ignominious tenth spot with a $14,810,200 bump.

Jackson whistled to Pruitt and pointed to the radio in his hand. "He's back."

Pruitt took the radio. "Calling to turn yourself in already?"

"I'm good, thanks. But I do have some good news for you. As a good-faith offering, I will be releasing more hostages. All but twenty-five."

"That's a start. How about we round down and make it all but ten?"

"In time, in time . . ."

It being 8:08 p.m., and an overcast evening, the grounds were nearly pitch black. I figured I should be able to sneak my way back across campus to the mailroom if I was careful. That is, if these guys didn't have night-vision goggles. I couldn't remember either of the two men I fought carrying a pair, which made me feel a little better. At least until I thought about what they were carrying. Guns. Large ones. More importantly, lots of bullets. Actually, even one bullet sucked. I tried to picture what they had on them when I took their guns. There was that thin black case they each had, but that couldn't have been big enough to hold night-vision goggles. Or could it? The only night-vision goggles I knew were the bulky binocular-looking things you see in the movies. But if every other piece of tech kept getting smaller, why not those too? Who knew, maybe night-vision goggles were no bigger than a pair of those thin circular John Lennon throwbacks that Reece wore. Those cases could easily hold a pair. *And if they do, I'm dead.*

I thought about other options. The gate was being watched, but maybe I could try to sneak over the stone wall somewhere. But that would mean having to believe the wire and the little metal grenade things they had strung up were nothing more than decoration.

Beyond that, I had zip.

I climbed out of the crawl space above the theater and crept down the back stairs leading to the service entrance where they loaded in the sets. I slowly pulled the sliding door open and peered out, then eased my way along the outside wall to the northeast corner of the building. I couldn't tell if anyone was scouting the green, but things had seemed to settle in as they awaited the deadline, so hopefully they weren't being as vigilant. I sprinted across to the science building and then slid along the side of that wall. One more open crossing, and I'd be at Bartlett Hall, where the mailroom was.

Just as I was about to run for it, I saw a light flicker to the right. I slammed my body back up against the wall and waited. A flashlight banked from side to side, scouring the grounds. On one sweep I saw the light reflect off a rifle lashed with a strap over the right shoulder of whoever was coming toward me. The light patch swung in my direction but stopped about thirty feet from me before swinging back the other way. I pressed up against the wall even harder, as if it would actually do something, like it would make me seep into the stone wall by osmosis.

The light swung back toward me, this time, maybe fifteen, twenty feet. My breathing stopped. This was it. Another couple feet and I'd be exposed, nowhere to run, thirty feet of stone wall to either side. Trapped, a wall already behind me, perfect for a firing squad.

I waited for the gunman to turn the light directly on me. *Would I hear the gunshot? Or is the end simultaneous?*

CHAPTER SEVENTEEN

"I have got to piss so badly." Weav was squirming in his seat.

"Just ask them to let you go," Sean said.

"I'm not going to be the one."

"What, you think they're going to shoot you for having to take a leak?"

"Hey, you never know. I'm not taking the chance."

"You'd rather piss yourself?"

Weav shrugged.

"Look, they aren't touching you." Sean nodded toward the screen with the ransom tallies. "You could piss all over this stage when you're going to be netting them nine figures. You know what's gotta be way worse than being up here?"

"I don't know. Nothing?"

"Not being up here."

"How you see that?" Weav asked.

"Haven't you always kind of wondered who were the richest kids here?"

"No."

Sean shrugged. "Hey, I'm just saying what everyone else is thinking."

"I wasn't thinking it."

"You tell me . . . you don't think there's a few of them," gesturing toward the auditorium seats, "who aren't embarrassed —at least inside—that they aren't up here with us?"

"That's dark, dude."

Sean was kinda joking, but not really. He bet some of the guys out there were actually a little jealous. "Gun to their head, you know they'd admit it. I bet Callahan is probably wondering how he can get these terrorists to look a little deeper into his parents' portfolio to get them to reconsider."

"I'd trade with him in a heartbeat."

"You'd be stupid to. If they're going to sacrifice anyone to get out of here, that's what the others there are for. I guarantee you. We're like a collectible. You keep your Avenger action figure or whatever it is all plastic-wrapped and in mint condition so you can resell it. You don't mess with it and get your grimy fingers on it. Everyone out there . . . they're the ones that get played with and no one cares if Captain America's arm breaks off. You just get a new one. Expendable."

Sean wasn't sure he really believed this, but it made him feel better saying it. If he was right, then great. He'd be safe, *and* he'd come out of this sounding like a badass. Fake it till you make it, his father was always saying. Yeah, he was freaking out a little inside, but why let anyone else know that? And if he was wrong and they were as expendable as the others, he had a plan for that too. His father was always saying, "A man makes his own opportunity and doesn't leave it to anyone else." You control the situation; not vice versa. He needed to ensure the best odds of survival. And the one thing he had was information. He wasn't saying he would necessarily use it, but—his eyes trained on Ms. Dixon—if it came to it, he wouldn't hesitate to play his immunity idol. He wasn't about to leave his existence on this planet to chance.

～

I was pressing myself so hard against the side of the building, I could feel the sandy grit of the bricks cutting into the back of my scalp. Holding my breath, I waited for the next swath of flashlight to frame me, pinned to that wall. The only question was, would he take me down on sight or bring me back to the auditorium where there was a bomb ready to go off? You know your day's gone to shit when you find yourself hoping for the latter.

Turned out there was a third option. The gunman swung his flashlight back to his left and by the time he swept the beam back to the right, he was past me. I remained out of his sightline as the beam lit up an area maybe twenty feet beyond.

I waited a beat until the light disappeared and then ran the rest of the way along the science building and across to Bartlett Hall. Garvey, not known for his punctuality, had trusted me with a key to open up the mailroom in the mornings when he didn't get the early jump on the day (i.e. Mondays, Tuesdays, some Wednesdays, most Thursdays, and definitely Fridays). When I put my key in the lock, I was surprised to see my hand shake. I hadn't really stopped to think to be scared, but my body was hard-lined with adrenaline. This wasn't just a shot from heightened nerve impulses to the adrenal glands kinda rush though. I figured this was probably some of that adrenocorticotropic hormone the physiology textbook talked about. Something shooting from the pituitary gland, kicking off production of cortisol from the cortex of the adrenal glands, giving me that jolt of glucose that long-term stress elicits. Knowing it was just a natural physical response didn't make me feel any better. Scared shitless was still scared shitless whether you knew the science behind it or not.

I slipped inside and locked the door behind me. I didn't dare turn the light on, but I knew this place well enough that I could feel my way through the mailroom by touch. Even in the midst of all this, I realized what a sad statement that was.

Kira watched as more hostages were led out of the auditorium. Row by row, the men with the guns ushered the students and teachers out the door, and presumably off property and into the arms of relieved loved ones. When it was her turn, she stood up with the others, but hung back as they all headed for the door. She was watching the group on stage. In addition to the ten kids who were being bid on, the gunmen had added another dozen or so frightened mid-schoolers. It was like they had plucked out central casting extras for a scared-senseless scene. They'd also chosen a few from the administration. There were Headmaster Harkin, Mr. Wilson, Ms. Pratt, and Ms. Dixon. For these thirty, it was beginning to sink in that they weren't being released along with all the others, and she could see the panic within them rising again, each person's fear compounding the next.

Except for Braydon. He remained motionless. Kira watched as Ms. Dixon went to him, taking her place holding his head up in the chair and stroking his hair. His face had darkened through two or three shades of purple. He'd gone from a sheen of watered-down Welch's to overripe plum.

"You gotta get him some help."

The gunmen all ignored her. Kira said it again louder, and added, "You're going to kill him."

Reilly looked in the direction of Kira, standing defiantly as the other students and teachers pushed their way toward the door. He smiled. "Well, yeah, that is the idea. Maybe not him, but a few of you all in general. If I didn't seem capable of wantonly offing anyone I please, it would sorta take away my leverage with the people with guns and assault vehicles out there who would love to bull-rush in here, now wouldn't it?" Reilly waited to see what this girl had to say next. He always enjoyed this part: the moment when someone decided to try to—*be a hero* may be too strong a phrase—try to attempt to do the right thing. You could see it in their faces, they never quite expected to make a stand; it just came out of them. And you never knew who it would be either. This girl with the large eyes lasered in his direction would not have been his first guess. *Not that I'm sexist,* thought Reilly a little defensively. She just looked too small.

"You need to let him go," she said again. Reilly could see her hands shaking, but she was trying to cover up whatever fear she had. Her face was steady and her lips pursed, the bottom one with a slight indentation in the middle that gave off the hint of a seeming smile, even if she didn't mean to. He liked this girl.

Maybe I am a hair sexist, Reilly thought. *Whosoever desires constant success must change his conduct with the times.* Machiavelli probably didn't have this scenario in mind when he wrote that, but Reilly thought he'd probably agree it wouldn't hurt to change his expectations. Especially given Pruitt's reputation.

Looking at the screen above, he shook his head in mock disapproval. "Eighth place for our little friend Braydon. His parents aren't exactly lighting up the board. Hey, look on the bright side; before he has a chance to die, I may have to kill him first."

Landry grabbed Kira's arm and shoved her back into the group of others being released. Halfway to the door, she stopped and turned back toward the stage. "I'll stay."

Reilly smiled and crossed his arms. "Oh, you will, will you?"

"Switch me out with him."

To be honest, Reilly would have been happy to get rid of the purple kid. It was always a hassle having to deal with injured or wounded hostages. The Barcelona take had nearly gone to shit because Trotter had shot one of the hostages and the cops felt forced to bum rush the place. The only reason he hadn't sent this little Violet Beauregarde out with the others was he didn't want to appear worried. Now he had an out of sorts.

"You're not some scholarship kid, now are you? I'm going to need a girl with a rich mommy and daddy if I'm going to trade out our little Concord grape over here."

"My dad runs Glenrock Financial."

"Ding, ding, ding . . . we have a winner. Preston, radio over and tell them they're going to need to invite a couple new party guests."

CHAPTER EIGHTEEN

I had never actually used the Ham radio before, but I'd watched Garvey do so. I'd always had an image in my mind of a shank of ham. That that's what Garvey and his loner buddies talked about over the radio—ham and maybe sausage-related topics. I knew it was probably some guy's name, like Joe Hamm, the inventor of it or something, but it was one of the few things I had never bothered to look up. I did know enough that it wouldn't be jammed along with the other electronics. The lone analog device within fifty miles, probably. I didn't know whom to call, but I could at least convince someone to call the police and pass the message to the cops gathered outside the gates.

"Testing, testing . . ." I whispered. "Uh, one, two, three?"

The radio crackled. I waited. Nothing.

A little louder this time: "This is Garvey calling out. Anyone there? Anyone?"

More crackle. But no voices.

"This is Garvey. Anyone? Anyone? This is an emergency . . . anyone?"

~

It hadn't taken long to get the Harrises to the trailer. As soon as the hostage situation chyron scrolled across Kira's father's screen, he and her mother had gotten in their car and driven straight up from Manhattan. The trip, normally two hours, had taken Mr. Harris an hour twenty. For the last few hours now they had been penned up in the holding area the authorities had set up a half mile up the road leading to St. Frederick. That is, until they were plucked from the hundreds of other worried parents and brought to the trailer where Pruitt apprised them of the situation. As soon as she explained the perverse bidding war, Pruitt spotted something on Mr. Harris's face. A flicker of grave concern. Rightly so, of course; his daughter was now one of the ten in the most immediate danger of losing her life. But it wasn't that that caught Pruitt's attention. The flicker had happened after the initial shock. Husband and wife both reacted to the shock of it, but then a moment later, as though an aftershock to an earthquake, something rumbled across Mr. Harris's face. If Pruitt had to put a voice to the looks, the first was, "Oh no, my daughter's fucked." The second: "Oh no; *I'm* fucked."

"Pruitt, you need to hear this," Jackson said. "Patch him through."

Over the speaker, a man's voice spoke rapidly: "And then he said I needed to . . ."

"Sir, hold on please. This is Agent Pruitt. Can you back up?"

Pruitt picked up the handset and took it off speaker. She didn't want a roomful of parents to go bonkers if the news was bad.

"Yeah, I don't know if it's a prank or not, but I figured it wouldn't hurt to pass it on just in case."

"Tell me exactly what the man said."

"You can ask him yourself. I still got him on the line. Let me put the phone next to the speaker."

A slight crackle of static, and then the caller's voice off-speaker. "Go ahead, son."

Pruitt was surprised when the voice came through, surprised that it sounded like a teenage boy, not the teacher or security guard she was expecting. Surprised too at the tone. Not calm exactly, but not freaking the eff out as most would in this situation. Instead, he sounded like an adrenalized teen, a high school basketball player in a tight playoff game, trying to explain something during a third quarter time out. Speaking faster than she imagined he normally would, but not panicked. Excited, really.

"Look, don't hang up. This is real, I swear. I'm at St. Frederick Academy. They've taken it over. Maybe fifteen guys. There's a bomb. You need to know there's a bomb."

"Where?"

"I don't know. Haven't seen it, but I think I heard them talking about it. Someone needs to get in there fast."

"How do you know this?"

"I overheard it."

"And how are you able to freely run around . . ."

"Look, I know you don't believe me. I don't want to be here doing this either. But I heard it. There . . . is . . . a . . . bomb. I am not fucking with you."

Jackson had been listening in and now mouthed to her, "It's bullshit. A trap."

Pruitt muted the call. Jackson continued full-throated, "If it's them, why do it now after letting some hostages go? What's the gain? He sounds like he doesn't even know they are being released."

Pruitt shrugged, then toggled the call back on. "Okay. What's your name?"

The voice paused long enough that Pruitt was sure whatever came out was going to be a lie.

"Mike. Phillips."

"Why aren't you telling me your real name, Mike?"

Pruitt wasn't the only one wondering this particular question at this particular moment. So was Reilly, who was hearing this exact same conversation. In fact, he had been privy to everything said in that trailer since the moment he had sent the radio over for them to initially contact him. You'd never know it looking at it, but the handheld radio was really two radios. The device itself and a transparent silicon wrap that picked up sounds within twenty-five feet and sent them back via a unique wavelength directly to Preston's laptop.

Reilly grabbed Principal Harkin from his onstage chair and put a gun to his head. "Radio. Where? Tell me now. Where is there a radio here?"

Harkin stuttered, "The, the . . . student union. They have a, a student radio station . . ."

"Not there. We took that out. Where else?"

"I, I don't know."

Not the profoundest last words ever uttered, but they would have to do for Principal Ronald A. Harkin, because Reilly pressed the trigger and sent a .38-caliber bullet slicing through temple skin on its way to ripping apart the meat of the Head-master's brain.

As Harkin fell to the ground, Reilly forcefully grabbed Kira, who had instinctively run toward Harkin as he fell. Wrenching her toward him by the hair, he turned her head around and faced the remaining hostages. On top of the thirty on stage (make that twenty-nine and in serious danger of quickly becoming twenty-eight) there were still about fifty left in the auditorium, waiting for their rows to be led out to safety. He yelled out, "Anyone else know where there's a radio on this campus?"

Silence, save for some whimpering from those still in shock from seeing their principal's brain matter spray across the stage. Reilly raised the gun to Kira's head.

"Anyone?"

"I do."

Reilly turned toward the voice coming from the far left of the theater. Garvey, his hand raised, said, "I know where it is."

~

I tried to think of something, anything that would convince them of the bomb. I couldn't blame them for not believing me. I would think it was some sort of trap too. It would be a reasonable smokescreen, having one of the hostages pretend to call. Add a deterrent to keep the cops from raiding the place. And by stumbling over giving them a fake name, I likely only solidified the cops' thinking. But there was no way I was giving my real one. I had to assume these guys were monitoring and hearing everything, and if they had my name, they may connect it to my mother. Working that assumption also meant my time was short. If they were monitoring, it might only be seconds before they found this place.

"Look, I know there's no reason to believe me, but if I'm right, these guys aren't just holding hostages, they . . ."

A loud bang echoed behind me. For a second I thought it was a gunshot but quickly realized someone was in the next room slamming something into the locked door.

I leapt up on the desk and stepped over the radio, just as a gunshot cracked behind me and the lock was blown off the door. I shoved the screen from the lower part of the open double hung window. The administration probably hated having to re-do all these nineteenth-century window frames to get up to code with the larger egresses wide enough a two-hundred-pound firefighter with full gear could fit through. An expensive new regulation meant to save lives. And it just did. Mine. Had it still been one of the small original openings, I'd never have shimmied through quickly enough before the gunshots came.

Small pieces of white wood flew into the air as a bullet hit the window framing a half second after I slipped through. Rolling to the right, I heard two guns spraying bullets out the window. I leapt up and ran, turning momentarily to glimpse one of the men leaping onto the table and slipping cat-like through the window. It was the basement guy.

I ran. There was no thought, no consideration, just instinct. Oddly, one thing did cross my mind as I ran for cover from two men bent on killing me: *How does running work?* My feet moved one after the other, but when was the last time I'd thought about the process itself? When I was three and learning to run, maybe? After that it just was. Like breathing. Or chewing. Where else in my life was I doing that? Where I learned something and then just did it without thought or consideration for whether it was the correct way? I also thought I used to push myself to run as fast as I possibly could when playing sports. Nope. Have a guy whiz a bullet by your ear next time you're running track, and I'll bet you'll knock a few ticks off your 400.

I heard a gunshot behind me. And another. And then a third coming from my left. A second shooter. There was one plus to hearing gunshots ripping toward you: seeing as the bullet's getting there about 1,000 miles per hour quicker than the sound itself, not hearing it means it's already buried inside your skull.

I immediately pivoted, broke right, and headed for the history building. Taking another quick look over my right shoulder, I could see Basement Guy gaining on me, and about twenty feet behind him, another one. To my left, maybe seventy-five feet away, was a third. Whenever I used to see guys in movies ripping off gunshots while chasing someone, I always thought it seemed farfetched they never hit their target; but no matter how good one might be with a gun, hitting a moving target *from* a moving target is apparently a whole lot harder than it looks.

Or so I hoped.

Twenty feet from the history building door, I had a thought that would have been more helpful a few seconds earlier, before it was too late to do anything about it: *It's eight at night; won't this door be locked?* If I aborted and turned right or left now, though, the gunmen had the angles on me, and I would never make it around either side of the building.

I two-stepped the eight granite stairs leading to the landing in front of the big oak door, reached for the handle, and hoped.

Liz knew she couldn't react. It would only bring attention to her and possibly reveal to this Reilly psychopath that she was related to the kid he was after. Knowing Cade, how hard-headed he was, if Reilly had her to dangle, who knew what he might do. *But you try not to react, not cry out, not scream bloody murder when it's your little boy that is likely at the wrong end of the gunshots that have been echoing across the grounds.* She didn't know for sure, but Reilly had sent his men out the door after someone, and who else would be using Garvey's Ham radio? A shiver had run through her when Reilly had answered his men's question of whether to take whoever it was alive or not: *"I . . . don't . . . care."*

The gunshots seemed to her to be moving away from them, so at least they must not have gotten him at the radio and he was on the run. She had faith in Cade; he was tough. Fearless. Too fearless for his own good sometimes. He had a coldness to him that he would sometimes sink into, and he'd get that look in his eyes. *But really, can you blame him?* she thought. *Considering what happened growing up?*

But he wasn't always cold. Nothing made her happier than when the soft side showed itself. Like when just the two of them would go into the city to see her sister. He would still switch sides of the street halfway across to be on the side of her that the cars were coming from. Somewhere he had learned that it was the chivalrous thing to do—in the event the car didn't stop, he would be the one to take the brunt of it. Seemed like something that might have worked when some Victorian-era Miss Manners came up with it back in horse-and-buggy days. But a 4,000-pound SUV? Both people were probably getting squished, but still, it always broke her heart when he did it. That said, she hoped that right now this soft side was nowhere to be found. If he had any chance, he needed that angry side, that side of him he had been trying for years to push back, to bury. That side his father put there.

Javier couldn't wait to get his hands on this little shit who had embarrassed him in front of everyone. *If Reilly thinks I'm a moron already, he's going to think way worse if he finds out this is some kid and not at least some token security guard.* As he watched the kid leap up the stone steps toward one of those ancient-looking wooden doors, Javier thought, *Cornered.* The kid was cornered and now Javier could put a bullet in him and end this, hopefully get to him before Landry and Franklin did so he could empty a clip in the kid's face, making him unrecognizable as a teenager.

In front of him, the kid yanked open the front door. *Lucky break for him that we were searching all these buildings earlier,* thought Javier, *otherwise they'd all be locked up for the night and I'd have a sitting duck standing there on those front steps. So be it.* Kid's luck was only going to extend his life another thirty or forty seconds.

Javier yelled to the other two men, "Franklin, north side. Eyeball the back exits. Landry, hold the front." He opened the door and entered. Listened. There were footsteps pounding up the stairs above. *There's something nice about knowing the guy you're chasing definitely doesn't have a gun,* thought Javier. You didn't have to move cautiously, all head-on-a-swivel; you could just pick up the pace and go for it. He took the staircase three steps at a time. At the second floor he heard the footsteps above him continuing higher. *Where's he think he's headed? Sure, going up is away from me, but that puts off the inevitable for only so long.*

At the top of the stairs, Javier scanned the hall and saw only one of the classroom doors was closed. No surprise, it was locked too. He stepped back, lifted a leg, and slammed his boot into the door just below the handle. The framing around the lock plate splintered, and the door swung open. Across the classroom, he saw the kid sprinting toward a tall glass window.

No . . . fucking . . . way.

As Cade propelled himself through the glass and plummeted to the ground below, Javier maneuvered through the desks and chairs. He peered out the shattered window and looked down at the body sprawled out flat. Motionless. *Now there's an optimist for you,* Javier laughed to himself. *Fucking kid thinks he's going to leap out a fourth floor window and walk away. A dumb optimist, but an optimist nevertheless.*

CHAPTER NINETEEN

"You can't roll in there on the word of a scared hostage," Jackson said, hitting "scared" with extra emphasis. "We don't even know if he knows what he's talking about. Whether he is a set-up."

Pruitt, Jackson, and two HSA agents had huddled up in the corner of the trailer, the three men arguing their respective cases to Pruitt, who listened silently.

"This guy isn't going to blow them up," one of the HSA agents said. "He thinks he's Robin Hood. He just wants to stick it to these rich guys."

As they debated, Senator Hastings pried his way into the scrum. "You had better not be thinking about doing anything stupid before we get my son out of there." He looked directly at Pruitt. "You can do whatever you want after 8:30 when he's out of there."

"Sir, we're working on it. We're going to continue negotiating for more releases . . ."

"The ones you got released don't do us any good."

Pruitt didn't much expect him to care about anybody else, but she figured he could at least show the pretense of caring what happened to the other hostages not rich enough to be related to the people sitting in this trailer. She looked at the total tally so far. $783 million. Enough to buy their kids' freedom.

Well, save for one. The unlucky family bringing up the rear in tenth place.

Pruitt looked out into the group of parents at the couple whose daughter had been switched out for the asthmatic kid. The Harris family. The fact they were in a distant tenth place wasn't out of strategy or cheapness. Something was amiss. She had sensed it when they had arrived, and it now became obvious as the father had spent the last thirty minutes pleading desperately into his cell phone. And the look of horror that had settled on Mrs. Harris's face as she came to grips with the reality her husband had just shared with her. The last thirty minutes had shattered all belief in her world. The 7,000-square-foot Greenwich home? The Aspen chalet? Costa del Sol? They may have owned them in name, but as her husband had just made clear, the debt was staggering. Debt he had accumulated due to some shorts that went sideways. Ditto the brokerage accounts she thought they had.

And now here they were; they could sell all their houses, cars, everything they had and it wouldn't do a thing. In fact, they would *owe* money. Greg Harris had been on the phone trying to call in favors for the last thirty minutes, but it had only gotten them as far as $8,302,431. A staggering amount, yet not enough to keep them out of last place.

Pruitt never thought she would say this about someone with eight million dollars to spend: *Those poor bastards.* In twenty-eight minutes, they would lose their daughter Kira.

These others, though, they would be able to buy their children's lives. And all for a drop in the bucket for them. *But after that?* Maybe he really would blow up a bunch of innocent kids. The kid on the radio sounded believable. Gave a fake name, but it made sense he wouldn't want his name out there if anyone was listening. Meant he was smart. And he was too calm to have been someone coerced into it if this was a ploy on Reilly's part. *But strategically, if we go in, it's going to be a bloodbath,* she was certain. *Wait it out, and maybe it really is just the one poor family out of these ten that has to be sacrificed. Sure, it sucks for them,* Pruitt thought, looking at Kira's parents, *but one casualty and a large payout? That beats turning this into a Waco . . . or, worse, a Horace Junction. We need more info. More time.*

"We're going to wait," she said.

"Good," snapped Hastings. "You just saved your career."

"Do I look like I give a shit?"

Inside the auditorium, Reilly handed the headphones back to Preston. The bugged radio they had sent in must not have been next to Pruitt and the others, because he couldn't make out everything, but he'd gotten the gist. It was what he figured. No way they would chance raiding this place on the hunch of a scared security guard. But one thing did worry him: how'd the security guard know about the bomb? Either his guys were chickenshits or incompetent. The first meant Javier or Trotter gave it up when they got beaten up. If the second, then his men somehow let this guy into the auditorium or he overheard them somewhere.

Experience told him, when in doubt, assume incompetence.

Over the Bluetooth he heard Javier say, "We got him."

"Bring him in."

Reilly heard a laugh, and then Javier saying, "We're going to need a spatula."

Liz's eyes hadn't left Reilly since she heard the gunshots. She had been trying to read him for any indication as to whether Cade was still alive. So far nothing. What she would give to have one of those earpieces Reilly and all the others had.

"He's going to be alright." Liz turned her head to see the words were Kira's. With the men preoccupied, Kira had gotten up from her chair and was now squatting at the edge of the stage. "He's going to be alright."

"You think?"

"He's smart. If any kid in here could escape these guys, it would be Cade."

As they talked, they saw a few of the gunmen return. The men's urgency from before seemed to have dissipated. Liz's face went ashen.

"It doesn't mean he's . . . that they've . . ." Kira tried to reassure her, but something caught in her throat. Dread. "Maybe, maybe they caught him and are bringing him here. Maybe he's not . . ."

Liz fought back her tears, but her body quivered, the emotion needing to escape her body one way or another.

"It doesn't mean they killed him. Maybe they only caught him and . . ." Kira said again, the welling in her eyes contradicting the hope in her words.

❧

"Fuck if I'm telling him," Landry said.

Javier looked at Landry and Franklin, both of them with that default dumb look they always gave him. "Are fucking kidding me?!" Javier said for the third time since he and the other two had arrived at where the body should have been. Instead of a splattered kid, in front of them was only a patch of fresh blood and a large divot in the grass, probably where a shoulder or knee landed first. He shook his head. "Two feet." If the kid hadn't propelled himself out the window as hard as he had, he'd have landed closer to the building. And if he had landed two feet shorter, he'd have pancaked on the concrete sidewalk. But instead, grass. And despite the blood on the grass, this kid had somehow walked or, more likely, limped away.

And because Javier had said over the radio to Reilly that he had him, Landry and Franklin had taken that to mean Javier had him captured upstairs. So rather than circling the building and spotting Cade before he could limp off, the two men had gone inside and met Javier on the way down the stairs. They'd inadvertently given him even more time to make a getaway when the three of them took their time walking around the building, never thinking the kid wouldn't be there.

Landry jammed his finger at Javier. "You're telling him. You're the idiot who jumped the gun and said you had him."

"I'm the idiot? Didn't you hear the window shatter?"

"Figured you shot it."

"Well, what'd you think I meant when I said I need a spatula?"

"What the fuck's a spatula?"

Javier fumed as he activated the Bluetooth. *Great, these two screw the pooch, and who's Reilly gonna blame? This should go real fucking good.* "Uh, boss," Javier said into the Bluetooth. "We have a little problem . . ."

On the other end of the communication, Reilly took it in as Javier explained the situation. Reilly yanked the Bluetooth out of his ear but stopped himself as he was about to heave it against the wall. Instead, he reminded himself, *Breathe, just breathe; see the other side.* But God did Reilly want to kill Javier right now. Even his therapist would say, "Shoot that dumb shit." How he would love to do exactly that; wait for Javier to come back to the auditorium, and then right there in front of the others, put a bullet into his neck. Like they did in the movies to show what a crazy MFer the boss was. Then again, it's pretty self-defeating, thought Reilly; he couldn't imagine anyone had ever done that. It'd be stupid to short yourself a guy. Maybe next time, he should over-hire like the guy teaching the CEO class he took years ago. Hire an extra couple people so that you could fire one or two to set an example so as to keep their coworkers on edge. He liked the sound of that. *Gotta remember that for next time.* Team up fat, so he could shoot the dumbest one in the neck. That'd keep them focused.

~

All I wanted was to find a place to lie down. Preferably for the next, oh, three to five days. Maybe a week. Even lying supine would still hurt, but not as much as limping across the grounds and getting into the science hall had. Every time I winced with pain from one body part, I noticed another flare up. My right shoulder, which took the brunt of the fall, had screamed out when I'd reached for the door to the building. Then there were the cuts to the side of my head, the area I wasn't able to cover with my arms when I busted through the pane of glass. *Pain of glass is more like it.* That's the kind of dumb joke Kira loved, and it made me feel a little better thinking about her laughing at my groaner.

The salty blood flowing into my eyes was making it hard to see. But on the plus side, thanks to the limp, I couldn't move fast enough for it to be a problem. I must have done something to my knee. I could still run on it, but only in a herky-jerky manner as I dragged that leg along behind me. I hoped it was like when playing football and you got your bell rung. You'd get up and limp your way back to the huddle, but once the snap came on the next play, the adrenaline kicked in and for the immediate future, your injured body part disregarded the nerves broadband-ing pain signals to your brain. After the whistle, the pain would shoot back, sure, but you could make it through the game, eight second bursts at a time. Hopefully, I'd have it when I needed it. At the moment, I highly doubted it. Ankle, knee, shoulder, ribcage, head, ear, two fingers on the right hand . . . any and all of these may well be broken and/or dislocated. And I was losing blood. At a certain point, adrenaline could only override so much.

I dragged myself to the second floor, poking my head into rooms as I went. I didn't dare turn on any lights for fear of being seen, so I searched in the near-darkness, feeling around when necessary. On the east side of the building, some of the light from the giant floodlights leaked in. I bent down to avoid giving off a shadow on the wall and crawled into Professor Archibald's office, where I found a bottle of Advil in the desk drawer. I poured all of them into my palm, seven of them, started to put some back, then thought better of it and popped all seven in my mouth. I swallowed them back with the cold dregs of the professor's half-full coffee cup still sitting on the desk, probably from when he had gone to his window to see what all the commotion was about.

I gagged and did a sitcom-worthy spit-take, spewing the coffee and Advil onto the floor. Hazelnut. I would have preferred the salty blood taste to this. Hazelnut creamer; why would an adult do that to themselves? Viscous and sickly sweet. I'd only had coffee once, but I liked to think if I did decide to make it a habit I wouldn't drink it like some candied milk a ten-year-old would love. For the second time in the last minute or so I was reminded of Kira. Her busting my balls for eating a Hershey bar rather than the dark chocolate with some kick to it that she liked. I'd worked my way up to 70 percent, but she was in another world. 90 percent or higher. Like bitter chalk, if you asked me.

It seemed odd timing to me that I kept being reminded of her as all this shit was going on around me. As I thought about it, though, I realized it wasn't odd. The odd, or maybe embarrassing, part was that this was the norm, not the exception. Things were always reminding me of her. Or maybe I had it backward. It wasn't that coincidentally random things were connected to her. Rather, whatever's hovering around your brain was bound to search for excuses for you to think about it more.

After scooping up the slimy Advil off the floor and swallowing them back with another swig of kiddy coffee, I searched the other desk drawers and wall cabinets looking for Band-Aids or gauze Mr. Archibald might have kicking around. A long shot that didn't pan out. There was a workout bag in the corner, though. I pulled out a sweaty T-shirt with the slogan "Do You

No?" and pressed it against the cuts on my head, hoping the pressure would stop the bleeding. I took a long drag off the half-filled water bottle at the bottom of the bag, swished it around my bloody hazelnut-infused mouth, and squirted some on my face, trying to clear the blood that had trickled into my eyes.

As I sat there with the T-shirt to my head, waiting for the blood to stop flowing and start coagulating, I considered what to do next. I knew I should be freaking out more. I was cornered; they may not have known where I was, but they knew to look and that I couldn't have gone far. What could I possibly do now? There was a Volvo key fob sitting there on the desk, likely left behind when Mr. Archibald was wrangled up with the others. I could sneak to the staff parking lot, find his car maybe and . . . and what? Try to smash through the gate? I doubted it worked the way it looked on TV with balsa wood or core form or whatever they built sets out of that always conveniently splintered into a million pieces when a stunt driver blew through. I put the fob in my pocket anyway. Of the crappy ideas I'd had, it was the best so far.

The other best option would be to just hide. I'd seen them sending out hundreds of hostages; odds were my mother was in with them. In that case, she was safe and hiding was an option.

But if for some reason she wasn't one of the ones that got out, then she was as good as strapped to a bomb.

Again I wondered: would they really use it, or was it just a bargaining chip? If I were them—knowingly surrounded by cops —I would have definitely planned the escape, maybe demanded a copter out of here, and then, in order to keep them from tracking me, threatened to blow them all up if I was followed. But in that scenario, you have to let the cops know you have it, and based on those cops on the radio, they hadn't. Which meant they planned to use it as a distraction. And what's more of a distraction than blowing a bunch of kids to bits?

No one could do that, though, could they? Maybe not, but would I bet my mother's life on this? Or Kira's? Was I willing to wait it out under the assumption that they must have only planned to use the bomb as a bargaining chip and not a distraction? And even if it was for negotiating purposes, a lot could still go wrong. Back against the wall, these didn't seem like the type of guys to refrain from using any and all means to save themselves.

As soon as the rich kids being bid on were released, the rest of them, my mother included, were disposable pawns. If she was in there, I had to get her out. An idea came to me, but I knew it was not likely to work. Still, slim chance or not, at least I'd have something if it came to it.

This building used to be one of my favorite spots. I hadn't been here all semester, but I used to sneak in after hours and play around with things, try out experiments I had read about that Mr. Archibald would never let me attempt. Rightly so. Like any teenager, I liked to watch things blow up. Add this chemical to that one. A drop of mercury in a solution of potassium chromate in this beaker. Dump it into barium chloride in another. See what happens.

Now I was going to have to see if I could put them together in a way that actually worked. I could always bluff, but I was pretty sure I was going to have to back it up at some point.

Reilly and Javier looked over Preston's shoulder at the aerial shot beaming in from the drone.

"I'd bet there," Javier said, pointing at the screen.

As they talked, Collins brought Sean over to Reilly.

"Kid says he has something important."

Reilly ignored him.

"Look, I think maybe we could help each other," Sean said.

"Is that right?" Reilly said without turning around. "And by me helping you, I presume you mean, letting you go?"

Sean had been content to wait it out. No way his father

couldn't call in enough chits to ensure he wasn't the tenth kid. But that was before they started talking about a bomb. He'd decided he needed out before anything got out of hand. Maybe the bomb was just their insurance policy. Well, he had one too.

"Yes. In exchange for some important information."

"Let's hear it."

"And you'll let me go?"

"I'll still have thirty odd other hostages in here. I'm sure I can spare one."

"It's not the security guard you're looking for."

"And you know . . . how?"

Sean nodded. "If I tell you, do we have a deal?"

"On my honor."

"Cade. Cade Dixon."

Preston typed the name in and a picture of Cade popped up.

"A kid?" Reilly glared at Javier. "A *kid*?"

"Hey, he sucker punched me. Must be an old photo too. I think he's bigger now."

"He better be an ROTC student, for your sake," Reilly said.

"He was 4-H," Preston said, more than happy to pile on Javier, who was always on him for being a nerd.

"What the fuck's a 4-H?" Javier barked.

"I don't know, I think cows and stuff," Preston said. He typed, then, "Stands for Head, Heart, Hands, and Health."

"That's stupid," grumbled Javier.

Seriously? Reilly thought. *These two are debating the merits of 4-H? Now? It never ends. I wonder if every manager in this country has to deal with this kind of stuff. Hundreds of millions of dollars on the line and these guys are going at each other like children.*

"Want me to send everyone the photo and have them look for this guy along with the security guard?" Preston said.

"There *is* no security guard." Unbelievable. Reilly couldn't get over how the stupidity never ended. Even Preston. *The guy can create algorithms in his sleep but he can't figure the unlikely odds that two different people choked out two of our men in the same manner?* "Forget the guard."

Reilly went back to looking at the drone image, searching the surrounding grounds for signs of movement.

Sean tapped him on the shoulder. "So?"

"So, what?" Reilly said without turning.

"Now it's my turn."

"Oh, sorry, I forgot." Reilly pulled out his handgun and pointed it at Sean's face. All the bravado Sean had earlier washed away in an instant. All that was left was a scared boy begging for his life. "You can't do this. I, I . . . my dad . . . he, my dad is a Senator, he can get you what you want. I, I. . . you can't do this."

"You're right." Reilly turned the gun toward the first row of seats and shot Garvey in the thigh.

The place erupted in screams.

Watching the chaos and fear on all the faces, Reilly said to Sean, "You know it was actually providential that you came over here when you did. It was just getting to be time to put people on edge again. You never want them to get comfortable. Humans can be like animals; they adjust to the new normal. Stasis sets in, so you need to shake them once in a while to control the emotions you want in them." He patted Sean's quivering cheeks. "Like these."

"We had a deal," Sean whimpered.

Reilly pointed the gun back at Sean. "Oh, you really did actually believe me?" Reilly turned to Preston. "Would you ever trust me?"

"Fuck no."

Sean, desperate for anything to get him out of this, wailed, "Please, I can help. I swear."

"How can you help?"

"Her!" He pointed to Liz. "Get her on the radio. He will have to surrender."

Reilly looked at the secretary who had tried keeping him from the files. Looking now at her petrified face, he thought, *Of course.* He shouldn't have even needed this sniveling rat to tell him. Reilly replayed the scene at her desk in his head. She must have had a picture of her boy there; every mother does. Reilly didn't have a photographic memory, but he'd trained his mind to pick up every detail, even the seemingly insignificant. He knew it was in there somewhere. "You." He waved Liz over with his gun. As she walked toward him, the image crystalized in his brain: the picture frame of the little boy holding an oversized trophy. He'd knocked it over when he smashed her face into the keyboard. "Tell your son to come inside."

CHAPTER TWENTY

The science lab was one of the few spots on campus that didn't look like it was built two hundred years ago. Even the new buildings at St. Frederick were constructed to look like some colonialists had built it. Probably cost them three times as much as had they just built it normal. The lab, though, was a shiny steel and glass oasis. I guessed emulating the 1800s was fine for English lit. Not so much the time period you'd want to invoke when it came to scientific knowledge.

On the large metal table in front of me, I'd laid out a bunch of open packets and bottles. I poured the white powdery substance into a beaker half-filled with yellow liquid, capped it, and put it in the gym bag I had taken from the professor. Inside the bag I already had three other capped beakers.

As I prepped, my resolve to follow through on this had pretty much dropped to zero. It was a dumb, suicidal idea. And if it came to it, deep down I doubted I'd have the guts the way Kira did to stay behind with Braydon.

As I reached for another empty beaker, a loud squawk reverberated from out in the hallway. A second squawk and then a voice. "Caaaaade . . ."

I dove for the floor and scrambled behind a storage cabinet.

"Caaaaaahhhhhhduuhhhhhhhh, I've got someone who'd like to speak with youuuuu."

It took a second to realize the voice wasn't coming from someone in the hallway, but rather the intercom system. "You seem like a smart kid, so I'm sure you've figured out why I'm reaching out." They talk about a voice from above. Well, here was one about to answer my question. "And there's probably no need to go into the details of what will happen to your mother —pulling her fingers off one at a time, peeling the skin from her lips, letting her bleed out, etcetera, etcetera—if you don't turn yourself in right now."

"Don't!" I heard my mother scream over the intercom. She must've been further from the microphone because it sounded fainter than the man's voice, but significantly more urgent. "Cade, stay where you are!"

"Awww, your mommy doesn't want to see you."

The chill that had run through me upon hearing his initial threat now intensified. Like suddenly stepping into a walk-in freezer.

"Well, Cade, I do. If you're not in the auditorium in five minutes, your mother will . . . like I said, you're a smart kid—I think you know the rest."

One would think that deciding whether to walk into a building full of hostages and their heavily armed guards would take some debating, maybe a little pro and con consideration, but in fact, it was one of the easiest decisions I ever made. Not in any brave sort of way, just in a "Do it, and maybe your mother lives; don't, and she dies" kind of way.

I had my left arm raised in surrender as I limped through the door of the auditorium. The right arm I couldn't lift above my head without a searing pain shooting through the shoulder that had taken the brunt of the fall. The guy I'd turned myself in to outside the science building led me toward the stage, the tip of his rifle pressing into the back of my head.

The first thing I noticed was the smell. Piss. The room reeked of it. They must have been making everyone pee in the corner or something. I coulda told them that was going to be a problem. All anyone did anymore was hydrate. Every kid on campus was constantly taking hits off a water bottle like they're trekking across the Sahara.

I watched my mother. She tried to speak, but nothing more than a barely audible "no" came out, no louder than a breath. She started toward me, but a guard yanked her back hard by the forearm.

I had seen the hostage situation earlier from above, but now, up close, even with the numbers whittled down, the dread and fear in the room were palpable. And no wonder. Lying on the floor in front of them all was Headmaster Harkin in a puddle of congealed blood. It looked like the thick purple ooze that seeps out the crust of a hot pie. Garvey's animal-like moans probably weren't helping either. They must have shot him too because he was pressing a blood-soaked sweater against his right thigh. The younger kids looked catatonic. The older ones merely freaked out. And none more than Sean. *What happened to him?* The guy looked like he was in tilt mode, his eyes watering, snot bubbling out his nose.

Above them, I could see the ransom tallies on the auditorium screen. Taking in the ten columns, I'd say there had to be nearly a billion dollars. At the top of the list was the Baker family with $283 million, Ally Baker presumably off the chopping block. Same went for Reece, his parents having reached $170 mil, and thankfully, Weav, his parents in the $150 range. After that, I was a little surprised to see there was a relatively steep dive. *These families have to be worth more than that, right? They would push it all to the center of the table, wouldn't they?* Knowing my mother, if she were one of them, every penny she had would be there. I couldn't fathom someone might strategically try to pay the least necessary to still save their kid, playing it like the ultimate financial trading scenario. I thought of the Warren Buffet saying I once heard: "Only when the tide goes out do you see who was swimming naked." Maybe some of them were cash poor, and now we were just seeing who was bare-assed all along. Maybe that's why the Cardoza and Harris families only had . . .

Wait, *Harris*?

I looked up at the stage and saw her seated with the group of ten. When I had walked in, I had first scanned the hostages that weren't on stage, assuming Kira would be with them. When she wasn't, I figured they'd released her. She hadn't been in the group of ten when I was in the attic; what was she doing on the stage now?

Braydon. He was gone. They must have chosen to keep her instead. Or, more likely, she chose. Of course she would. I could totally picture it. Her not just volunteering, but her demanding they get Braydon help, and that she'd take his place.

Some people did good things because they wanted you to know they did good things. Kira just did them. Naturally. Whether it was wanting to be a therapist. Or her summer job lifeguarding (which she did even though I was pretty sure she was rich enough to be the one lounging around the pool all day). Or being the one person I knew who almost never talked about herself but asked ten questions of you to every one coming her direction. If I was being her armchair psychologist, I would argue it was because of her brother. Her whole being came from this. That night we had all stayed with her grand-mother up in New Hampshire, she had told me about how he had been in and out of the hospital their whole childhood. There were two responses to a clinically depressed brother who might try to kill himself again at any time. You either shut down or you did what she did—decide you were going to fix him. And if not him, you would fix anyone you could. I remember sitting there across from her, me hopped up on coffee for the first time, wanting to tell her how special she was. But I didn't. It's funny; I'd love if someone told me they thought I was special, but the idea of voicing those words about someone I like seemed embarrassing to admit. It's bizarre that saying something nice was embarrassing. I wish I'd been able to tell her this quality was maybe the thing I loved most about her. But not now. Right now this desire to help others was what had had put her on this stage. Taking the place of another. In last place. Seventeen minutes until that psycho killed her.

Looking at her, though, you'd never guess she had a thing to worry about. Those eyes that always seemed one size too big for their sockets seemingly piercing through me as she looked at me and . . . I'd almost swear there was a hint of a smile. Probably just that cute indentation on her bottom lip that gave her a perpetual expression of good cheer, the one that made her look to always have a Mona Lisa–like glint of a smile. I knew it was her default expression, but I had always pretended the smile was for me. This time, though, maybe it was. A relief at seeing I was still alive. *And given the fact I'm probably going to stop being alive in about three minutes, screw it; I'm going with that assumption.*

The head guy, Reilly, hopped off the stage. As he started toward me, I thought in a sort of out-of-body way, *Funny, this guy is about to kill me, and I'm wondering if a girl I've had a crush on for years is smiling at me. Three years now I've had this crush and done nothing about it. Never had the nerve to tell her the half of how I felt. And as it's looking now, apparently never will.* I made a mental note to myself: in retrospect, asking someone out on a date didn't seem as daunting as it did before trying to negotiate the release of one's mother from some guy ready to blow up a roomful of innocent people.

As Reilly closed in on me, something made him hesitate. He must have caught the just detectable rank smell in the air. He turned to the guy who had brought me in. "You didn't search him, did you?"

"Uh, I didn't think I'd need to. It's a kid. You think he's got a gun?"

I saw Reilly's eyes go to my chest, and I wondered if he could see the slight bulging around my ribcage, something I had feared the guy I had turned myself in to would notice but hadn't.

Reilly grabbed my mother from the guard and wrapped one arm tightly around her throat. "What's under the shirt?" he barked.

"You're a smart kid. I think you can figure it out."

To be exact, what was under my shirt was piperidine, malononitrile, 2-chlorobenzaldehyde, and methylene chloride. Breaking one of those beakers taped to my chest wouldn't amount to much. Two even. But breaking them all at once was another story. Theoretically I knew the chemistry behind it, but as for the application . . . well, I'd never actually tried this before.

"Show me or I snap her neck." Reilly tightened his grip on my mother's throat.

I tried divorcing myself from the feeling rushing through me. A coursing fear telling me to unstrap this contraption, lay it on the ground, and hope this guy let her go. I remembered this feeling well, from back when I was seven, eight, watching my dad wrap his hands around my mother in a similar manner. I would try to do anything my father wanted in hopes he would let her go. I lifted up my shirt, taking particular care not to jostle the beaker filled with the methylene chloride, the volatile color-less liquid taped to the center of my chest.

"And I'm supposed to believe that's a bomb?" Reilly laughed.

"You're supposed to believe there's enough of a possibility it's a bomb that you let her go. Maybe I messed up my ratios. Or I've got the wrong combination. You could take the chance . . ." Trying to sound sure of myself, I spoke as slowly as I could. "But so you know . . . I did get an A in Chem." (Full disclosure: I might have had that line chambered when I walked in). "If you let her walk out the gate, I'll do the same. Taking these beakers with me. And you won't have to worry about the 50 percent chance I'm not bluffing." I always thought Sun Tzu was just cocky bluster that assholes used to rationalize bad actions, but this one time the dude had a point: *The supreme art of war is to subdue the enemy without fighting.*

Reilly looked at me. Probably trying to read me. I wondered what he saw. Gun to his own head, he'd probably say I was bluffing, but he also had to figure I was right: why take the chance over a school secretary? Reilly didn't need her. Or me. *Get these two off the property and move on.* That's what I'd be thinking.

"Ferland. Take these two to the front gate and let them go."

"Nope," I said, "I don't trust you. Your guy takes her there, but I stay. When they let you know on the other side that she's safe, then I walk out of here. Till then, I'm a bomb that doesn't leave your side."

Reilly looked at the guy who had brought me in and said dryly, "You don't even think to pat him down, yet this teenage kid knows enough to keep his leverage?" He shook his head. "Take her to the gate."

The Ferland guy grabbed my mother but she struggled to get free. "*No!!!* He won't let you go!"

"Trust me," I said.

"No . . . he won't let you go," she said, her voice trembling. "He won't let you go . . ."

I avoided looking her in the eye; I didn't want her to see that, yeah, I kinda agreed with her. "Take her out," I said as firmly as I could.

She struggled, but Ferland was too big and easily dragged her thrashing body out the door. As they left, I heard Sean plead, "What about me? I told you how to get him. We had an agreement."

That scumbag. I shouldn't have been surprised he sold me out. Then again, who's to say how I would have reacted in that situation, my life being bid on as I sat helplessly. Sure, he was a dick, but now, hypothetical gun to *my* head, I'd have to admit I wasn't any more pissed at the guy now than when I had found out he'd kissed Kira before and I hadn't. Were my priorities a little tweaked right now? Yeah, sure, but you tell me the weird places your mind goes the next time you're standing next to your crumpled bloody principal and have at least three guns aimed in your exact direction.

"Really? Still? You *still* think I'm going to hold up my end with you?" Reilly said, sounding truly surprised.

"You did with him."

"You shoulda strapped some colorful glass thingies to your chest." Reilly then looked at me. "You have some big ones on you. Fucking with me like this."

I ignored him and said to Preston, "Do you have video of out there? Put it up."

Preston put the video feed of the front gate up onto the main screen. On it, my mother and Ferland came into view. They stopped as Ferland yelled something inaudible. In response, the cops on the other side backed up and the gate opened. My mother didn't move and instead yelled something at Ferland. He tried to shove her out. She wouldn't leave and instead grabbed at his arm, pleading to him. Finally, Ferland dragged her by the shirt, and flung her out the gate. She tumbled to the driveway. Before she could get up and run back in, two cops rushed in, grabbed her, and whisked her away.

"There you go," said Reilly, arms folded. "Your turn."

She was safe. I was shocked it had worked. My mother was on the other side. Pissed, sure. But safe. With the cops. And in two minutes it was beginning to look like I might be too. All I needed to do was back out the door and walk away. Except . . .

Except that theoretically Reilly could have me shot once I was outside the auditorium and away from them. I was guessing Reilly wasn't the type to care if the guy escorting me to the gate got blown up along with me.

"Well?" Reilly said, making an out-with-you gesture with his hand.

I hesitated. What was my other option? I needed a hostage

of my own until I got to the gate. Someone who Reilly actually cared stayed alive. None of the kids or teachers. Reilly himself, sure, but there was zero chance he was walking outside with me, putting himself in danger. Maybe Preston? Everyone needs an IT guy. But that was a long shot.

I took another scan around the room, hoping to come up with something. All I saw was a couple dozen scared, unhelpful faces looking back at me. If someone didn't do something, they very well may all go up in the explosion Reilly may or may not have planned. I looked at the ten students seated onstage. Any chance one of them was worth it to Reilly? Enough to get me to the gate? Maybe Ally or Reece. They were both high on the list, worth way more to him than me. Could I really do that? To be honest, I half expected these beakers to explode any moment. Could I really grab one of them and put them in danger too? As I looked at the ten, I caught Kira's eyes again. Bomb or no bomb, she was doomed. Tenth place is a death sentence, and with only fifteen minutes before the deadline, it was looking like her parents were never climbing out of that hole.

It hit me what I had to do.

Before I could change my mind, I ripped the beakers from my chest, squinted my eyes shut and smashed them to the ground in front of Reilly, who instinctively dove backward. Who wouldn't when expecting something to explode in your face? Which the beakers did. But not in the way they all probably expected. There was a loud bang and a gray plume of smoke. Before Reilly and the others could react, I lunged toward Kira, my eyes and mouth squeezed shut.

As I pulled Kira back, the tear gas started to take effect on the others. I had hoped I wouldn't need to try it, that the bluff alone would work, and I'd never have to see whether the combinations of powders and liquids would actually synthesize the way they were theoretically supposed to. But apparently I'd gotten it right, 2-chlorobenzaldehyde and malononitrile producing a condensation reaction catalyzed with the piperidine and then weaponized and dispersed with methylene chloride.

Everyone on the stage was in a state of disorientation, coughing fitfully and rubbing at their eyes as they watered uncontrollably. It looked like Reilly was in the worst shape, having gotten the brunt of the shattered beakers.

I yanked Kira by the arm and led her toward the wing of the stage. Moving as fast as I could with someone who couldn't open their eyes, I dragged Kira behind the big velvet curtain, shoved aside the wardrobe rack, and slammed my hip into the emergency exit bar leading out the back of the stage. Pulling Kira up against the storage shed behind the auditorium, I pressed a hand over her mouth to muffle the coughs as I waited for the gunmen who would inevitably be running out the door after us. Unable to breathe, naturally she struggled, but I pressed tight. She struggled more, and I was forced to press harder. When they finally ran by, I let go and she was overcome by a cascade of coughing and hacking.

"Let's go." I grabbed Kira's hand and pulled her off into the dark.

CHAPTER TWENTY-ONE

On the other side of the gate, the cops had spiked to high alert, getting in formation as they readied for the order to storm the place. Inside the trailer, the parents huddled nervously, watching—but unable to hear—Pruitt and Jackson debate.

"Call it and go," Jackson said.

Pruitt shook her head.

"The kid must've been right about the bomb. We gotta go now," Jackson said with more force.

"If that was a bomb, we'd know it," Pruitt said calmly. "That was something else. Not big enough to blow anything up."

"I don't like it."

"I don't like to wait either, but it's the right call. Get them on the radio."

Jackson toggled the radio Reilly had sent. "What's going on in there? Is everyone safe?"

They waited. Nothing. Jackson looked at Pruitt. "We need to go."

She shook her head.

Jackson barked into the radio, "What's the status in there?"

More silence and then a crackle. "That wasn't us," Reilly said, his voice sounding raw. "No one has been hurt. That was the kid."

Hastings yelled out, "Show us our kids! I need to see my son. *Now.*"

"They are fine. For now." Reilly coughed through these last words, anger rising in his voice. "But I'm changing things. There are now two on the chopping block thanks to that little prick. The lowest two bidders both die. And I'll keeping adding more if anyone tries anything again."

When Reilly clicked off, Pruitt said quietly to Jackson, "The kid has her."

"What?"

"The boy." She shook her head. "I don't know what happened in there, but they don't have the Harris girl anymore. He wouldn't have added the other. And there wasn't a gunshot, so they didn't get the boy either."

"You think the kid . . . what?"

"I don't know. Get me the mother."

Once Liz had been brought to the trailer, Pruitt and Jackson stepped outside, away from the other parents.

"Liz Dixon? I'm Britt. How are you holding up?"

"My son. What do you know about my son?"

"Far as we know, Liz, everyone is still okay."

"He should be here by now."

"What do you mean, he should be here?"

"He had a bomb or something wrapped around him and he . . ." Liz couldn't finish the sentence; once she said the word bomb her throat had felt like it was starting to clamp shut. She could only assume the noise they had just heard had to be whatever it was he had wrapped around his chest, had to be what exploded.

"We are still sussing the situation, but we have reason to believe everyone is still alive." Pruitt couldn't be sure, but she could hear something in Reilly's voice. It was an anger that came from embarrassment. Someone had bested him.

"He has to be . . ." Liz said, tears slowly filling her eyes.

~

Javier would love to say it to Reilly right now. Oh, would he love to. *Who's the idiot now? Who let a kid best whom?* He would even throw in the "whom" just to give it an extra jab at Reilly who always used that fucking word—just to make them all feel dumber, Javier was pretty sure.

Instead, Javier said, "Want me to turn the power back on out there?"

"We can't. You're going to have to find them in the dark. They're little kids; I think you should be able to find a couple scared kids."

Hey, I'm not the one who let "a couple kids" escape. Oh, Javier'd love to say that too. But based on the seething, Def-Con 1 scowl on Reilly's face, Javier figured he'd holster that thought for now.

~

Kira was still having difficulty seeing, her eyes watering from the tear gas. We needed to find somewhere to hide and let her eyes adjust.

I had watched the gunmen who had run past us enter the cafeteria next door, so I figured, rather than run from them, I'd go where they'd already searched. As I led Kira toward the cafeteria I could feel the intensity of her grip, the fingertips pressing into the back of my hand.

Entering from the rear, I saw a truck backed up against the loading bay and had an idea. Maybe a way out. Right now there wasn't enough time to try it, but maybe when Kira's eyes cleared up.

Once inside, we snuck through the back office and into the

storage area. I looked around at the racks filled with large insti-tutional-sized jars of condiments, boxes of cereals, and other food items. I was looking for something, anything, that might be useful if we ran into one of these guys, but I'd chosen the wrong building for that—potato chips, chocolate sauce, mustard, risotto, corn starch—all great if I was planning dinner, maybe, but nothing I could crack someone across the head with.

On the far side, I pushed through the swinging door that led into the kitchen. Maybe it was because I couldn't see much in the dark, but the smell of cleaning chemicals was overwhelming. When I washed dishes at Corrsero's I used to come home reeking of that smell. Even after showering, I'd lie in bed smelling that odor of metallic citrus that the floor cleaner gave off.

I leaned Kira's head over the sink with my left hand, and cupping my right, I splashed warm water up into her eyes. Instinctively, her hand went to her eyes, trying to rub the irri-tants out. I pulled her hand back and tried to splash more gently. After a minute or so, I stopped and watched her blinking rapidly while trying to resist rubbing the tear gas further into her eyes. I didn't realize it at first, but I had been running my left hand over the back of her head. In my mind, I was doing it in a comforting sense, but now looking down at my hand, I realized I came across more like someone petting their dog. In my defense, it was the first time I'd touched a girl's hair probably since pulling a pigtail in kindergarten.

Still blinking rapidly, Kira put her hand below the motion-sensing towel dispenser. I took it as a good sign that she could see well enough to find it. As she patted her eyes with the paper towels, I scanned the room looking for something more useful than Ruffles and Hershey syrup. Something kitchens are never in short supply of.

Knives.

Sharp knives.

Working at Corrsero's I was always fascinated watching the

sous chefs chop vegetables. The tap-tap-tap of a carrot being diced at lightning speed, the chef always careful to tuck the fingertips in so that if she missed, she wouldn't lose a digit. I knew just how sharp kitchen people kept their knives. One of them had told me it's not the sharpest knives that are dangerous. It's the dull ones. A dull blade slips.

I yanked the largest handle out of the knife block and unsheathed a stainless chef's knife, the business end of it a glistening twelve-inch blade about two inches wide, the steel curving to a razor sharp point. Could I sink this into someone's gut? I could never see myself shooting someone with a gun, but for some reason a knife seemed plausible. Maybe it was the thinking that a bullet kills and a knife only wounds. I knew this was illogical, that this Amazon jungle machete of a cooking knife could just as easily take a life, but I hoped if the time came, I could convince the safety on my brain otherwise. Besides, my only other option at this point was what? Bonk 'em on the head with one of these frying pans like some cartoon character?

"What the fuck was that?"

I turned to see Kira looking at me, those big eyes of hers now bloodshot and incredulous. These were the first words she'd said since we had run from the auditorium. They came out of her like they would a two-pack-a-day smoker, her voice dry and hoarse.

"Uh, tear gas. Sort of."

"No 'sort of.' I can vouch for that."

"Cool."

"Cool?"

"Well not cool, but, well, I didn't think it was going to work, to be honest."

"I thought you had a bomb."

"I was hoping they thought the same."

I pushed open the swinging door leading from the kitchen into the dining area. At the other end of the room was a set of stairs leading up. "Where do those go?"

Before Kira could answer, a light reflected off the dining room windows. Her response time was better than mine, and she shoved me to the floor and dove next to me. From the floor, we could see a bright light outside, moving toward the east side of the building.

We scrambled between the cafeteria tables on our hands and knees in the opposite direction of the light. Just as we reached the door leading to the bathroom hallway, the main cafeteria door banged open. Kira and I ducked through to the hallway seconds before a bright beam of light swept the room.

Once in the hallway, we scrambled to our feet and ran past the bathrooms and toward the emergency exit. Bleating alarm giving our location away or not, we had no choice. I shoved the push bar and the door swung outward. Silence.

I always knew those "Do Not Open" signs were bullshit.

I didn't know which one of us started running first, but the other followed suit and we raced across the lawn toward the nearest building, the gymnasium. Ducking into the first door, we scurried around the lacrosse nets, archery targets, and other gym class gear stored in the equipment room. I scanned the room looking for something I could grab to replace the kitchen knife. I still wasn't certain I had the nerve to thrust the blade into someone. The hockey sticks looked unwieldy. The javelin, comical. Bow and arrows, great in theory, but aside from never having used one before, it also seemed the type of thing where I'd be gunned down way before I could ever load and shoot an arrow.

A bat. I may never have the guts to shoot someone with a gun or stab them with a kitchen knife, but I figured a nice thirty-two-inch wide-barreled Mizuno, I'd happily take a cut at one of these dicks with that. But wherever Coach Rayley stored the baseball gear, it wasn't here.

Once we'd crossed through the room, we slid quietly into the hallway of coaches' offices. "I know a spot," Kira said, her voice still roughed up from the tear gas. "Up here."

I chased after her through the stairwell door. We wound our way up, and then stepped out onto the running track that circled the gym from three stories up. Kira started running clockwise. Half a lap around, she stopped at the stretching area.

"Give me a boost."

I looked at the ceiling above and saw the two-foot square hatch I'd never noticed before when I'd run on the track. I set the knife down and put my hands together. Kira stepped on them and a laser of pain shot along my entire right side again, the result of my earlier fall. If you can call jumping out a window a fall.

As I lifted her, Kira pushed the hatch up and to the side and then pulled herself through. I leapt and grabbed the corners of the opening and tried to pull myself up into the attic area. The pain flared along my side again and my right arm gave out. Kira reached out and grabbed my armpit. As she yanked I couldn't help but yelp as I was momentarily blinded by the flash of pain in my shoulder. She pulled again, this time getting my right arm and shoulder up over the edge. With my left arm, I pulled myself the rest of the way up and in. Kira slid the hatch door back into place.

"How come you know about this?"

"One of my friends works the front desk and has a key to the building. A couple of us used to sneak up to the roof on clear nights and star gaze. Watch your step crossing to the ladder," she said as I followed her along the open framing of the attic, careful not to step on—and through—the Ruxol insulation sheets laid in between the floor joists. We climbed the metal rungs attached to the wall and pulled ourselves up onto the roof. On a different day, in a different world, this would be amazing. Kira and I sneaking up to the rooftop, a clear night so you could see Mt. Rollins to the east and Lake Canopy to the north. I could picture the two of us leaning up against the three-foot-high parapet that ran around the roof's edge, peering over to watch unsuspecting students below. Or maybe lying on the roof side by side, pointing out constellations and making out like we were in some sappy romantic comedy.

Tonight was not that night.

Tonight we sat against the three-foot wall and ducked out of sight, scared and uncertain of what to do next. For now, it was simply this: hide and hope. Hope that in their search, these gunmen would never consider we could have found our way to the roof of the gymnasium. Who knew, maybe we were safe and could wait it out here. I'd actually believe it too . . . had I not just remembered that, like an idiot, I had forgotten to pick up the kitchen knife after lifting Kira into the crawl space, and that the knife was now sitting on the edge of the track, directly under the hatch. It might as well be a blinking arrow pointing toward us. It was too late to go back for it now, though. Anyway, maybe I was just being paranoid; they'd still need to put a whole bunch of two and twos together to find us here. We were likely as safe here as anywhere. Particularly Kira, who had been sitting at number ten on the list and so was at way more risk back there. Which triggered a sudden thought. The same thing that Kira said at almost the exact instant it came to me. If this were the aforementioned rom-com it would be cute, a moment of simpatico.

Again, *tonight ain't that night.*

"They're going to kill somebody else in my place," she whispered. Since we'd left the auditorium we hadn't thought anything but *Go! Run!* But now, as the adrenaline subsided, we had both remembered what we had run from. "Eric. His parents were the next ones above mine. They're going to kill him instead, aren't they?"

Although I was thinking that very same thing, I said, "I don't think so."

"What makes you think that?" she said with enough hope in it that it hurt. Enough to get me to make something up I didn't believe.

"If I were them, and someone had just come in and set off a

bunch of tear gas and escaped with one of my hostages, I'd be fast-forwarding to my end game and getting out with whatever cash I'd gotten as fast as I could."

This seemed to relieve her. At least until her next thought, which also ran more or less parallel to mine. "Yeah, but what do you think their end game is? You said something about a bomb."

My mother was safe. Kira was probably safe. Same for me. I had told the cops about the bomb . . . which maybe there wasn't even one. Or if there was one, maybe it was only going to be used to bluff. An insurance policy. Not to be a selfish dick, but none of this was my responsibility anymore. I had done everything I could. I wasn't leaving this roof till this whole thing was over. "There's nothing we can do about it."

CHAPTER TWENTY-TWO

8:27 p.m. Three minutes to the appointed time.

Nearly a billion dollars on the board. "One *billion*," Reilly said to himself. Literally said it aloud to hear the "B" on his lips. It was an insane amount. He wanted to pace, he really did. But with everyone in the room watching him, he couldn't. It was a tell. A weakness. Worse, a cliché. But frustration really did elicit a desire to pace. And he was more than frustrated that his guys hadn't found the two kids yet. He wasn't worried about anything they would do. Rather, he worried what this loose hand was doing to the mindsets out there. In the trailer. Would the earlier commotion set off a panic and a chain reaction? He had this whole thing planned to the smallest aspect, and now this.

Counterintuitively, he needed the cops to think everyone on this side of the wall was safely under his control. The counterintuitive part being, two loose kids might be seen from the cops' vantage point as more dangerous than everyone contained. Like any situation, people craved order. They craved the authoritarian figure who had things in control. The minute they see chaos, the revolt comes. A perfectly executed plan devolving into an uncontrollable situation.

Reilly had been listening to the bugged radio and no indication was given yet that they were contemplating storming the place, but he couldn't be certain.

"Reilly." Preston was holding up the sphere.

Of course he's calling. He must be losing his shit after that mess. Reilly would have preferred having Preston tell G he wasn't available, but G was no different than anyone else out there. He needed to be comforted, like a little child. Told that Reilly had everything under control and that this was just one more step in the process. Nothing to concern himself with. Nothing to panic over and ruin the whole thing.

Reilly took the sphere from Preston and said, "Yes?" He could already guess the first two questions out of G's mouth. The answers to which were: "Relax, I have it in control" and "Everyone that you care about" respectively.

"What the fuck?!" G's voice came through as a hard whisper.

"Relax. I have it in control."

"Are they safe?"

Two for two, thought Reilly as he said, "Everyone that you care about. There was a loose end of sorts, but—"

"Someone radioed out. About a *bomb*. What the fuck?"

Reilly knew that G had the same access to the tapped radio as he had, but he had been hoping he might not be in a position over there to be monitoring. "Relax. There's no bomb. It's a scared kid trying to do anything he can to get the cops to do something. He's—"

"A kid? You have a loose kid?" Two, to be exact, but Reilly figured this wasn't the time for exactitude. Again, Reilly could anticipate G's next words. Some variation on, "This is what I'm paying you dumb fucks for?" But this time he was wrong.

"Kill him. Kill him now. Whoever it is that is ratcheting everyone up out here. They're going to do something stupid."

You control chaos by inflicting some of your own. That's what Karamov had taught him. As soon as G hung up, Reilly picked up the radio connected to the trailer. "Change of plans. And it comes with good news and bad news. I'd ask you which you'd like first, but it's never any fun telling you the bad first. You wouldn't really enjoy the momentary reprieve you think you're getting when you hear the good news." Reilly stopped, realizing he had been unconsciously pacing the stage while he talked. "I'm extending the deadline until 9 p.m. Whoever ends up in the last two spots gets another thirty minutes knowing their little ones are alive." It was an enlightening experiment, Reilly had come to realize. He was right that pitting these ultra-rich against each other would result in way bigger a ransom than he may have otherwise gotten. But interestingly, once it had become apparent that there were two obvious laggards, the other eight had slowed. The only two still nudging upward these last ten minutes were the Weavers and Martells. Reilly didn't have kids of his own, but from all the bluster he'd heard from friends that did about how they would trade their own life for their kid's, he was surprised at the noticeable drop in urgency when the odds started to look good. These parents were willing to lay their money out there to save their kid. Just not all of it.

Still, a billion dollars was nothing to sneeze at. Well, a billion minus—Reilly looked at the second-place number on the screen above: $183 million. Even considering that deduction, $800 million or so was still an insane payday.

"So, that's the good news. Now the bad. I've decided since there's no real contest anymore for low men on the totem pole, we need to up the ante. A billion five. That shouldn't be a problem, should it? A Hampton house here. A Cessna there. Just a few more electronic transfers in the ether. At least it better not be a problem. If it is, and you all together can't crack a billion and a half by 9 p.m., everyone's tyke is toast."

Reilly stood in the middle of the stage. Control. He had taken control. Even thrown some alliteration their way. *That's showing command of the moment,* he thought, smiling. This would change the narrative. Not only that, he just now realized, but he didn't feel like pacing anymore.

~

It was strange. Hidden up here on the roof, knowing we were probably finally safe, I actually felt the least safe I'd felt over the course of this whole thing. It was the lack of control over what happened next. Sitting there, waiting it out, doing nothing other than hoping none of the men bothered looking here. We couldn't even peek over the side of the parapet to see what was going on below, see if they were still searching. If we were spotted, we were trapped. Dead.

All we could do was wait. Wait for it to be over. Or wait to be found.

"How do you know how to make . . . make whatever that was. Tear gas?"

"Sorta. There wasn't any propylene glycol, but I was able to use methylene chloride instead."

"Oh, well that explains it." She shook her head slowly. "*What the fuck?*"

"I'm not one of those kids that was planning to blow up his school or go on a shooting spree," I said defensively, seeing how it looked from her eyes. "I just . . . I was just, I don't know, interested in, well . . . it was something I read."

"Well, that's a relief." For what I was guessing was the first time since this all started, Kira laughed. "I hate to ask what else is on your reading list."

We sat shoulder to shoulder, backs against the parapet. Neither of us spoke for a few beats until Kira said, "Let me ask you something." She paused, and I thought of all the things she might want to ask. If I had to bet, "How fucked are we?" would have been the two-to-one Vegas favorite.

"Do you spy on people?"

"Well, no. I mean, I have. Not on random people or

anything." The more I spoke, the worse it sounded. "I do spy on classes. Long story."

"I knew it!"

"You did?"

"Yeah, when you were on Reece about that GXC Holdings thing. Plus, it's weird—you're going to think I'm crazy—but I sometimes get this feeling now and again that I'm being watched."

"I'm not a stalker or something. I do it to make money."

She gave me a look. She was right; that didn't make it sound much better.

"So I can write papers to sell."

"It was a nice feeling actually. Like being watched by someone protecting you."

Here I had spent the day doing all sorts of crazy shit I would never have thought I dared to do, yet still, even with a perfect lead-in, *still* I couldn't get up the nerve to say the one simple statement I'd been wanting to say for ages. That I liked watching her. I'd had zero problems leaping on that guy or walking into that hornet's nest with just the beakers taped to me, but I wasn't brave enough to say what I'd been thinking for years? *I like you. I think you're the friendliest girl I know. The most interesting girl I know. The smartest. Prettiest. Nicest. Sure, if one wanted to piss on things, one might point out I don't exactly speak to many girls and so the competition for those positions is limited, but still . . .*

"You ever hear the theory that you are the average of the five people you spend the most time around?" Kira asked. "I used to think about it when I had those thoughts that I was being watched. That maybe this ghost or whatever was one of my five. I wondered how that might affect me. What it turned me into."

I ran a quick tally in my head: My mother. Garvey, I guess. Weav. And maybe my MMA instructor. I don't even have five. You could make the argument Kira's my fifth but any time spent with her is me above her, staring down at her classes.

"Who are yours?" she asked.

"You don't want to know."

"So, what's the plan?"

"If you hadn't noticed, I don't know what the eff I'm doing."

"It looked like you did in there. How do you not panic? You looked relaxed almost."

Funny she thought that. *She* looked the calm one. "The things that panic me are different. Have you ever been punched in the face?"

"Uh, no."

"It's amazing how a punch to the face washes away the panic. I think it's why I like MMA so much."

"That sounds kinda insane."

"The first one may freak you out. But by the tenth time you've been whacked, you disassociate, and there's almost a weird serenity about the situation that settles in. Whatever it is, it works."

"Oh." Her face turned grim. "You're not talking about your martial arts stuff, are you . . ."

I didn't respond. That was unfair of me, I knew. I could tell by the look on her face she had made the connection to my father, and that she was feeling sorry for me. I hadn't lied—I really had built up a useful tolerance to getting smacked around —but, yeah, I probably wanted her to feel sorry for me. But it had the opposite effect on me as I thought; I felt terrible making her feel terrible.

I tried to lighten the mood. "He used to call me Spurt."

"Why Squirt?

"No. *Spurt.* It was his way of reminding me I wasn't planned."

"Oh, like . . ."

"Yeah," I laughed. "Like that. For years I didn't even know what it meant. Thought it was his way of saying sport. At some point as a kid I was reading some magazine I'd found, and I saw the word in context. After that all his comments about trading three seconds for eighteen years made sense. It also made a lot more sense why he did what he did. No one sets out to be the guy who punches his wife and kids. I guess for him, I don't know, he felt boxed in. He didn't want a kid. Never would have married my mother if he hadn't gotten her pregnant. Maybe trapped people lash out; I don't know."

"I'm sure people feel trapped about a lot of things. They don't all take it out on others."

I'd never really told anyone the whole story. Not even Dr. Phelan. Maybe I'd never get a chance to tell anyone. I wanted to, but it just felt too surreal, or maybe pointless, to be talking about this on the roof at this particular moment. Instead, I shrugged.

"I'm sorry," she said, putting her hand on my forearm, and again I felt bad for making her feel bad. Besides, she was the one who should be upset. Better to have one dick of a parent and one amazing one than two apathetic ones. She'd never said as much, but you don't dump your seven-year-old kid off to boarding school and never visit if you care.

"That was probably the bravest thing I've ever seen," I said.

"What was?"

She honestly didn't know. "Braydon. Volunteering to take his spot."

"Anybody would have done it."

"No way. I know I wouldn't have."

"You just walked into a room with a tear gas thing taped to your chest."

"Yeah, but that was for my mother. There's some self-interest. You did it because it was someone who needed help, not someone you wanted to help. There's a big difference."

"Remember that concert we went to? We all stayed with my grandmother."

Uh, yeah. Only the best twenty-one hours of my life. "Up in New Hampshire?"

"When my parents sent me here, she would come visit me on all the parents' weekends. Come to my hoop games. She was my closest friend. I don't blame my parents; they just weren't kid types. But I don't know what I would have done without her when I was younger. I've never seen anyone come see Braydon."

"But still."

"It's sort of out of self-interest too."

"That's one way to look at it." The other being: she's basically amazing.

She was silent a moment, then she said, "Why do think they wouldn't pay to get me out?" The words came out barely audible, as they might when you said the words as you realized for the first time that your parents would put a price on your life. I wondered what that was like for her, watching that number just sit there as she saw the tallies for the other kids skyrocket. "I don't blame them for not wanting me at home."

"Have you ever heard the saying, 'Not until the tide goes out, do you know who is naked'? In all the big market crashes, there were inevitably people who were exposed when it all started falling apart. Madoff, that type of guy, that during good times no one questioned things, but then when withdrawals came calling, they were shown to have bogus books."

"You think my dad was running a pyramid scheme?"

"Maybe not that, but something. Something wasn't up and up." I shrugged. "Coulda been totally legal, but they may have been leveraged to some level they couldn't handle when something went sideways, and now don't actually have the ability to pay more."

"So my parents are frauds . . ."

"Better that than cold-hearted and not willing to pay for their daughter's safety."

I looked at her, but I couldn't tell whether that made her feel any better. When she didn't say anything, I asked, " Do you know the song 'Sweet Things'? It's . . ."

Just as these words were coming out of my mouth, I saw it.

Movement out of the right side of my eye. I grabbed Kira and shoved her back against the large rooftop HVAC unit.

Fuck, fuck, fuck . . . we were idiots to come up here. We trapped ourselves.

The gunman hadn't seen us yet. He would have—and we'd both probably have a bullet lodged in our brains right now—but for that slight flicker of light, just enough to turn me in the direction of the trap door lifting open, the moonlight licking off the metal handle. Now, with our backs to the HVAC unit, we sat motionless, hoping the gunman didn't cross the rooftop toward us. I considered what would happen next: in less than ten seconds, the gunman was going to peer around one side of this HVAC unit and that'd be the end of it. Of us.

Unless . . .

Unless I could guess right on the 50-50. The only chance was if I could get a second of surprise by sneaking around the unit in one direction and come up behind the guy as he discovered Kira.

Left or right. 50-50.

Nothing I'd read was going to help me here. This was pure fate. Or faith. Choose wrong and we were both dead. Choose correctly and there was hope.

I pressed Kira's shoulder, hoping she understood it to mean "Stay put," and then I inched my way around to the right, my back tight up against the cold, vibrating steel. My whole system had been running on about 10,000 RPMs, so until now I hadn't realized the air had chilled as night set in.

When I reached the corner, I took a calming breath and edged around the 90-degree turn. No sign of the gunman. I inched toward the next corner, peered around, and saw the back of him as he moved slowly toward the next corner, the one where he was about to find Kira. I had a second, maybe two. I stepped faster, disregarding my attempt at keeping totally quiet. The gunman lowered his rifle at Kira, motioning her to stand. As she did, I took the last two steps and launched myself, leading with my shoulder, just the way Coach Phillips had taught us. Well, Phillips never said to launch into a head shot with its attendant fifteen-yard, hitting-a-defenseless-receiver penalty, but the occasion called for it. I felt the point of my shoulder blade strike cheekbone.

On contact, the rifle fell from his hands and clattered a few feet to the right. He stumbled but didn't fall. I felt like I had hit him twice as hard as any padded wide receiver I'd ever drilled going over the middle, so even given his fifty-plus-pound advantage, I thought I would have at least knocked him to the ground. Instead, I was the one laid out on the roof. Before I could get up, he grabbed me by the scruff and unloaded a right fist into my cheekbone.

People have been conditioned to think a punch in the face is the ultimate knockout. Sure, if you get one just right, maybe catch their jaw hard enough to propel it forcefully into the upper teeth and send the brain sloshing against the inner wall of the skull, that can do it, but more often than not, when you throw a punch, it glances off an area you didn't expect to hit, since, surprise, the other person is trying their mightiest to get out of the way of said punch.

Even this guy wasn't above winding up with a big right-hand wheelhouse, going for that knockout punch. Maybe it's how satisfying it feels to connect and knock someone cold. Or maybe he didn't expect much resistance from a civilian. Particularly a seventeen-year-old one. But I had absorbed worse, and I was able to ride the punch and then return serve by crashing the heel of my right foot into the side of his right knee. If I recalled correctly from Anatomy, I probably just ripped the quadriceps tendon from the kneecap, caving in the patella. His crumpling to the ground in screaming agony was a good indication I was right. A right cross to the jaw may well be satisfying, but there are two other underrated areas: the knee and the throat. Crush a fist or a foot forcefully into either of those, and your opponent is floor-bound.

Whenever I wrestled at the gym, I could only take moves so far. You were allowed to hurt but not injure, so some moves I knew in theory but had never fully unleashed them. I felt a strange rush of excitement at the chance to use all I knew and not worry about the consequences of injuring my opponent. There were consequences if I *didn't* inflict damage. Even in the midst of this life or death exchange, I was aware of the thrilling feeling at having the safety clicked off.

I leapt onto the guy's back, grabbed his arms in a double wristlock, and wrenched them back. The cracking sound of shoulder bones reminded me of biting into a chicken wing before sucking out the marrow. I wrapped my legs around his neck, but just as I started to squeeze, he rotated to his left, got the leverage, and flipped me onto my back. Now it was his turn to place a chokehold. With both paws tightly wrapped around my neck, he pinned me to the ground. I had gotten lucky the first two times and somehow had choked out both guys. This time, I was on the receiving end.

I felt my internal pendulum swing from excitement to sheer panic. I had read people who survive near-drowning speak of the ecstasy of the sensation. And of course there were the tales of autoerotic asphyxiation that guys always joked about. But I was beginning to think that was all bullshit. Nothing about this felt remotely ecstatic. In fact, I was in full-fledged panic mode, writhing on the ground, trying to dislodge the guy's arms, but as I weakened from the lack of oxygen my arms did little more than flail.

My life did not flash before my eyes. The only thing that did flash was the car crash that Christmas. Ironically, just as I was about to take my last breath, my brain flashed to the time I thought I didn't want to take it anymore. And now, as things did appear to be ending, I was seeing the moment again, and I thought: I was wrong. Way wrong.

Live.

I want to live. I yanked his body to the right as hard as I could, but in my weakened state I was unable to toss the larger man. I thrashed again, trying to rock him forward in order to put his center of gravity to a tipping point. He barely budged. I tried again and again, each attempt weaker and less effective, and realized that it didn't matter what I wanted; there was nothing I was going to be able to do about it.

CHAPTER TWENTY-THREE

If Pruitt had her choice, these parents would never have been in the trailer. It was only adding to the chaos, especially after Reilly's last announcement. But it wasn't her choice. It had come from the president himself. But really it was Senator Hastings and a couple of the others. She knew they had put in calls to the president demanding they be involved. It made you wonder how the president ever got anything done what with rich donors calling in favors. Regardless, now she was babysitting a bunch of wealthy, freaked out parents.

Back in the old days, back when people would miscarriage every second kid, Pruitt figured, this ransom idea would never have worked. Back then, people assumed kids were going to die: that's why you had eight or ten and you even bought life insurance on *them,* not you, because you'd be losing a farm hand if one died. No matter how salient a point it may be, she thought better of sharing it with Hastings, who was in her face again.

"Sir, I wish I could . . ."

"I don't care what you wish," Hastings barked. He gestured toward the group of parents. "We need to see the kids."

"Sir, I can . . ."

"You tell that guy in there we need to see the kids are alright after that explosion."

With the other parents vehemently voicing their agreement, and the situation in danger of getting out of hand, Pruitt decided on the least bad option. She picked up the radio and said, "Reilly."

After a beat, Reilly answered, "Yeeeeesss, my dear?"

"Put the kids on camera. We need to see the ten are all okay."

"You *need*? You don't get to need anything. If I decide to do something, I will do it."

"*Can* you put them up? The money is already in the bank accounts. No clawing it back now. They just want assurance everyone is . . ."

"All ten are alive and more or less well."

Does everyone have to interrupt? That was the biggest thing that drove Pruitt crazy. Men had an innate ability to interrupt a woman way more than a fellow man. Even men under her. Point it out, though, and you're a whiny girl. She wouldn't mind being interrupted if they actually said something worth interrupting for.

"And the boy? The one who got the woman out?"

"Who cares?"

"I do." As she spoke, Pruitt caught eyes with Liz. She couldn't decide if this woman's kid was a brave SOB. Or an insanely stupid SOB.

"He's alive . . ."

Pruitt watched Liz let out what probably felt like the first breath she'd taken in the last twenty minutes. The momentary relief was quickly squashed when Reilly continued, "But only until I find him."

⁓

It was over.

I hadn't given up—the will to fight back was still there—but with the gunman choking off all air, my body had lost the ability to respond. My thrashing had slowed, and now all I could do was swing meekly at his face, with as much force as a ninety-year-old grandmother grazing a child's cheek. Terrifying as it may have been to have this man sitting on my chest, squeezing my throat shut, there wasn't a thing I could do to keep him from killing me.

But there was someone who could.

In my blurred vision I saw Kira behind him, the rifle he had dropped now in her hands, hesitating, trying to overcome the built-in defense mechanism against slamming a gun butt into the back of a human skull. I wanted to will her to do it. To telepathically egg her on. Convince her that *this guy on top of me thought so little of you, like you're some frail little girl who wouldn't fight back, that he completely disregarded you while he attacked me. Fuck this guy.*

Whether she was thinking something similar or she convinced herself some other way, I watched her lift the gun above her head and rear back for extra leverage. She swung down and forward, catching the gunman in the crown of the skull. Kill-shot? No. Unconscious and future CTE victim? Bullseye.

"We have to get off this roof. Someone must know he came up here," Kira said as she sat me up. I could see in her eyes that she was locked in. The moment had crystallized for her. Just like getting punched in the face, cracking a dude with the butt of a rifle will do that. Like a straight shot of Adderall. She had told me once how her parents made her take it for years. At first she had loved the feeling the pill gave her. Focus. That uninterrupted train of thought, a bullet train of thought. She said she used to picture her ideas ripping through the countryside like those 150-mile-an-hour bullet trains streaking through Europe. Her parents had her on it for the SAT prep and paper writing, but what she liked was the daydreaming. Not necessarily what the pharmaceutical makers had in mind, but she liked to sit and think after taking her dose. Let her mind zero in on whys. She told me she could sit for hours with her eyes closed thinking about why she was here. Why she did what she did. Why she wanted to be what she hoped to be.

And now I could see something similar. Like she was layered in on the moment. I could picture her bullet train of thought whooshing up the track toward the next moment. If she was like me, and the focus was as sharp as it got for me after a fight, she might not have known what to do, but she wouldn't be worried for a while. Focus pushes fear to the back and moves your intentions to the forefront.

"What're you looking for?" I asked.

She had crawled over to the concussed gunman and had pulled back his jacket to search the inner pockets.

"There must be a unit that connects with the earpiece," she said as she tried to plug his Bluetooth into her ear. She pulled out a flat case that looked like an old-fashioned black metal cigarette case you'd see in a black-and-white film. She flipped it around in her hand but it didn't seem to have any buttons or latches.

"The other guys had one too."

The earpiece fell from her ear. "It's too big for my ear. Here. See if it fits you." She handed me the Bluetooth and the black case. "This must be the transmitter or whatever."

I pressed the earpiece into my ear. On the edge of the case I found a slight overhang on one side and snapped it open expecting to find buttons or a screen face. Instead, there was a syringe. A small, thin syringe filled with yellowish liquid.

"The others had *that*?" she asked.

"I don't know. They each had the same case."

Kira felt around the jacket for another pocket. "Here we go." She pulled out a small transmitter and handed it to me. I shoved it and the case into my pocket. "Let's go."

"Where?"

I pointed to the Bluetooth device now lodged in my ear. "Wherever they aren't."

∼

"Can I just say this is bullshit," Hastings huffed, to no one in particular. He took a deep drag on his cigarette, held it, and then exhaled like he was trying to blow out a 110-year-old's birthday cake. He and Bill Weaver had stepped outside to smoke after Reilly had hung up. It wasn't so much the cigarette he wanted; he just didn't want to stay in there and hear that Cardoza woman losing her shit anymore. Reminded him of Dorothy. But more than that, he was embarrassed. He couldn't be sure, but he thought he had heard Sean's voice in the background when they had Reilly on the radio. His own boy blubbering worse than any of the others.

"They are doing what they can," Weaver said. "They can't just go blasting in there."

"No, I'm not talking about her or the rest of the cops. The terrorists. And their 1 percent bullshit. Everyone hates the 1 percent. But they all wanna be it. The minute this thing is over, every one of *them,* the terrorists, is a one percenter. Fucking hypocrites."

Hastings and Weaver had met before. Chatted about having kids together at St. Frederick. Some canned small talk during a meeting in his congressional office, Hastings recalled. Weaver wanting his approval on some weapons contract with the Saudis. And Hastings wanting a check. Nothing illegal. Or personal. Just an unconnected campaign check from a loyal supporter.

Hastings took another deep pull and exhaled as he said, "Everyone's the 1 percent."

"How do you figure that?"

"You could be a thirty-grand-a-year school teacher in America and it puts you in the top 1 percent of the *world's* population. I don't see them giving away their money or clamoring for me to tax them their fair share. *Fair* share." He shook his head. "Since when is paying millions in taxes not a fair share?" *It's not like people in this country save any of it either,* he thought. Hastings remembered a report his committee got once: median net assets for the bottom 50 percent in America? *Negative $233. Total.* He couldn't believe it the first time he saw those figures. Thought his aide had messed up. *That's 150 million people and none of them can save a nickel. We're number one worldwide in income and number twenty-five in savings.* Hastings realized he was getting worked up over nothing, something totally irrelevant, but it felt good to vent when your son sounded like he had just wet himself in front of everyone.

The trailer door opened and Hastings instinctively hid his cigarette. When he realized it was only Chris Taylor, he took a deep drag. As he let it out, he said, "They get a picture on Facebook of you puffing away and some idiots won't vote for you. Social media is killing me."

"Actually, it's probably *saving* you then," Weaver said.

The cigarette seemed to relax Hastings a bit. "Chris, how much you in for?"

"As much as it takes."

Easy for Taylor to say. Hastings had heard the figures on his last year-end bonus after that Burke Tech takeover. *I definitely got in the wrong business.* And Weaver? Even less danger of being the lowest bidder. He had seen the contracts Weaver had gotten from Hastings and the others on the Appropriations committee. He didn't know what Weaver's cut was, but even 2 percent of a $17 billion contract for some next-gen stealth bombers and enough ordnance to bomb the country du jour three times over was a pretty nice payday. No wonder he was so calm. Try being a senator and making do on $170,000 a year. If it wasn't for Dorothy, he'd be in that tenth slot. Without her family's side of things, he'd be Harris. *Now there's a guy who musta gone full Madoff,* Hastings figured. *That's gotta be embarrassing. Dead fucking last.*

"What's so funny?" Taylor asked.

"Nothing. Nothing. Just thinking of something." *Dead last. Yeah, more ways than one.*

~

Back inside the trailer, Mrs. Harris was apoplectic.

"We believe that Kira is still alive," Pruitt said with a voice that made her sound more assured than she actually was. In truth, she'd have given it only a hair over 50 percent chance the girl was still alive. Because Reilly hadn't been willing to show the ten kids, it meant he hadn't found her and Cade yet. Or he had, and she was dead. Pruitt would bet the former, but didn't rule out the latter.

"We think she may be with the boy," Pruitt said.

"That boy is going to get our kids killed," Mrs. Collier said.

"We are . . ."

"You get that kid to stop. Now," John Stringer, another parent, chimed in as he took a step closer to Pruitt, standing over her, looking like he wanted to poke a finger in her chest. *Is this guy seriously trying to power stance over me?* Yet another man accustomed to barking orders and never getting pushback.

"Sir. I'm going to need you to sit down and let us deal with this . . ."

"I'll sit when I'm ready to sit. You put me on the radio with them . . . the terrorists in there. This has gone on too long."

Pruitt didn't say anything, just looked him in the eyes. She had learned over the years that nothing throws a guy off like a little silence and eye contact from a woman who doesn't give a fuck.

"That kid's a danger to all of our children," Stringer said, less forcefully than before, more plaintively this time.

Behind him, a voice said sharply, "That *kid* tried to save everyone's life in there." Stringer turned to see Liz staring him down. "He could have just hid out, saved his own skin. But he found a way to radio out to warn everyone about a bomb."

"There's no bomb," Stringer scoffed.

"He saved me. Cade is . . ."

"Great. Great, he saved you," Stringer said. "Saving his mother doesn't do us any good. Actually, it only seems to be making things worse." He pointed at the Harris couple. "These two have a daughter who has likely been killed because of his recklessness."

"Sit," Pruitt growled. Stringer's head whipped back around to Pruitt. There was a flash of fear, just a moment, before he caught himself, but she could tell she'd gotten his attention. Slower this time, she said, "Sit." Captain Lowry would be proud. Whenever she wanted to verbally punch some overbearing guy, she would channel Lowry's voice, the voice that had barked away at her during her time at Fort Sill. You want to hear authority in a voice, get ordered around by a Black Ops trainer. "Unless you get the President of the United States to tell me different, you are going to sit down and you are going to let me handle this." She waited. He didn't sit, but his power stance was growing flaccid. "Got the Oval Office number? No. Well, when you do, get back to me. In the meantime, over there." She wanted to add, *And apologize to this poor woman whose son is, who knows, maybe dead, but braver than some mouthy CEO with a few leadership retreats under his belt.*

CHAPTER TWENTY-FOUR

I don't know how it never slips out. In the movies they're always cramming a handgun in the back of their pants and running off, but I'm not buying it.

I had put the case in one pocket, the transmitter in the other, then loosened my belt and tried the handgun-in-the-back-of-the-pants move. But when Kira and I leapt from the hatch onto the indoor track, the gun slid through my waistband and got stuck between my inner thigh and pant leg. Thankfully it didn't go off. I'd feel pretty stupid shooting myself like that New York receiver did when his handgun slipped down his sweat pants in the VIP room of some club.

"Hold up a sec." I undid my front button, dropping my jeans, and pulled out the handgun.

"Briefs?"

"What? Oh, uh, I didn't pick them out," I said, realizing a little late that the "my mother bought my underwear" excuse didn't sound much better.

I held the gun out to her, barrel aimed at the floor. "Do you think you could shoot someone?"

She shook her head. "Sorry."

"Me neither." I hid the gun under one of the stretching mats off to the side of the track. Taking the gun had seemed like a good idea, but in reality, I knew, even face to face with someone else with a gun, I couldn't bring myself to shoot anyone. Which weirdly made me feel like I was letting somebody down by not having the balls to do it. It wasn't an issue of being against guns per se; it was the prospect of having the guilt of taking a life. I didn't think I could handle the aftermath.

I followed Kira as she ran toward the stairwell.

"Did you see the knife on that guy?" Kira asked.

"No."

"He must've picked it up, but I didn't see it either when we were looking for the transmitter."

She was right. It wasn't where I had left it. *So where was it?*

"We need to find a way out the gate," she said.

"I don't see that happening."

"Then we need to find a better place to hide."

"I know one spot they'd never find us. But we'd have to get all the way across campus."

At the bottom of the stairwell, I turned toward the front door.

"Wait!" Kira said. "Back this way first."

One billion dollars. Funny how already that seemed like such a ho-hum number to him. Reilly had been paid well over the years by G, but tops he'd probably cleared twelve mil over his career. A billion should seem more remarkable. Maybe it was the fact it's merely a single-letter difference and three little added zeros. Oddly, in a way a million seemed more to him, because growing up he had always thought he wanted to be a millionaire.

Reilly stood over Preston's shoulder watching the footage from the local news shows as Preston fielded updates from the men. He wouldn't admit it to anyone, but he was kicking himself for not having put up more cameras around the place.

Not that anyone would have anticipated some kid running loose, but still. He prided himself on his prep, and this he hadn't accounted for. Now he was left with the newsfeed to see if their cameras had picked up any movement.

His mind returned to the thought of the billion dollars. Whose wouldn't? Back when he was a kid and he dreamed of being a millionaire, he had thought of all the things he was going to buy, like the guy in Barenaked Ladies who sang about the llama and the lifetime supply of Kraft Mac and Cheese that he would spend his million bucks on. Young Reilly had dreams of BMX bikes and pellet guns. Now that he'd gotten those millions, nothing much had been fun about the spending. A house? More trouble that came with it—the upkeep, lawns to mow, busted pipes, all the other headaches. And luxury items? As Gertrude Stein would say, "A car is a car is a car." But a *billion* dollars? Now that's gotta change one's mind.

Preston turned from the laptop and looked up at Reilly. "Nothing. No one's seen them yet. Avery's the only one I haven't heard from. Maybe he's on them."

"When did he last confirm?"

"Ten, maybe. Could be searching one of the basements. These radios don't pick up great there."

"Try him again."

"Avery, radio check. Confirm."

In the silence as they waited, again the billion drifted to the forefront. *Maybe buying the proverbial island wouldn't be such a bad idea. No other idiots around to ever have to deal with.* Not that the full billion was his, though. G was cutting him in for 8 percent of whatever they pulled. Close to $80 million at this point. $120 if they got up to the billion five. Ten times what he'd made over his career. And sure, it's tax free, no bullshit income tax and OASDI, but he still felt he was getting the shaft. The bidding war was his idea, and look how well it had turned out. He'd done everything from planning to executing, and all G had to do was sit back and collect.

"Nothing," Preston said.

Just another reason I deserve more, Reilly thought. *G bankrolled this and he was supposed to supply top-line tech for us, and we can't even get the radios to work properly.* Not exactly a reassuring thought when they were going to be relying on those little syringes. Sure, he had tested and retested the system, but if it failed, it was going to complicate things. And who's left with his ass hanging out? Not G.

Which was why Reilly decided, *What's mine is mine,* and he determined his was the entire 1.5 billion dollars. His guys would all be dead once the day was out, so you could add those shares to his. And G? Reilly had a plan for him too. Reilly had all the access codes to the bank accounts. Once he got G out of the picture, there was no one else to claim it.

"I got a bad feeling, boss. Avery's still not answering. Every minute we're here, more chance for shit to hit. Let's take what we got."

"Not yet. They're not done bidding it up. But get everyone prepped; I'll make the call shortly."

I was pretty sure these guys had maps of the campus. Every building. Every pathway. But there was one place that wouldn't be on it. The old tunnel at the graveyard where Sean and the other Dead Poets Society wannabes met up. Like most every corner of this campus, I had been in there before. Not as a member—they sure were never asking me to join, not that I would have accepted anyway. I'm with Groucho Marx, but it wasn't just that I never wanted to be a part of a club that would have me. I didn't want to be a part of any club that would have lame prep school legacy kids who find snorting crushed Ritalin off a casket encasement the height of rebellion. Still, I had gone out to see what they kept there. You needed the old-timey skeleton key to open the metal door that sat at the back of the

Wentworth tomb. It had taken me most of one afternoon a couple months ago to find the key, but I had eventually discovered the false wall where it was hidden. I used to go out there now and again until Sean and Reece found me there one day and got all territorial.

If Kira and I could just get to the cemetery, we could grab the key and slide into the tunnel, and we'd never be found.

Great plan, sure, but we still had to get across campus.

"What are they saying on the tooth?" Kira asked.

"They've fanned out looking for us. The guy you took out hasn't responded and they've called for him a couple times. We'll know when they find out." I indicated the earpiece. "This'll go dead."

"Can you tell where the others are?"

"One is searching Grayler Hall. Another Barnes."

We slowly stepped out the gym equipment room door and inched our way along the outer wall. From here we would need to make the eighty-foot exposed run to Jefferson Hall, cross Hampton Road, circle around behind the library, and then run, exposed again, up the slight hill to the cemetery on the far east end of campus, just inside the high surrounding wall. We could always try to get over the wall instead, but those mini-grenade things they wired all along the top of the wall were enough of a deterrent even if I didn't know exactly what they were.

"Shit."

"What?"

I pointed to the earpiece. "There are two guys covering the east side. We'd be picked off if we made a run toward the catacombs." I tried to think of another option, but my imagination just stood there, scratching its head with a dumb look on its face and empty thought balloons floating over it.

"I bet there are keys in there," Kira whispered as she pointed to the van labelled Crowley Distributing that was parked next to the cafeteria. "Trin said she saw a bunch of them jump out of there when all this started. I bet the keys are in there. Why would you bother to take them out if you're about to kidnap everyone?"

"Probably." She was right; we could hop in and make a run for the gate. "There's only one guy manning it now. If we drove slowly, he might think it's one of his guys and wouldn't react until we were right up on him. And then we barrel through the gate?" I said more as a question than a suggestion.

She did the same with her answer. "Maaaaayyyybeeee?"

We snuck back to the cafeteria and edged around to the loading dock. I slipped open the door to the Crowley van and looked inside. No keys in the ignition and none behind the visor or in the drink holder or anywhere else. Kira had even less luck with the Northern United Foods truck: both doors were locked. We tried the third truck, but that was locked too. *Who'd they think was going to steal their trucks?* Unfortunately, now my imagination kicked into action and began thinking of all the things that could be locked inside or reasons they may need to use the trucks later.

The locked doors also did one other thing. They reminded me of the fob in my pocket. I didn't know which car was Mr. Archibald's, but it had to be sitting in staff parking. To get there we'd have to expose ourselves crossing the main drive unless we cut through the garden the administration had just put in. They'd torn down an entire three-story building to grow broccoli and raise a few chickens so the parents could feel good about their kids eating farm-to-table or something. Anyone doing the math could figure there was no way a half acre of veggies and a dozen chickens was supplying 700 kids with Caesar salads and omelets, but I'd begun to realize that, as adults were wont to do, they hadn't done it to be effective; they'd done it to give the impression of being effective.

Staying as low as we could, we crept along the farthest edge of the garden until we reached the parking lot. I pressed the fob.

Nothing.

We snuck through the rows of cars, careful to keep our heads out of sight. Every fifteen feet or so, I pressed the fob. There was always the chance that when the fob triggered the correct car, we would in essence be sending up a flare. If it was one of those cars that gave just a quick blink of headlights, we'd probably be fine, but if we landed one that lit up like a clown car, we were screwed. Each time I pressed the fob I reflexively flinched, anticipating the worst.

Nothing.

We tried another row, and I pressed the fob.

Landry saw the flicker from a distance. He had been walking back toward the auditorium, so he hadn't gotten a good look, but off to his right, he thought he'd seen a light. Just a split second, like someone had quickly flicked a light switch on and off. His first thought was a flashlight, but he could swear he saw a tint of orange in the flash.

He turned and looked in the direction of a parking lot. It didn't make sense anyone would be out there, but they hadn't had any luck finding the kid who had kicked the crap out of Trotter and Javier anywhere else. He clicked off the safety and headed toward the cars. Landry really hoped it was the boy out there; he'd love to be the one to put a bullet in him so he could make make fun of those two, that dick Trotter in particular.

When the engine kicked on, he froze. It was dark and the driver hadn't turned on the lights, but Landry could see movement. A car backing out of a parking spot and moving up the row. He squinted, trying to get a better look.

The car turned and headed toward the parking lot exit. When it got to the road, the blinker came on, then immediately off, like the person behind the wheel had turned it on out of habit and then immediately realized, probably not exactly necessary given the circumstances.

As the car turned onto the road, it crept toward Landry. He

took a look behind him. The gate was more or less a straight shot, maybe three hundred feet away. *Was this freaking guy going to try to make a run for it?* Landry sidestepped to the edge of the road and waited. The car was still two hundred feet away. Landry pointed his gun at about the twenty foot mark, readying to unload a hail of bullets into the car once it reached that point. The driver'd be dead before he hit the gate.

The car continued creeping toward him. At about a hundred feet, the headlights kicked on. Landry had been looking directly at the car so the sharp contrast from pitch black to high beams momentarily blinded him. He squeezed his eyes shut, opened them, and squeezed again trying to clear the sun-spots. He could hear the rev of the engine, the driver apparently hammering the accelerator. Landry squeezed his eyes one more time. Sun spots or not, he could see well enough to squeeze off a hail of bullets into the windshield and the driver's side window as the car barreled past.

The car veered to the right and hopped the curb onto the grass lawn. Instead of ramming the gate as Landry presumed was the driver's wishful thinking, the gray Volvo bounded across the lawn, the wheels leaning right, and slammed headlong into the stone statue outside the auditorium.

"Talk to me. Whadda we got?" Pruitt said as she came up on Jackson, who had taken up position by the gate with three of his men.

"Someone T-boned a car. Probably making a run for it."

"What were the shots?"

"Can't see. The construction lights make it impossible to get a good look. But likely, they emptied a couple cartridges into the face of whoever was stupid enough to try."

"I want eyes on. Swing the drone in."

As Pruitt said this, the Satcom phone buzzed in her pocket.

The one she carried for one caller and one only. A caller you didn't let roll to voicemail.

∽

It's not often you get immediate confirmation on whether a decision you made was right or wrong. Usually you batted the choices around in your head, eventually deciding on one, and then at some point in the future you discovered whether you chose wisely or not. As Kira and I had watched the windshield shatter and the car fill with bullets, for once I could take immediate comfort in knowing we had chosen correctly. Had we made a run for it in the car, rather than putting a rock on the gas pedal before bailing out and sending the Volvo off in the direction of the gate as a distraction, we'd right now be bullet-ridden and face-planted against that statue. And as we had hoped, the headlights must have covered me when I jumped out because the guy who shot up the car never looked my direction as I scrambled across the garden to where Kira was waiting.

From listening to the radio chatter over the earpiece as we circled back behind the cafeteria, I'd gathered that they were all headed toward the sound of gunshots. We waited at the edge of the cafeteria until the last flashlight beam jogged past us and toward the others outside the auditorium.

We waited another beat, and when no one else passed, we sprinted across the open space toward Jefferson Hall. I'd seen Kira play soccer and basketball, but I hadn't realized until now, running beside her, just how fast she was even with that thing strapped over her shoulder. As a matter of fact, I wasn't running beside her; I was chasing her (although, if she were to decide to rub it in, I would point out that only one of us had recently jumped out of a moving car. To which she would probably counter: it was more a roll than a jump, seeing as the car hadn't picked up any speed yet).

We slipped the side door open and made our way through

the first-floor hallway of Jefferson, Kira figuring that it was still better to stay indoors and out of sight when possible. At the other end of the hall, I slowly pushed open the towering front door, above which was cut into the granite, "There is always room at the top. Daniel Webster 1847." Whenever I was on my mail route and would see these quotes chiseled into stone around campus, I thought, *You had to really commit to sharing your motivational quotes back in the day.* It took more than a Pinterest image of an ocean vista and a cute quote like the one I'd seen on Harkin's screensaver. Back in the old days you had to break out the masonry tools to share your don't-sweat-the-small-stuff wisdom.

"Was it a bad day? Or was it just . . ."

Just what? I hadn't read the whole quote when I was in Harkin's office earlier. Maybe: "Was it a bad day? Or was it just your fault"? Unlikely. What exactly was this motivational saying that had touched Harkin enough to turn it into his screen saver? And what did it have to do with a giant wave crashing on the rocky shores of the Northern California coast? And more importantly, *Why am I again so caught up on something so inane when I have a few more pressing issues to deal with?*

From the doorway we were looking out at the east side of campus, toward the far end of which was the graveyard. In front of us was Hampton Road, a small one-way street that cut through this end of campus. Not much more than a glorified pathway that was originally put there for horse carriages. But when you're afraid some unseen dude might be about to take a sniper shot at you, running from one side of that road to the other seemed as daunting as sprinting blindfolded across one of those eight-lane highways in Los Angeles.

We looked at one another, she nodded, and we sprinted across the road. I wondered if she was unconsciously squinting like I was, anticipating a gunshot at any moment. Once across the road, we ran up the lawn toward the Dean's house. Make it past there and then all we had to do was run across the soccer field and up toward the graveyard behind it. Halfway across the lawn I heard an odd whirring sound overhead, and I looked up. As I did, I caught a toe on a sprinkler head that was nearly invisible in the dark. Tumbling to the ground, I landed on my bad shoulder and yelped in pain.

Kira stopped and turned back.

"Go, go, keep going," I whispered, wincing, my head swiveling around to see where the whirring sound was coming from. She grabbed my arm and pulled me up and toward the nearest building, the Headmaster's house.

We edged along the west side of the building. That had to be a drone I'd heard. And if it was Reilly's, we were seriously screwed, although I hadn't seen sign of one from the footage they had running on the auditorium screens earlier.

"Must be theirs," Kira whispered while indicating in the direction of the police compound. She was probably right. Made way more sense it would be the cops outside, wanting a view of what was going on over here.

"I haven't heard anything on the radio yet, so you're probably right."

At the far side of the building we again peered around to see if our path was clear. I had started to run when Kira grabbed my shoulder and yanked me back. I pressed up against the wall next to her and looked in the direction she was pointing. Up on the ridge along the stone exterior wall a light flickered. The light moved slowly along the top. Even though they'd wired the wall, they must still have been running regular sweeps around the edge of the grounds. At the pace he was going, it would be a good five minutes for him to walk that whole section of wall before we'd be clear to make a run for it. But by now they had to know we weren't in the car and they'd be out looking for us again. We had to get out of the open.

~

Pruitt stood outside the crisis trailer, talking on her phone. "I believe they will try and take a handful with them. They've asked for two Cyclops copters." A beat, then, "No, Mr. President. I have no idea how they do." As she spoke, she watched a guy climb out of a restaurant delivery vehicle with a "Lotus Indian" sign on the roof, his arms loaded with bags of food. She shook her head. They'd been here five hours and the crew had already ordered pizza, Chinese, and now somehow found an Indian place out here. The address on the door said Chitsworth. *Really?* Chitsworth was a good forty miles away. Her guys must've paid him an extra fifty bucks to bring it all the way out. Happened every time they were on a job. They knew it was going to be expensed, so they loaded up on takeout. "We'll try to track them, but as you know, those birds can go dark."

As the President said something on the other end, Frost opened the door to the trailer and waved Pruitt in urgently. She held up a finger and continued into the phone, "No, they'll have them swept for any tracking devices. You'll have to be okay with the pretty good possibility they get away. And the money has already been deposited and moved through at least three accounts. Trail's gone dead. Whether we get these guys or not, whoever is running this thing isn't doing it from in there. He or they are moving that money around as we speak."

Frost waved urgently again. "You gotta see this."

She covered the phone. "Dude, it's the President."

"There wasn't anyone in the car."

"Mr. President. Uh, I'll have to call you back." Pruitt never got used to dumping a call with the President.

Once inside the trailer, Frost pulled up the drone image. As he backed up a few frames, Pruitt said, "Where we looking at?"

"The Dean's house. But here . . ." On the playback, one of the two runners looked up and just as he did, tumbled to the ground. "They're alive. That's the kid. And the girl there in front of him. They weren't in that car."

Pruitt usually didn't much root for anyone in these situations. She'd learned the hard way that if you were going to do this kind of work, you needed to desensitize yourself. Even now, she didn't feel a particular emotion, but when Frost said they hadn't been shot up in the car, she did find herself with a tinge of that feeling she'd had as a kid watching the Celts. She may not have been emotionally attached to the two kids, but she was rooting for them. And at the moment it felt like rooting for the winning team.

CHAPTER TWENTY-FIVE

I hadn't realized it until we were inside Headmaster Harkin's house and forced to wait, but, wow, did I have to pee.

I wouldn't have thought in situations like this you'd ever be thinking about doing something as normal as taking a leak, but I suddenly had to go. Bad. "I'll be back in a second."

"Where you going?" Kira asked.

"Uh, I'm gonna look around."

She gave me a quizzical look.

"See if there's anything we can use," I added.

I walked upstairs and looked for the bathroom. I could have found the one downstairs, sure, but here was another thing I'd never have thought would occur in situations like this: that I'd still be embarrassed to have her hear me whizzing loudly into a toilet bowl in an otherwise silent house.

As I peed, I looked around the Headmaster's bathroom. The requisite potpourri in a bamboo basket. *New Yorker* and *Car & Driver* magazines next to the toilet paper dispenser. A stubby candle and matchbook on the back of the toilet. I picked it up and took a whiff. Vanilla. It reminded me of something Weav said once. Someone was worried about having to speak at assembly and Reece gave the guy the "imagine the audience naked" trope. Weav said, no, what you really need to do is imagine them all taking dumps. His theory being, *how threatening can anyone be when they are,* as he put it, *grunting out a deuce.* Maybe Weav was onto something. Picturing Headmaster Harkin up here on the can, lighting a match to cover the smell from his family, did kind of taint my image of him.

I tried this theory on Reilly and the others.

Nope. Still scary motherfuckers.

Next to the toilet was a cup holding two toothbrushes. I pictured Harkin and his wife side by side as they brushed their teeth. I remembered Kira once telling me about how her parents every night shared an orange, drank cocoa, and then would brush their teeth in the bathroom together. She always thought it was romantic seeing them flossing simultaneously. I guess as long as they weren't sharing the same string, there is something kind of sweet about still doing anything together after twenty years of marriage.

I tried to picture Kira and me standing here flossing together. I'm not gonna lie; I kinda liked it.

"Oh, sorry."

I whipped around and saw Kira standing there.

"I thought you were looking around."

"I was," I said defensively, as though it was somehow insane to need to go the bathroom. I saw her glance at the candle in my hand.

"You got some other tear gas type plan with that?"

"Uh, no. It's vanilla."

She gave me that crinkled up quizzical look of hers.

I thought about telling her about her and me flossing together. But rarely when something made its way from my brain out my mouth and into a girl's ear did it come out the way I envisioned it, and I was pretty sure telling a girl you were fantasizing about flossing your gums together would be one of those times.

"I think we need to . . ."

I put my hand up. "Wait." I pointed to my earpiece, and we stood in silence. "Oh, no."

"What?"

"They know."

"Know what?"

"Where we are."

We sprinted out of the bathroom and hopped down the stairs. As we got to the ground floor I could see flashlights headed in the direction of the Headmaster's house. By the time we reached the door, it was too late. The lights were only fifty feet away and closing fast. If we opened the door, we'd be walking directly into their gunsights.

Maybe the reason she felt such pride right now, thought Liz, was all these parents in this room had been questioning her boy's efforts. Her boy who not only saved her, but risked his life to save the Kira girl. He may act the standoffish type, and there were times you would've thought he was angry at everyone, but no matter how hard you tried, you couldn't hide your true persona. The fake nice types were often hiding a mean, bitter streak. But no matter the cynical facade Cade sometimes put on, she knew he had a heart. A huge heart. *Screw these parents. As if some money or privilege gives them the right to speak ill of my son. The girl's mother, now her I don't blame. Her daughter is number ten. But these others whose kids will end up getting released, and yet they are still angry at my boy?* She was willing to give them the benefit of the doubt—everyone was on razor's edge worried about their kid. She was willing, that is, until Hastings, upon seeing the drone footage, had said, "Do something with that piece of trash; he's going to get our kids all killed."

"My son is ten times the man you are. I don't care who or what you are, or what you can do to me, if you ever so much as look at him wrong, I will sic him on you."

"What?" Hastings barked. "How dare . . ."

"And you don't want that. Your little squash games or whatever you play aren't going to train you up to handle an arm bar." And yes, she did actually know what an arm bar was—hyperextending the crap out of someone's elbow—thanks to watching YouTube videos of MMA fights. It had given her the shivers watching them, but she had wanted to know what had interested him so.

Hastings grabbed Liz's arm. "Get this woman out of this trailer. She has no business . . ."

As her balled-up fist landed on Hastings's right ear, Liz thought, *Huh, that's what throwing a punch feels like.* She'd been on the receiving end of many a balled-up fist from Cade's father, but this was the first time she'd felt how knuckles to bone feel, rather than the other way around. *Perhaps that was a wee bit of an overreaction*, came her next thought. Perhaps. But also, maybe, just *maybe* there was a little repressed anger toward another man who also used to grab her by the arm and tell her what to do. Either way, she had to admit, it felt pretty exhilarating to watch a grown man whimpering and whining to Pruitt that she needed to "arrest this crazy woman."

Pruitt's hint of a smile was pretty good indication that nothing of the sort would be happening. She watched Pruitt turn her attention back to the computer screen. Liz didn't know it, but with ten minutes to go until the deadline, Pruitt had a decision to make. Storm the place and try and save the last two kids on the list or sacrifice for the rest. Pruitt would never tell the parents, but it was a simple decision to make. For two kids she wasn't going to chance losing dozens more in an unconfined shootout. *Simple*—that is, if that were it.

But the bomb. Or the potential of a bomb. She knew the boy wasn't lying but while he had said what he thought, what he thought might be wrong. And if they had one—*I would too if I were them*, she thought—it would be their bargaining chip. But if that was the case, how come Reilly hadn't even let her know he had it to play?

Her instincts told her Reilly knew there was no walking out of here unless he had a massive chip to play. And if that chip was a bomb, that meant he planned on keeping them all wired to it until his escape route was clear and he was off the grid. If that were the case, then what incentive would he have to blow them all up if he was already gone? It would only intensify the hunt for him. A heist with a massive ransom taken from the filthy rich? Who cares. It's off the news radar in a couple days. Dozens of dead innocent kids, teachers, and staff? The public blowback would be so massive the manhunt would never stop. Reilly had to know this. He had to know a bomb as tactic is one thing, but a detonated one with all these kids was an insane idea. He had to.

Didn't he?

As Javier crept toward the front door of the Headmaster's house, he motioned for Revere and Landry to search the two nearby buildings. The two kids were likely hiding out in one of these three buildings. Thanks to the bugged radio, Preston had picked up voices talking about what was on the drone footage, but they hadn't been able to see the images. The last they heard was the kids were in the vicinity of this cluster of buildings.

All three had their rifles shouldered as they fanned out. Javier couldn't wait for his payback. Already, the other guys had been giving him shit for getting jacked by a seventeen-year-old kid. He was never going to live this one down. Which was bull-shit; it wasn't his fault the kid had caught him off guard. Sure, he may have been half-assing the recon mission, but could you blame him? Was he really to be expected to anticipate a teenage kid willing to fight back? And one that had the skills to do so?

Every other one of Reilly's operations they'd been on, the initial sweep was nothing more than digging out cowering civilians pissing themselves in the corner. Javier had to be the one to get the lone person who decided to fight back.

This time, he'd be ready.

Javier slipped the door open and slowly entered the living room, sweeping his gun side to side, the light on his rifle illuminating shelves of books to the left, a couch and reading chair to the right. As the beam of light passed by the doorway leading into the adjoining room, something caught his eye. He jerked the gun back in that direction and lit up the room. He could see a desk and chair in what looked to be a home office. He didn't see anyone, but he could feel it. That tingle he used to get on recon missions outside Krandeer. You couldn't see them, but you knew they were there hiding behind that busted wall or pile of rubble. Do this gig enough and you literally feel it. *Then again, I didn't feel him last time, right before he sucker punched me; maybe I've been out of the real shit too long.* Maybe, but even Javier had to admit he just hadn't been paying enough attention before. Civilians would wonder how you could be lackadaisical while walking around with a gun ready to put a bullet where it needed to go, but honestly, Javier figured, it was like any other job you'd done too long; you started to slack off. But, like any job you'd done too long, when you did actually focus, you were eminently better at it than anyone else. And right now Javier was razor focused on whatever had just rustled ever so slightly behind that desk.

Javier eased into the adjoining room, his head on a swivel. No way he was going to get jumped again by that kid. This time he was prepared. Gun drawn. Eyes open. Attention paid. Last time it never occurred to him he was going to find any resistance. This time he had the advantage. He knew the kid was in here. The kid didn't know what the fuck was on its way.

What was that? Javier could swear he heard a slight reverberation and then the sound of a quick puff of air. He would have heard a third sound too, had his nervous center not instantaneously mainlined his blood stream with adrenaline and dopamine the nanosecond the arrow pierced his skin and sank deep into his thigh. Had his body not over-ridden his pain centers in the shock, he'd have heard what sounded like a Phillips-head screwdriver being plunged into a ripe cantaloupe.

His first thought when he looked down at the half arrow sticking out of his right thigh: why did his leg have one of those gag arrows Steve Martin wore on his head sticking out of it?

His second thought wasn't so much a thought as it was a reaction to a sudden screaming jolt of pain now that there was an arrow lodged in his thigh, rubbing against the femur and the surrounding nerve endings. Every instinct in his body was begging him to yank it out, but he had enough sense to know that would only make things worse.

He pointed his gun in the direction the arrow had come from and let off a round of bullets. They rat-a-tat-tatted, sending hunks of books and desk panels into the air, but no sounds of a kid screaming in pain. Just silence. He'd probably gotten a kill shot. Good, he thought; he didn't want to have to explain how some teenage boy had speared him and then gotten away again. However, if he thought that ribbing was bad before . . .

. . . it was about to get worse.

Reilly felt the buzz in his jacket pocket. G again. He had known the minute the drone spotted the kids, it was only a matter of time before he got another "What the fuck?" call from G. And here it was.

He held the sphere in front of his mouth and said curtly, "It's controlled."

"You fucking kidding me? They are freaking out here. If they decide to go in, this whole thing is fucked."

"I have it controlled. If anything, they are confused. They are going to want to find out more before doing anything. The longer things go, the less likely they rush us. They always either go immediately, which they didn't, or they go siege mentality, waiting it out till the end. It's never middle ground. They aren't coming in."

Reilly really did feel like a middle manager. First it was juggling the inanities of his underlings and now it was reassuring the micromanaging boss man above. "We only need them to hold off another twenty minutes. By then, we'll have started. Trust me; they aren't rushing this place in the next twenty."

I couldn't believe she'd done it. Even earlier when she ran back to the gym equipment room and strapped the bow and arrows over her shoulder, to be honest, I never thought she'd be able to shoot someone if it came to it.

Sure, like millions of other girls her age, Kira had read every *Hunger Games* book and grown up on *Brave* and *Narnia* and begged her mother for archery lessons. She'd even read *Zen in the Art of Archery* I don't know how many times. But actually doing it? Unlike all those millions of adolescent Katniss wannabes, Kira had actually just gotten the opportunity to put it to use.

There were a lot of reasons to love a girl. I knew quite a few, as a matter of fact, but one I'd never considered until now was this: when there's a guy spraying bullets in your vicinity, you wanted a girl who was clutch. I mean, it's one thing to have an arrow lined up, ready to shoot as a guy with a gun entered the room you're cornered in; all you had to do was merely let go of a string. But it's a whole other kind of focus to quickly string a second arrow—after having been *shot* at herself—draw it back, aim, and stick this arrow dead nuts in the guy's upper torso, causing him to tumble backward and to the floor. I'd always known she was clutch watching her play sports—the one you wanted taking the last shot—but this was a whole other level of clutch.

Once she saw the blood start to gush, though, her whole tenor changed. Up till then she probably hadn't been thinking of it as trying to kill someone. It was a target, a bullseye that if she missed, was going to take *her* life. Knowing that she herself might die had a way of removing any dilemma. But now she dropped the bow and her body started to shake. "Did I kill him?" Kira said softly.

"Let's go. Let's go!"

"Did I kill him?"

"We gotta get outta here."

She didn't move. I couldn't blame her. If I'd probably just mortally wounded someone, I'd be a little wonky too. Still, we had to go now; I was pretty sure he wouldn't be the only one looking for us.

As I grabbed her arm and tried to get her moving, the guy she had shot reached for the gun he had dropped when the second arrow hit. He was struggling, and I could see blood leaking out his mouth, but he was able to draw the gun toward him. I rushed him and raised my foot to jam my heel into the side of his head. He lunged forward and wrapped his arms around my leg, pulling me on top of him. As we fell to the floor, he tried to say something into his Bluetooth, but it came out in a gurgle. Maybe he couldn't speak, but he had enough strength to get his other hand on my head and slam it to the floor. Again he tried to speak into his Bluetooth. I swung at the side of his head and clawed the earpiece out. Pushing me back, he reached into his jacket and pulled out a handgun.

Behind him I could see Kira trying to string a third arrow, but the way she was now shaking, I'd have a bullet in my head before she'd be able to. I flung my right arm out toward his leg, but I missed my target. He pointed the gun toward me, but before he could pull the trigger, I flailed my arm out once more, this time catching the arrow lodged in his leg. With a hard downward yank, I wrenched the arrow, tearing through flesh.

He screamed and instinctively reached for the leg wound, dropping his gun in the process. I pushed myself away and stumbled to my feet. Kira and I ran out of the room and toward the back entrance.

"Wait. This way." The back door would have aimed us out toward the graveyard where we needed to go, but my instinct said since this guy had come through the front door, anyone else with him would have been circling to the back.

We were leaping off the front porch steps when I heard a crashing sound from the back side of the building, like a foot had bashed in the lock of a door. We ran across the lawn and hooked back around Jefferson Hall. I looked over my shoulder, but couldn't see anyone.

How long are they going to keep looking? Once they have the money, they'll want to make their escape, so at that point who cares about us two? Maybe if we can just keep moving . . .

But the longer we stayed outside, the more likely we were to be seen. Inside we had a chance.

The Administration Hall was adjacent to Jefferson, so we ducked in and ran along the first floor past the offices and the conference room that had been modified last spring into the campus safe space. I heard what sounded like a half grunt, half laugh from Kira running next to me. *She's way more relaxed with all this than I am,* I thought. *That, or it's nerves.* Either way, I swore I heard her laugh.

A couple doors before the end of the long hallway, we slipped into one of the offices. Inside, I closed the door and looked around for a hiding spot.

Behind me I heard the door open back up. I spun around, thinking somehow the gunmen had magically appeared at the door, but it was Kira who had reopened it.

"They won't be as likely to search a room with an open

door," she whispered. "They'd assume anyone running from them would hide behind a closed door. At least I would."

Add that to the list: divergent thinking.

On the far side of the room was a closet. We ducked as we passed by the windows and stepped into the closet. Again, Kira pushed the door back open. Halfway this time. If someone were to enter the office and peer around, they wouldn't have a direct view of the closet without walking all the way over to this corner. They'd see a half-open door, and if Kira was right (not to mention Tversky and Kahneman and their *Framing of Decisions* psych book I was guessing she was working off of), the gunmen wouldn't bother searching. It made theoretical sense; I mean, they did get a Nobel for it. But theory has a tough time convincing human nature, and human nature was screaming at me to slam the door shut and hide.

"What were you laughing about? Back there."

"Safe space."

Yeah, the idea of teddy bears and bean bag chairs did seem a little ironic right about now.

"Wanna know my trigger word?" Kira whispered. "*Trigger*. The one these guys are going to shoot us with."

"I feel like you've been waiting for a chance to say that."

She half smiled.

God, she's cool.

"What're they saying over that thing?"

"Nothing. It's silent. They must have found the guy I took it from. Changed the frequency or something."

"We need to find out what they plan to do."

"No, we don't."

"If they really do plan to use the bomb, the police need to do something about it. If they think everyone is going to get traded out, they will just wait it out. And it'll be too late."

"What if the bomb's just a precaution?"

"What if it's not?"

"We did as much as we could." If my mother was still in

there, would I say the same thing? No. I would try and do some-thing. But she wasn't. And neither was Kira. If I knew for a fact everyone in there was going to get blown to bits, sure, I'd do something. But on a "maybe"? Screw that. At this point, I just wanted to get through it all. "There's nothing we can do." She was looking me in the eyes. I added, "Right?"

"No."

"Do what then?"

"I don't know. There has to be some way."

Thing is, she was right; there was a way. I had an idea of how we could find out a whole lot more. I just wasn't going to tell her. I had realized it when we were running through the gym earlier and I'd noticed the intercom speakers. Pretty simple, really. But I hadn't wanted to bring it up because I knew she'd say, let's do it. The psychology buff in her would also say, maybe I ran us into this particular building because subconsciously I knew we should. But even if we did find out what they had planned, I had no idea how to let the cops know once we did. But you try saying no to her.

In the end, do you want to know why I decided to tell her? Birthday cards.

Every year she made me a homemade birthday card, not an e-card, but an honest to goodness construction-paper card, with a printed-out picture glued to the front, with some goofy pun. And inside, instead of the generic one-sentence "have a great day" or "thinking of you on your birthday," would be written a full page note. Sure, she made them for other friends too, but ever since she gave me the one for my fourteenth birthday, the one with the picture of her, upside down, her legs around a branch of the Hawthorne tree, with the words "Hang in there" in blue marker, ever since then I looked forward to my birthday the entire month leading up to it, waiting for the card. Aside from my mother, I'd never received one from anyone else.

Was I sappy?

Definitely.

Did I realize how idiotic it was that I would do anything this girl wanted or needed? Even something as foolish as what we were about to do?

Sure.

Was I now going to still do it?

I'm guessing you know the answer.

CHAPTER TWENTY-SIX

Reilly toggled the radio connected to the trailer. "Are the transports ready?"

"They're set for you in the field outside the east gate," Pruitt answered.

"I want them on this side of the gate."

"It's a tight landing there, so . . ."

"Are we really going to go through some charade where you tell me you can't land them over here and I say no deal, and you say blah blah blah? I'll save you the stupid back and forth: the pilots each land on the green, or you aren't getting the kids."

"I need assurance on the pilots' safety."

"They aren't coming with us."

On the other end of the phone, Pruitt was struck by this comment. These Cyclops stealth birds were relatively new. Reilly had to have inside intel to even know of their existence. When he had asked for them, she was suspicious, and now, not needing pilots? He had someone capable of flying one? Actually *two* guys capable. Either he had no idea what he was getting into . . . or he knew exactly what he was getting into. She doubted highly it was the former. And the latter made her wonder just how high up this guy was tied in.

"I need the kids, everyone," Pruitt said. "Out of the building."

"You'll get them. You have my word." Reilly always loved saying that. *My word.* As if. "I'm taking five of the ten with us. The other half will stay with the group in the auditorium. When we're safe, I will release them."

"No deal. I need them all. You don't leave with anyone."

"Again, Ms. Pruitt, do you really want to spend a chunk of your years on this planet going around and around on a point you know is moot? You either let me leave with five or I just start eliminating one after another. Thirty or so is a bit messy, but I'm guessing you'll come to your senses before I have to run through too many."

"We trade the kids for my guys. Five for five."

Silence on the radio as Reilly let her counter hang in the air. After a sufficient pause—one long enough they might think he was actually debating the possibilities rather than saying what he had planned all along—he said, "Okay. Send them in. Stripped. I don't want them carrying anything. Soon as the birds and your men are in place, I send you the five kids. The others you collect when we're out of here."

Reilly toggled the radio off before Pruitt could respond.

Preston looked at him. "We're trading them out?"

"It's irrelevant. Gives them something to chew on for now, so they don't pay attention to what they should. Soon as the trade is being made, initiate the transmission."

"Gotcha."

"And send Landry the code. I'll tell him when."

"I thought that was Plan B."

"Consider it Plan A1. You can never have enough confusion."

~

We heard the footsteps before we saw the flashlight.

Inside that closet, with not even a single coat to hide behind, Kira and I listened to the footsteps coming up the hall in the direction of the office. A click, click, click sound echoed closer. It seemed so exaggeratedly loud, I'd swear the guy was wearing tap shoes. From where we were we couldn't see much, but a sudden flicker of light made us both flinch. It quickly went dark again, and a moment later we heard the door to the office across the hall open. There was a beat during which he must have been searching the room. We heard the muffled sound of another door opening. Probably the closet door in that office. The same matching closet we were huddled in here. If he did the same search in this office, we were done. But it was too late to run. I looked at Kira. She was looking back. I wondered if she was trying to silently impart the same thing I was.

The clicking footsteps reached the door to our office. Through the half-open closet door, we could see the flashlight beam light up the room. It swept left to right and back again. A pause. Maybe Kira had been right. Maybe he was going to pass right on by and . . .

The footsteps entered the room. Based on the direction of the beam of light, the gunman seemed to be headed toward the desk. Another pause. The light swung around the room and toward the wall where the closet was. The half-closed door would hide us from this angle, but a couple more steps and he'd see us. We both stood dead still, neither of us daring to even breathe for fear of making a noise. I could feel the blood pulsing through my ears. To me it sounded like an oil gusher exploding out from a busted well. I felt my head start to spin. I knew it was just low oxygen in the brain, a side effect to anxiety, but for a second I wondered if I was going to pass out before he even opened the door and started shooting.

It was likely three seconds total the guy was in the room, but it felt like ten minutes before the room went dark again and the disembodied footsteps continued up the hallway. I wanted to shout, "You're a freaking genius!" but instead just looked at her, my eyes bulging, and mouthed, "Wow."

We waited silently in the closet until they had searched the rest of the building. When we heard the front door close, we waited another minute and then snuck back out into the hallway.

I had hoped Kira would forget about trying to alert anyone, but the first thing she said was, "How are we going to let them know?"

I didn't answer, but she was staring at me, and after a second, said, "Let's hear it."

Crap.

～

The A/V room, where they kept the school intercom system, was on the second floor, down the hall from the registrar's office. It had been put in after Parkland as a warning system, but since each building was now connected, they also used it for campus-wide announcements. Last April Fools' Day, Weav and I had tapped into it and Weav, who did a great Headmaster Harkin impersonation, read off a bunch of completely insane announcements.

So it's not like this was going to be breaking in *Mission: Impossible* style. Anyone with a few coding classes could get in and post goofy photos on the auditorium screen or on any of the other units hard-wired to the system. More like *Mission: Fairly Doable*. All one needed was direct access to one of the hardwired stations. Preston, or whoever had tapped in from the A/V system at the auditorium, would have definitely taken precautions so that none of the cops on the outside could hack in wirelessly. Anything like that would be encrypted. But maybe if you were figuring the cops were never going to have access to one of the physical portals because you had the entire campus sealed off, you may not bother monitoring the portal access.

And the fact they had tapped into the intercom in the science building earlier meant they hadn't cut the line. Which also meant they never thought to account for an insider tapping into *them*.

The administration must have changed the password after our April Fools' prank, because 1223334444 no longer logged me in. It took all of one guess before I was able to get in with 4444333221. Kira stood at the edge of the window watching the front door to the building as I searched around for a way into the auditorium A/V system and from there, Preston's laptop, which hopefully was still hard-wired to the system.

I had the auditorium screen mirrored to our computer within minutes, and on screen I could see the ransom tally of the ten hostages as well as footage that must be coming from one of the news trucks. A little more digging and I had the sound. The speaker blared, " . . . until we turn around. Get Franklin to check them."

"Turn that down!" Kira yelped.

"I'm trying!" I hit a few keys. Their radio transmission continued to blare from the computer.

I'd never been able to find the volume button on any computer. I tried another key, but it only got louder. I hit the key to the left of it and slowly the sound softened until it was barely audible. I kept it as low as I could while still making out what they were saying. After about a minute, Kira whispered from the window, "Anything?"

"I don't know. They're talking about getting the copters set. They have two coming in, I guess."

"Anything about the bomb?"

"It's not like they're going to conveniently start talking about how they plan to blow the place up."

She gave me a look.

"Sorry, I didn't mean that to come out as sarcastic as it did."

As I continued to listen, Kira came over and joined me. The two of us leaned in to hear. Voices jumped on and off the frequency, updating locations, and at one point we heard our names mentioned, the search for us apparently still on.

"What's that other guy saying? In the background."

Kira leaned in closer. "I can't make it out. There's a woman's voice too."

"Did you see any women with them when you were in the auditorium?"

"No."

I focused in on the female voice, but I couldn't make out the words. Whoever it was, they weren't talking into the Bluetooth. It sounded like they were somewhere in the background. Or coming off a monitor in the background.

Kira and I sat and listened. My forehead was maybe three inches from hers and I could smell citrus. Probably the lotion I always saw her rubbing on her arms and hands, not that I ever noticed dry skin. Then again, the fact she was always applying may have accounted for this. It smelled orange-y but was probably some Ecuadorian guava fruit extract or whatever they make that stuff out of. Whatever it was, it had an aromatherapeutic effect. I sat and listened and breathed it in slowly, each breath bit by bit calming my agitated state.

I had mirrored in Preston's screen, so while we listened we watched what he was doing on his laptop. He seemed to alternate between confirming bank transfers and continually updating the encryption code. They were taking no chances. This coding was way above anything I knew, but I gathered the other side must be working on cracking it. With the alterations every thirty seconds or so, though, the cops would never have a chance to crack it before a new one was created. I searched through the audio software, but only found the one line active. Wherever the female voice was coming from, it wasn't over their system.

In order for Preston to find me, I knew he would have to be specifically searching for someone hardwiring their way in. But why would he? He'd never have assumed someone had access.

That said, if he was, or if I was flat out doing this wrong, then we were cornered. "The longer we stay here listening, the more chance they're going to discover we're in their system."

"Just a little longer."

I figured I'd give her three minutes. After that, sorry, but not our problem.

The chatter continued but still nothing of consequence. Then Preston came on, relaying an updated radio frequency. They must have been switching them up every few minutes since they discovered we had taken one. I entered the frequency into the Bluetooth, and suddenly the chatter was back in my ear. "Let's go. I've got the radio back."

I was moving the mouse to click us out when Kira grabbed my hand. "Wait. What's that?"

On the computer where I had the audio screen up, a second line had appeared. Toggling over, I brought that communication to the forefront. It was the Reilly guy. We listened as he explained the copters were on their way. He sounded like he was reassuring someone. That all was under control.

The guy on the other end spoke in clipped sentences. He didn't sound happy.

" . . . that was unnecessary."

"It doesn't change the timeline," Reilly said calmly.

"If I don't authorize, you don't do it."

"You want me to give it back?"

"Don't be a smartass."

The guy's voice sounded vaguely familiar; who knew, maybe one of the guys I overheard when I was above the auditorium. But if it was one of the gunmen I'd heard before, why talk on a separate line from the rest?

The voice continued, "If you fuck me on that, what else are you going to fuck me on?"

"Relax. I am . . ."

"No. Get the first five out now. After that, I don't give a fuck."

The line went silent, so I toggled back to the other. Kira and I looked at each other.

"What was that?" she mouthed.

I shrugged. "Somebody over on that side?" I gestured toward the gate.

In my earpiece I heard Reilly's voice. "Base in ten. Everyone. Landry, switch the timer to twenty. Confirm when keyed in."

You know how you sometimes find yourself doing one tiny thing you wouldn't normally do, and then that leads to something just a hair bigger? And then maybe something slightly worse? And another and another? Whether it's shoplifting a pack of gum leading to holding up a liquor store or one tiny fib winding into a big tangled web of lies, at some point you're looking back and wondering, how in the world did I get here?

As I followed Kira into the lecture hall I'd been in the attic of earlier today, I wondered, how did I get here? How in the world did I get here? Each step I could rationalize, I guess. But this last one, taking the chance of getting caught as we had snuck over to the econ department at Carter Hall, was a lot harder to rationalize. And now I was keeping watch at the door as Kira ducked behind the podium up front. At each point, I wanted to just stop. Quit all this and hide. But I didn't. And now as she ran back toward me, the laser pointer in her hand, again I didn't say, *let's go hide. Get to the graveyard and wait all this out like sane people.* Instead, I followed her to the second floor, where she opened a classroom window and aimed the pointer in the direction of the trailer.

All these steps were bad enough, but playing this forward to its logical conclusion, this probably wasn't the last insane thing we would do today.

CHAPTER TWENTY-SEVEN

Whenever Pruitt heard gunshots, she always first focused her reaction on the sound. When the shit hit the fan, the brain went every which way, but she had trained herself, Captain Lowry had trained her, to pick out the location of the shot first, then react. React first, and your knee-jerk reaction very well may expose you even more. She'd seen it too often: guys discombobulated, reacting haphazardly, only to make themselves easier targets.

She was in the trailer when the shots went off. Five of them. Two guns. Pruitt yelled at Frost to keep everyone in the trailer. Its steel-enforced walls would stop these shots. M-27s, her ears told her. Gun drawn, she slipped out the door and dashed behind the nearest construction light unit. Whoever her men were shooting at, they'd have no line on her with the klieg lights in their eyes. She looked over at Aldridge and Ferris, ducked behind a squad car, their M-27 rifles pointed over the hood. The shots had come from them. From the angle of their rifles, she could see Aldridge and Ferris were aimed at the second floor of the stone building about a hundred yards away. At the one open window, presumedly.

"Ferris!"

"There was a laser sight. At the trailer. We returned fire."

There may have been a laser sight, but despite Ferris's reframe, she was certain he and Aldridge were not *returning* any fire; no one on that side had shot.

"Hold. Hold."

Pruitt watched the window. Ten seconds. Nothing. Another ten. Still no movement. Then, a door on the north side of the building opened. Aldridge and Ferris turned their sights in that direction. Two shadows tentatively slipped out the door and edged along the wall.

"I've got the shot," Ferris said.

Aldridge looked at Pruitt. "Take it?"

The two shadows slowly snuck across the space between the building they had just exited and the one next door.

"Hold up! Let 'em go." Pruitt stood and toggled her radio. "Get me that news truck. One closest to the trailer."

Tucked up against the corner of the library's east wing, Kira and I hesitated. I peered around the corner and looked across the soccer field and up toward the graveyard. It looked clear, but it was so dark on this side of campus, you couldn't be sure. When we had been listening in earlier it had sounded like Reilly had called all his guys back in, but with the cops having just shot at us, that might have changed things.

Couldn't really blame them, I guess. The cops, that is. We probably should have had the forethought to figure, you know, a blinking laser beam against the side of the trailer may just be misconstrued as a gunsight, not some girl who knew Morse Code because she and her brother used to send messages when she would camp out in their backyard as a kid. They were cops, though; we had figured they should know the difference. The recent hail of bullets that whizzed our way was a definitive indicator that, uh, nope, they couldn't tell the difference between a gunsight and a lecture class laser pointer transmitting a message in dots and dashes.

In their Occam's Razor reading of the situation there's no way the obvious reason for this was someone had escaped *and* knew Morse Code. How many teenagers do you think know Morse Code? .01 percent? It takes one with a real font of random nerdy skills. This was a girl who could ride a unicycle, of all things, so when she had told me she knew Morse Code, I said, "Of course you do." And when she said she was going to let the cops know we heard the guy say the timer was going off in twenty minutes, I said, "Of course you are."

They said twenty, but how long ago was that? Time was cratering; you could have told me it was 8 p.m. or 3 a.m. and I'd have believed either.

"They didn't see it," Kira said.

"Doesn't matter."

"There's got to be another way to let them know."

I peered around the corner again. I couldn't see any movement between here and the graveyard. If we were going to go, we had to go now.

"Maybe the timer isn't what we think it is," I said.

"What does that mean?"

"I don't know. Either way, we gotta hide. They're going to be coming for us. Think about it for a second; what else can we even do?" When she didn't respond, I answered for her. "Nothing."

~

"You were right," Jackson said as he and Pruitt watched the Channel 3 news cameraman play back the footage.

Jackson sounded surprised, thought Pruitt. He shouldn't be. It was more surprising that none of her men had thought to consider it before peppering the building with bullets. It was her first thought when they'd said they saw a blinking laser. Morse Code. The news crews had had their cameras trained on the campus, and her guess was right that the one closest to the trailer had the angle and was likely picking up the kid flickering a message.

It had probably been ten years since she'd any reason to use Morse Code, but like learning the fifty state capitals, it was something that stuck to the brain.

-.. --- -. .----. - / - .-. ..- ... - / - .... . -- .-.-.- / - .... . -.-- / .... .-

The problem with Morse Code was it's not a speedy language. As she watched the playback, the Dots and Dashes only got as far as *"Don't trust them. They ha—"* before the first bullet clipped the mortar about four feet to the right of the window. She watched as four more shots hit the side of the building, not one even clipping the window framing much less the three-foot-by-three-foot opening. Not that she wanted to see the kids getting a bullet between the eyes, but she did expect a little better from Aldridge and Ferris.

Ferris, who along with Aldridge was watching the playback over Pruitt's shoulder, beat her to the punch. "I aimed wide, uh, in case it was the kid."

"Yeah, me too," added Aldridge.

"If you thought it was the kid, why'd you start shooting?" Pruitt said as she watched the rest of the footage play out.

Ferris looked at Aldridge and said, "Uh, in case it wasn't?"

The camera angle didn't pick up the two figures she had seen leaving the building, but she assumed it had to be the two kids. If she had to guess, "Don't trust them. They ha—" had to have been meant to be "They have a bomb." *But the kid already told us that, so why go to all that trouble unless they had more to add?*

***.

Reilly circled his finger in the air. "It's time."

Preston typed one last command in his laptop and slammed

it shut. The other gunmen moved up front and joined Reilly and Preston onstage.

Each man, Reilly included, pulled out the slim black cases they had been carrying and opened them. Inside each was a needle that the men then jabbed into their thighs. They each pressed on the plunger flange, driving a viscous, yellow liquid stream into their leg. They put the needles back in their cases and slipped those inside their pockets.

Reilly rubbed the spot where he had stabbed himself with the needle. It felt like the muscles in that part of his thigh had touched up against a warm stove. He had known to expect it; when they did the trial run, the same thing had happened. Didn't mean it didn't still sting like a hive of wasps under his skin. *Small price to pay, though,* he thought, *considering the alternative.*

CHAPTER TWENTY-EIGHT

The instant we left the safety of the corner wall and began the sprint toward the graveyard, my first thought was, *If we are going to be taken down, it would likely be these first few steps.* But now, after ten feet, then twenty, with each strike against the ground, I felt our odds of escape increasing.

I looked at Kira running ahead of me. I wondered if she felt the same. Her eyes were locked in on the ground directly in front of her. Running full speed in the dark, one's eyes started to play tricks on you. A slight depression in the lawn could appear to be a rock; or a rock might look like a shadow. I expected at any moment to catch a foot on something and face plant on the grass.

As we passed the small grove of apple trees at the far end of the soccer field, we veered right and up the slight knoll to the cemetery. We ran through the cemetery gate, and both of us slowed as we maneuvered through the tombstones, making our way to the back, where the mausoleums were. I pulled open the old rusted door to the chamber with the name *Wentworth* engraved in large 1,000-point Tombstone font.

Whenever I used to come over here, I'd wonder what kind of person wanted to bury himself and his entire family at his prep school. Joseph Benjamin Wentworth the First, apparently. At the time, the guy was thought to be the fourth or fifth richest person in America. Or so said Google. That's saying something when Rockefeller, Carnegie, and Morgan had a lock on three of those spots. Every generation of Wentworths had sent at least a handful of JBW descendants to St. Frederick, including two current ones. Times had changed, though—not one of the current Wentworths had made the top-ten hostage list.

Wentworth's tomb was pitch black and since neither of us had a phone, we had to feel our way along the wall. You would think doing this would have creeped me out when I used to come in here by myself, but to the contrary, it gave me a sense of calm—that existential kick in the pants type reminder to appreciate things more during the time you have on the planet before you end up here. If there was anything that creeped me out, it was the incomplete birth/death dates. The ones where some patriarchal dude when he died had them chisel his wife and kids' names on the tomb too, each with their birth date, a dash, and then a space where the as-of-yet-unknown expiration date would go. Now *that's* creepy.

I had been in the crypt enough times that just by feel I knew roughly where I would find the crevice holding the skeleton key. Still, as I ran my hand along the stone interior wall, gathering cobwebs on my fingers and forearm, I couldn't help but shiver at the thought of my hand bumping into a corpse. I knew this was ridiculous, but pawing around an ink-black ancient tomb covered in spiders with the echo of bats fluttering in and out has a way of making one's mind shoot off on unhelpful tangents.

When I reached the corner where the key was hidden, I dropped to one knee and stuck my hand into the crevice between the bottom two rows. As I ran my fingers along the crack, one of them caught the metal key, and a surge of euphoria came over me. I tried not to get ahead of myself, but I felt the urge to blurt out, "We've done it. We've fucking done it!" The two of us had made it to the tunnel, unseen and un-followed.

During the run, and as we made our way through the crypt, I'd been listening to the radio chatter, but I'd heard no talk of the men chasing us. In fact, it sounded like Reilly had called them all back in. Whatever the gunmen were doing over at the auditorium, they weren't worried about us anymore. And with the copters now on the lawn, I was guessing they'd be leaving shortly. Still, in the back of my mind I did feel a tinge of worry —what if Kira was right?

But it wasn't our job.

With the key in one hand, I grabbed Kira's hand with my other and led her over to the grated metal door at the far end of the crypt. I inserted the comically large skeleton key into a metal plate and turned. The tumblers clicked, and I pulled the door open with a teeth-grinding screech as the old metal door scraped along the stone floor. Slowly, I led her into the tomb chamber, the spot where Sean and the Skull and Crossbones crew met.

As I closed the door behind us, I noticed that Kira's breathing had picked up pace. I'd been in here so many times I'd forgotten how creepy and claustrophobic it might be for someone inside a dark tomb for the first time. I whispered, "We're safe. We're good . . . we're good." Kira's breathing still sounded labored, the claustrophobic feeling likely piggybacking on the sprint across the campus.

I reached out toward the sound of the breathing and found her shoulder. I pulled her toward me and wrapped her in my arms. It must've been the absolute darkness that made it possible to do this, otherwise I would never have fathomed being able to so casually put my arms around Kira and hold her, let alone whisper in her ear in as calming a voice as I could, "Breathe . . . just breathe . . . we're good." Over and over I whispered it, as her warm breath blew on my neck.

All it took was the skin of her cheek against my chin and I lost all track of the fact I was in a creepy old crypt hiding from a bunch of ruthless psychopaths who would love to put a bullet in both our skulls. I felt Kira's torso press against me with each rapid exhalation. "We're safe . . ." Slowly the exhalations became softer and further apart. I would never admit this to her, but this was the closest I'd ever physically been to a girl. I'd never had a girlfriend. Never kissed someone at a school dance. Never even *been* to a school dance for that matter.

Again, I whispered in her ear: "We're good . . ." And we were. If we were to stay right here, no one would ever find us, and when this was all over, we'd walk out safe. Back to our lives.

And I would have done exactly that . . . except.

Except for Preston's words. I almost missed it; one short sentence lost in the rest of the chatter in my earpiece. But like how hearing one's own name spoken in a nearby conversation will pull one's focus, so too did the words I heard Preston say. Up until now there was the possibility we were wrong. Wrong that they intended to blow everyone up. We'd heard things and made assumptions despite the fact Occam would say the bomb was there as a bluff. That was the obvious answer. But when I heard Preston there was no denying it.

They were going to kill them all.

As soon as the second copter set down on the grass, the pilot stepped out and was led back to the gate where five of Pruitt's men were being searched and waved over with a surveillance wand by Franklin.

Satisfied, Franklin said, "Okay," into his radio, and the five men were handcuffed and led to the copter.

In exchange, Franklin led five of the hostages to the gate, Weav, Reece, and Sean all among them.

On the other side, their parents stood back by the trailer, the cops restraining them from running toward their children. Finally, when the kids were safely on the outside, the cops stepped back and the parents and children ran toward each other into a mosh pit of hugs, tears, and relief.

Off to the side, Kira's parents stood by themselves, both with a thousand-yard stare, unable to bear watching the happy reunions.

After reuniting with his son, Bill Weaver said to his wife and Weav, "I'll be right back." Mr. Weaver walked over to the parking lot, put his hands on the Harrises' shoulders, and said a few consoling words. When he was done, rather than immediately return to his family, he ducked into his tinted-glass SUV. Inside, he pulled out a slim black case. He opened it, took out a needle, and plunged it into his thigh.

I listened to the Bluetooth while I held Kira in my arms, her breathing now back to normal. An unknown voice said over the radio, "Confirm, eight, five, five," followed by Reilly saying, "Affirmative. You and Landry bolt them when it's done."

He is going to do it. The psychopath is really going to do it. And the cops weren't going to do anything to stop it. Even if somehow we got on the other side, they still were never going to take our word. And while we were begging them, the auditorium and everyone in it would be smoked.

Of course they would. *You don't bring a bomb if you don't plan on using it.* Maybe I was muddling things in the heightened state, but I swore that was like something I'd heard Professor Alvarez say when we were reading Chekhov.

What's thirty bodies blown up to these guys? And I said thirty, but who knew what the range was? Maybe the distraction would be bigger than I thought. Maybe they planned on taking out more than just the auditorium. Get the helicopters off the ground and then take out everyone on both sides of the gate. Now there's a distraction.

Which meant, the minute those copters left the area, not just the kids on the stage or the others in there. Everyone. Kids. Teachers. Cops. Weav. My mother.

We could go back and try and do something, but it would be suicide. I wanted to laugh: I'd thought about it once before, that Christmas night, so what's another time? That time, though, I didn't. Nearly ended up dead that night by accident anyway and would probably not have been disappointed if I had. But, this time, I wanted to live. I wanted to get through this and hug my mother and tell her I knew I'd been a pain a lot of the time. I wanted to get through this and ask Kira on a date. An old-fashioned date, sit across from each other with a sandwich or whatever you had on a date—I'd never actually been on one of those either. Never had to weigh the opportune moment to lean in for a kiss. And I wanted to sit and tell her the rest about that Christmas. My dad showing back up that morning. Me excited that maybe this was going to finally work out. I was already fourteen, so I should have known better, but I didn't and I got my hopes up. He literally couldn't make it through the day.

But this time when he grabbed my mother by the hair, I grabbed him. And this time when he swung at me, I swung back. And I hit him. I didn't know it until later, but I hit him hard enough that I broke my ring finger. And it should have felt great. I'd dreamed of doing exactly that for years. I'd finally done it. Knocked him to the ground. But as I stood over him, I felt nothing. Well, that's not exactly right. I felt ashamed. Actually, that's not exactly right either. I did feel ashamed, but that came later. After I had run out of the house and took his car. I didn't have a license, but my mother had taught me to drive. I was ashamed that I had run, that I had left my mother there with him in the house. I pressed the accelerator to the floor, and thought about doing it. It would be so easy, just a flick of the wrist and it could be over. A flick of the wrist and I'd veer off the road and slam into one of the cedars that lined Baxter River Road.

I'd never told anyone this, that I almost did it. Really thought about doing it even though I knew it would be a way more vicious thing to do to my mother than anything my father had done to her. Even so, I was ready to do it. I wanted to tell Kira, and to tell her before I could do anything, a front tire blew and the car swerved off the road. I ended up in the ditch, a little banged up, but not as bad as my father's car. And as you might imagine, a fourteen-year-old with no license smashing a car into a ditch at seventy miles an hour doesn't go over well with the cops. Hence, my probation.

To this day, I didn't know whether I'd have done it had that tire not gone first. That's why I'd always wanted to tell Kira. I wanted her to tell me she thought I wouldn't have.

I let go of her and leaned back. I wanted to leave with a great parting line. Something heroic sounding even. Or, at the very least, stoic so I didn't sound as scared as I felt right now at the thought of running back toward those nut jobs with the guns and bomb. Instead I said:

"I like you . . ."

Kira leaned her head back and looked me in the eyes. She squeezed my forearm and for a second I thought she was going to say, "I like you too." Instead she squeezed even harder and said, "Fuck you."

Now *that*, I did not expect.

"What'd they say?" She tapped my ear. "The tooth."

"Nothing."

"You wouldn't have said that unless you were thinking of doing something stupid."

"Look, if you wait in the tunnel there, there's no way they'll find yo—"

"No."

"No what?"

"No, I'm not going to wait. Like the fragile lil' girly."

"I didn't mean that. You're badder than I ever will be. It's just stupid for two of us to go back. At least one of us is safe."

"Fine. You stay here, and I go."

"Do you know how to dismantle a bomb?"

"Do *you*?"

"Well, no, but I'm sure you just need to cut a few wires. That whole "Do I cut the green wire or the black one?" stuff is bullshit. Some stupid movie conceit. I mean, just cutting the wrong wire couldn't make a bomb explode." I said this with a lot more assurance than I felt. "Right?"

She still had her hand on my forearm as we stood facing one another in silence. At least I thought we were facing each other. It was so dark in here I couldn't tell for sure.

"I'm going," she said, letting go of my arm.

"Wait." I reached out to pull her in, but in the dark I hadn't realized she'd turned already and when I drew her in, her back was toward me. In that second I thought it: I'd choked out two dudes already today; by now I'd have a pretty good idea of how to gauge the sweet spot on choking someone unconscious. Maybe I could do the same so she wouldn't come too. She wouldn't be out long, but hopefully long enough. I had few illusions we were going to be able to do anything about the bomb, so why sacrifice her too? This way one of us would make it. She was going to be globally pissed at me when she woke up, sure. But by then, at least it would be over.

I could feel my arm resting just below her neck, and again I had the out of body sensation of realizing I was about to choke someone out. This time, though, it was my favorite person on the planet I was considering.

Even in the pitch black she must be able to read me, because she suddenly pulled away and said, "You were going to try and choke me out like that other guy."

"No I wasn't."

"You were."

"Well, no." I let go of her. "I mean, sorta. I thought maybe . . ."

"And that sounded like a good idea?"

"Well, kind of. But now that I say it, it doesn't sound as . . . I mean, I probably wasn't going to. It's just that there's no reason both of us . . . hey, you would have done it to me if you . . ."

Clang!

My initial thought when I heard the bang of metal was that they'd found us. But it was my second thought that was the correct one.

～

"Landry, is it set?" Reilly said into his earpiece.

"Headed that way."

Reilly took his handgun out of his inner jacket pocket and put it in his waistband, then removed the jacket. *Let's see if these jagoffs can time it out right,* he thought. If so, he should be standing on the other side minutes from now, slipping off into rural Connecticut, no one the wiser.

He had no intention of getting on those copters. No matter the technology, no matter the hostages, the cops would find them. Aircraft couldn't disappear these days if you didn't want them to. Even these birds, the ones G knew to request. And with a billion and a half dollars at stake, he wasn't getting on that copter. His guys would be, but Reilly knew better. He'd be walking out. Between the bomb detonating and the E-78 transmitter, Beyoncé could walk out the front gate and no one would notice.

Reilly pulled on the other jacket he had draped over a chair. He checked his watch. *Eight minutes.*

CHAPTER TWENTY-NINE

Kira may have thought I was an idiot to consider choking her out, but she had agreed with me about one thing: it was stupid for both of us to go back and try to do something about the bomb.

I yanked at the metal bars, but the door wouldn't budge.

We just disagreed who should do it. And now I was the one locked inside while she must be halfway back across campus already.

As I felt around blindly, trying to find something to pry the door open, I listened to the Bluetooth. It was like waiting for that punch to come, an inevitable update that they had shot some girl as she tried to get back into the auditorium basement.

I slid my hand along the top of the sarcophagus and heard the clinking of glass as I must have knocked over some beer bottles Sean's crew left behind. I felt around where I'd knocked the bottles from and my hand bumped up against some books and loose sheets of paper. I could picture those idiots reading some Econ passages to each other like it was ancient poetry.

Books and bottles weren't going to get me out. But the next thing I grabbed might.

Feeling my way back to the door, I slid the flashlight

through the metal bars. It was one of those long metal ones you see cops with. The guys must not have been back in a while, because the batteries were dead. But that didn't matter. What I needed it for was to create a fulcrum point I could pry against. I pressed the far end against the wall and pushed. I was guessing whoever designed the lock all those years ago wasn't looking to do more than stop garden-variety trespassers and hadn't gone Fort Knox on the thing.

I was right. One good shove, and the metal nub popped loose from the strike plate.

Getting back across campus was easy. With no one looking for me, I was able to slip from the cemetery to the library, then past the green from building to building until I was on the back side of the auditorium. All the activity was out front. Two shiny black copters were sitting on the lawn between the auditorium and the front gate. While sneaking across, I had seen the gunmen checking the copters, running some sort of device around their exterior.

Over the Bluetooth, I'd still heard nothing about Kira.

I pulled at the fire door in the back, but it was locked. Trying the windows, I found one ajar. I was pretty sure I knew who had opened it. As I slipped inside, I dropped into the hallway leading from the dressing rooms to the backstage area. Running as silently as I could, I headed up the hallway to the stairwell and opened the door to the basement. I stood and listened.

Silence.

I climbed down the stairs and slowly opened the door at the bottom. Putting my ear to the slit between the door and the framing, again I heard only silence.

I opened the door the rest of the way and entered the basement. I'd never seen a bomb before other than in the movies, so I didn't know what to expect besides what they always showed: a big shiny husk attached to a mass of electronics with wires leading to it. And a clock, always a clock. A timer ticking down the seconds until the explosion.

The bomb was bigger than I had expected. It did indeed have a big shell, presumably holding the explosives. The electronics, though, were simple, nothing more than what appeared to be an iPad-like device attached to some wires.

But no clock.

"You scared the crap out of me."

I whipped around and saw Kira. She must've hidden when she heard the door open.

"I thought it was them."

"I can't believe you locked me in."

"I can't believe you were going to choke me out."

Point taken.

"There's no timer on this thing," Kira said, joining me next to the bomb. "I couldn't find anything to turn off."

I'd never really thought about it before, but of course there'd never be a big clock conveniently ticking down the waning seconds like they always show in the movies. There must be a way to tell when it would go off, though. I had heard Reilly say, *set it for twenty minutes*, but I didn't have a phone so I didn't know how much time we actually had. I tried to recall if I had noticed the time on the steeple clock when I had run by, but I couldn't picture it. It had to be getting close. And seeing as I could hear the rotor blades starting back up outside, probably too close.

The transmitter. I'd heard them discuss a transmitter. I had thought the one I'd seen on the cafeteria roof had something to do with jamming signals, but maybe it was to set off the bomb. Maybe we could get to that. Stop the bomb from being triggered. But that made no sense either; Reilly had said something about triggering the transmission right *after* the bomb went off.

I stared at the bomb. It was way too big for us to lug up the stairs and out of the auditorium. "Should we smash the iPad-y thing?"

"You think so?" she said, with about as much conviction as I had.

"I don't think anything."

"How about the wires. You said that's all bullshit."

"Well . . ." Now that I was staring at a real live bomb, I was a little less certain about my theory that ripping out the wires didn't do anything. Good or bad. I had learned a lot of things over the years in the thousands of books I'd read, but—shocker —I couldn't recall anything about defusing bombs. "I mean, yeah, that whole 'should I cut the green wire or the black wire?' thing makes for good drama, but if cutting a wire really could detonate a bomb, that seems like an incredibly stupid way to design these things, right? Wouldn't it explode if the connection on the *bad* wire of the two just randomly came loose then?"

"Maybe back in the day you had to wire dynamite that way or something; I don't know. But this thing's not going to blow everything to smithereens if you cut an arbitrary green wire. Right?"

"You'd at least probably write, 'Don't Cut The Fucking Green Wire' on it if it did."

We leaned over the bomb and peered inside. None of the wires had any writing on them, and I didn't see any dire warnings anywhere else about not cutting anything.

"Fuck it," one of us said, and Kira reached in with her right hand, and grabbed the wires connecting the electronics board to the main body of the bomb. She looked like she was holding a handful of thin black licorice. I felt myself scrunch up bracing for the impact, my body putting up a defense mechanism ill-equipped to do much against 200 or so pounds of high-grade explosives. Before she had a chance to rip the wires free, a loud bang echoed. I froze, my mind playing tricks on me that the bomb had exploded even though I was still staring at it. It took a second, but my mind caught up with the situation: a door.

I turned quickly and saw someone raising his gun toward us. We both dove for the floor behind the bomb, but this didn't deter the dude from getting off a couple shots in our direction. I couldn't believe this idiot was shooting directly at a bunch of explosives. While I may have had my doubts about the danger of pulling bomb wires, I had zero doubts that shooting a round of bullets straight into an explosive's casing was a fairly bad idea.

We scrambled on all fours away from the bomb to a spot behind some scenery sets left over from a recent play. Bullets tattered the painted plywood, leaving large holes in a background scene of a grand living room. Having seen *A Little Night Music* five times, I could tell you it was Fredrik Egerman's living room if you wanted me to be precise (you could probably guess who was playing Desiree Armfeldt).

The scenery was made of cheap quarter-inch plywood that could barely stop a staple, let alone a bullet. The gunman sprayed it from end to end, but we had already slipped beyond it and made our way around the stage furniture, which was stacked in a precarious pile. Kira shoved the pile over, and she and I cut back the way we had come. The diversion worked; the man turned his gun and sent a hail of bullets in the direction of the furniture, giving us just enough time to circle back and toward the door leading up to the box office front entryway.

As we ran up the steps, I said as fast as I could, "You go left, I go right. Whoever he doesn't follow, go back and pull the wires."

Once we hit the foyer, I broke right. I was halfway to the exit when a phrase shot across my brain: "Turn into the skid."

I'd heard the saying before, but never fully believed it. I knew it had something to do with losing control of your car on black ice. Rather than wrench the steering wheel and exacerbating the skid, you're supposed to turn into it. It's counterintuitive, but it's also the safest thing to do.

As soon as the gunman stepped into the foyer, I leapt out from behind the door and drove my shoulder into him, catching him off balance and sending the two of us crashing into a large glass display case on the back wall of the auditorium lobby. We smashed through the glass and landed on a pile of overturned trophies from decades past. He tried to twist around and trigger a shot, but I shoved the rifle back into him, pressing it across his chest like I was crossing a T.

He thrashed his head forward, head butting me hard enough that it knocked me off. As he reached for his gun and set his trigger finger, I grabbed the first thing I could, cracking him across the skull with a "1922 New England Prep League Champions" trophy, the bronze-colored head of the football player catching him squarely in the temple. Thankfully for me, they used to make trophies out of something more sturdy than the cheap plastic ones today. Then again, back then you only gave out one. Winner. You didn't have to buy Second Place, Third Place, and forty participation trophies to go with it, so you could splurge on real metal. A first place trophy from 1922 had more than enough heft to daze this a-hole.

"Was it a bad day? Or was it just a bad five minutes you milked all day?" Just as I was winding up for a second crack with the trophy, the missing part of the motivational quote from Harkin somehow dropped into place. I swung the trophy with my right arm, drilling him in the chin.

I shoved aside the supine body and climbed out of the trophy case. *No, it's a bad fucking day.*

CHAPTER THIRTY

A locked briefcase in his hand, Reilly jogged out to the copters and instinctively ducked under the whirring blades even though with these new military copters the blades were a good ten feet off the ground. He looked inside and saw the five hostages Pruitt had traded him, each one tied to a metal restrainer in the back of the copter. Trotter gave him a nod from the pilot's seat.

Reilly crossed to the second copter, ducked in, and slid the briefcase into the storage rack. He checked his watch. 8:58. Just about go time. The rest of his men were headed this way. All but Landry and Javier.

As he hopped back out, he pulled the small black remote he had in his pocket and enabled it.

On the other side of the gate he could see that Pruitt and her crew had left the trailer and were standing at the ready, waiting for Reilly and his men to lift off so they could enter and free the hostages. Reilly had thought of maybe timing the blast for when the cops were in there, but the pleasure of taking them out as well wasn't worth the risk of delaying the chaos.

The cops all had guns held at the ready, except Pruitt. He could see her standing there scanning, her head slowly pivoting, taking in everything, every aspect of the situation, reading, searching for details that might mean something. At one point, her gaze stopped on Reilly. They held eyes for a moment, Reilly a tight smile on his lips, Pruitt expressionless. He could see her catch a glimpse of the gadget in his hand, a small antenna visible to her. Her eyes darted around, looking, looking. *She's good,* he thought. *She's looking at the rooftops. Knows it's not a bomb remote, but rather something else, knows it's for a transmitter.* Her eyes stopped on the mushroom-style transmitter atop the cafeteria. *Well done,* he conceded. *But that isn't going to do you any good; you may know where it is and that I am about to activate it, but you have no idea—how could you?—of what it is about to do.*

He was enjoying this. Figured he'd give her another minute to stump herself.

Reilly watched Pruitt grab one of the sharpshooters and say something in his ear, pointing toward the transmitter. The sharpshooter raised his gun. Reilly suddenly realized he didn't have that minute. The sharpshooter put his eye to his sight. A minute? Reilly didn't even have three seconds.

He depressed the switch on the remote.

The first thing that made me realize something was wrong was the vibration.

After brushing off the shards of glass, I had been about to run back to the basement when it suddenly felt as though my head was vibrating. I'd have thought it was just the excitement of the moment, but then the sound struck. It was like a large metal sheet waving in the wind and reverberating as though it were coming from a distant echo chamber. But no, I realized; it was coming from inside my own head.

Then the nausea started.

One after another, people started dropping to their knees or stumbling aimlessly. Most of them clutched at their ears or temples, every one of them feeling an odd, disorienting pressure deep inside their skulls. To Pruitt, who was now on all fours trying to regain her equilibrium enough to grab the gun from the stricken sharpshooter, the sensation was of marbles rubbing against one another, a giant bag of them squeezed inside her skull, grinding marble on marble. She fumbled with the gun, trying to lift it. She got the sight to her eye, but her vision was a cascade of colors. She squeezed her eyes closed and opened again. For a second she could see what she was looking for—the cafeteria roof—but before she could pull the trigger, a white sheet of blinding light flashed across her vision and she dropped to the ground, writhing from the pressure against her temple.

All around her, others were doing the same. The cops. The parents. The kids. Dozens of bodies stumbling or rolling around clutching their heads.

The only people not affected were Reilly and his men, which was a relief to Reilly. At least *this* had gone right. He knew it had worked in the test runs, but until you were in the mix, you never knew. It had to work. They would be sitting ducks otherwise. Now, though? Now the copters could take off and he could walk out the front door and no one in a three-mile radius could do a thing about it.

Reilly could see G amongst the other parents writhing on the ground. Not a bad acting job. Reilly laughed. Knowing G, there was no way he would have subjected himself to the pain and discombobulation. He'd have shot himself up with the antidote needle too. But his son and Mrs. Weaver? Those two were writhing around for real.

Reilly had to give G credit. This stuff really worked. It was better than a weapon. Rather, better than a *conventional* weapon, because this thing was definitely a weapon. An unbelievable one. A sector of G's company had been working on it secretly. Reilly guessed Weaver Enhanced Technologies weren't the only ones.

The Chinese and Russians probably had something similar in the works too. A much better way to lay waste to an entire army than attacking the old-fashioned way. Take out their equilibrium, their cognitive functions, and who needed bullets and bombs? One weaponized wavelength, and he could do anything he wanted.

I'd been hungover twice in my life. This felt exactly like that, only if you weaponized it with a metal vise slowly squeezing in on your temples. I could do nothing but clutch my head and clench back the urge to vomit. My first thought was I'd been poisoned, but it couldn't be that; I hadn't eaten anything all day. Besides, I could see across the way that there were dozens others who had dropped. My next thought was that maybe they sprayed something in the air, but that wouldn't explain why there were some people still standing. Through my warping vision, I could see that the guys with guns hadn't been affected, but since they weren't wearing masks, it couldn't have been something airborne.

Another wave of the metal sheet echoed through my head, but this time I felt the sensation channel over my whole body, from my toes to my teeth, where it felt like I was clenching them around a cold piece of tin. I put my hands to my ears, trying to block out the sound. It didn't help. In fact it actually worsened, like I was somehow trapping the contagions inside my skull. As though some poison had entered my bloodstream and I was pushing it back in.

Through the pain and disorientation, a flash of awareness slipped through. The gunmen. They weren't affected. Which meant it could only be one thing.

The needle.

I fumbled to pull the case out of my pocket, the one I had taken from the guy on the roof. As I slid it from my pants pocket, it dropped to the ground. I was already on my knees and I leaned over trying to pick it back up, but my motor skills were going haywire. Flailing, I missed and fell forward on top of it. Rolling over, I reached out with both hands this time. I pulled it toward me and fiddled with the latch, but it was like I was trying to open something while wearing a pair of catcher's mitts. I squeezed the case with both hands and brought it to my mouth. Pressing it to my teeth, I got my front ones on the latch and pulled the case down, snapping it open, the needle falling to the granite floor. I grabbed it, but my hands jutted forward uncontrollably and the needle point jammed against the floor, bending to a 45 degree angle. I tried to bend it back, but it was too fine a task to complete with my nervous system in full tilt mode.

I pawed the needle between my palms and spiked it—bent point and all—into the thick of my thigh. Depressing the plunger partway, I felt a sudden warmth run to my foot and then back up toward my chest, like a gentle wave cresting to shore and rolling back out to sea.

I lay on my back, waiting, but nothing happened. I must have been wrong. Or maybe, I now realized, you needed to take the serum beforehand for it to have any counteracting effect. I reached to the needle in my thigh to see if I hadn't pressed all of the liquid into my leg. It was then that I realized the bent needle point had snapped off in my thigh. The casing, with about three quarters of the serum still in it, lay on the floor next to me. But now with the needle buried in my thigh, I had no way of getting the remaining serum into my veins.

I picked up the casing and shoved the business end in my mouth. Depressing the plunger, I squirted the rest of the liquid into my mouth. I swallowed, nearly gagging it all back up again. My mouth tasted of dish soap, as though having drunk from an un-rinsed glass.

The warm sensation moved down my throat and into my stomach, but even with the entire dose inside me, still nothing happened. I lay motionless on the ground, waiting, my mouth filled with the sudsy aftertaste. *Maybe taking it orally won't absorb it fast enough*, I thought. For all I knew, I could be dead by the time it did.

~

It reminded Pruitt of the time the Hummer in front of them dinged the IED and the whole left side of her vehicle exploded. That hollow, echoing sensation rumbling inside her head. The disorientation. But this was different. Even then she had more control over her motor skills. She had been able to climb over the seat from the back and press her hand against Private Russell's side wound until the medic arrived. Now, though, she was stumbling, couldn't get back to her feet. But she had to. She had to take out the transmitter. She would bet her life that whatever was happening to her, to the others, was emitting from there.

She clenched her eyes shut and opened again. The building with the transmitter atop it bloomed out at her in a kaleidoscope of bright colors. Lying on her side, she aimed the gun in the direction of the building. There was no way she would be able to accurately shoot at the transmitter using the sight, but maybe off of an establishing shot she could adjust enough to narrow in on it. The first shot missed the transmitter to the left by ten feet. The sound of the gun echoed inside her skull along with the sensation of a handful of steel ball bearings rolling around and around a metal funnel.

Pruitt readjusted her aim and took another shot. Still off, but this time only a foot to the right and about four feet too high. Always took three shots to truly aim a gun you'd never used before, she knew. As she aimed a third time, she felt the familiar sting of a bullet enter and exit her right shoulder. She still got the shot off, but it missed wide left, and the rifle fell from her grip. She rolled to her right as three more bullets ripped into the trailer behind her.

Jackson, from his perch on the ground to her left, was able to pull his handgun and, disoriented, fired a shot in the direction of the gunshots coming at Pruitt. He missed wildly, and Reilly ripped off a return barrage of bullets, one catching Jackson in the neck, flopping him sideways, facedown and motionless. Reilly's attention was pulled by Jackson just briefly enough, though, that Pruitt was able to roll behind an SUV and duck safely out of sight.

Safe, yes, but having failed to take out the transmitter. As the sensation in her head continued to worsen, she wondered, *what will happen once we're completely helpless? They can do anything to anyone.*

~

I couldn't get up. I was supine, shaking. It felt to me like my limbs belonged to someone else. I could see them shaking wildly, but I couldn't feel anything. Just warmth. But slowly that sensation waned and I couldn't even feel that; I just lay on the cement, shaking, unable to move. The serum I took must have been too late. My whole body felt like it was slowing down. I could count the heartbeats; they seemed to be three seconds apart. Soon, it was five. The next time, eight.

As I lay there I thought, *How did this happen?* It was like I was living someone else's life. One thing had led to another, and that led to another and somehow I was lying lifeless on the floor of the auditorium, a place where I had dropped off mail about ten hours ago. Ten hours ago I was bored sick of the mundane tasks of sorting internal memos for professors. And now? Now I was afraid I was going to die.

My foggy brain caromed back to a song I used to hear coming from Garvey's stereo. Some Tragically Hip song about a guy in his thirties who'd never kissed a girl before. I'd always felt sorry for Garvey after that. Maybe it was just one of many Tragically Hip songs he liked, but it also seemed the one he played the most. Even though I had never kissed a girl either, I was only seventeen and hadn't been too worried I'd end up like Garvey, alone with a Ham radio, never getting the opportunity. But lying here, my heart seemingly slowing to a stop, it was looking like that was going to be my fate too.

Weirdly, I was almost angry at myself. Angry that I could have spent my few years on this planet as such a complete and utter wimp. A million things I wanted to tell Kira and never did. And all the things that reminded me of her that she probably had zero idea about: headstands, Junior Mint cake, Plain White T's lyrics, Jeffersonville, L'Orange, palm tree cookies, tartar, all things pumpkin, Java U, the Dartmouth bookstore entrance, the Rest of My Life song, Christmas riddles, Choc-ola, St. Viteaur, sand for Christmas. On and on and on . . . all the things I'd never get to think about again. All the things I'd never get to do with her or tell her about. The anger dropped away and was replaced by sadness. And I thought:

I wasted it.

With my mind running over all this, I had lost track of the time since the last heartbeat. I had a sudden panic: maybe that was the last one. Last one I'd ever feel.

I listened closely. It was faint, a hint of a beat at first, and then, like a pair of defibrillator paddles blasting my chest, my body abruptly jerked upward. Immediately my heart raced, as though making up for lost beats. And the echo. The echo had dropped away. I sat up and looked around. The bright lights and the warped equilibrium were gone too. It was as though my whole body had restarted, and I was sitting there like nothing had ever happened.

I had always had a theory, but one I obviously had no way to test. In a way we were all computers, I had always figured, and one of the best fixes for a tweaked computer or malfunctioning modem was to unplug it and reboot, so why couldn't that work for humans too? I had read about doctors giving induced heart attacks as a way to scar and shrink overgrown ventricular muscle.

How about inducing a heart attack then in order to turn off the body so as to spark and reboot some part of the human body that is malfunctioning? Maybe for certain problems, a stroke, cancer, Parkinson's, you simply needed to wipe away the current state of our brain's software and start back up from scratch? Crazy as it sounded, I had always had a feeling this was going to be one of those things that years from now would be common knowledge, like *don't eat lead paint or medicate with leaches, you idiots*. No one would fathom that we didn't do it. This may not have been what just happened to me, but whatever was in that syringe had done the same. I had been rebooted.

I stepped outside and looked around. It was like surveying a battlefield—the cops and the news people, the parents and the kids, half of them clutching their heads or thrashing uncontrollably on the ground. The other half passed out completely. Or for all I knew, dead.

In Anatomy, we had studied the inner ear. Mr. Grady had lectured about the three separate ear canals. One controls side-to-side movement, another the up-down, and a third regulates tilting. Our own personal gyroscope. All it took was a break in communication between the brain and the tiny hair cells that float in each of the canals, and it could knock you off your axis, so I guessed it wasn't surprising they had discovered a way to discombobulate everyone's equilibrium with a particular wavelength. And the serum had apparently returned my equilibrium the way the Epley maneuver could jostle vertigo sufferers back to normal.

Above me, a copter flew off to the west. The remaining gunmen were loading into the second one as the blades began to rotate.

I felt completely helpless. Sure, I was physically fine again, but with everyone else at best a writhing mess, how could I get everyone out of the building in case Kira hadn't gotten back and dismantled the bomb? A second panic rolled over me. Whether she dismantled it or not, she didn't have a needle. What if this wavelength or whatever it was that they had disabled everyone with, what if it had the potential to scramble their brains permanently if left on too long? I realized I couldn't solve either problem without finding out where the wavelength was coming from.

I went back and grabbed the gun out of the busted trophy case. I paused and thought about bolting down the stairs to see if Kira had made it back to the bomb, see if she was alright.

She wasn't. That much I knew. And it was pointless anyway. I had to stop this thing.

When I had seen the transmitter earlier, and with the phones and Wi-Fi all down, I had assumed it was just a jammer of some sort, but that thing on the cafeteria roof must be doing this. I ran out onto the lawn and around the east side of the auditorium to get a better sight line of the cafeteria roof. As I raised the gun, something caught my eye off to the right.

A body.

A body lying underneath the open window I'd snuck in through before.

It wasn't moving.

She wasn't moving.

I raised the rifle and aimed at the transmitter. As I squinted at the sight at the tip of the gun, I could see the barrel shaking. I was panicking.

I needed to calm down. But no amount of diaphragmatic breathing was going to shake me from the complete terror coming over me: *she was dead.*

They killed her. Kira wasn't moving, not even twitching like I had been. The transmission, wavelengths, whatever it was, it had scrambled her.

I wanted to run to her, feel for a pulse, but I was too scared to find out. Besides, unless I stopped this thing, it was moot either way. So, despite the shaking, I aimed and pulled the trigger, but it wouldn't budge. I tried again. Nothing.

The safety. Sure, that much I knew, but where's a safety? I

turned the rifle over in my hands until I saw a small black switch. I clicked it, aimed the shaking rifle at the transmitter, and pressed the trigger.

A bullet blew out a window in the cafeteria, a good twenty feet from my target. I was caught off guard by the gun's kick and was nearly knocked off my feet. I steadied myself and tried again. This time the bullet came a little closer but still far off from where it needed to be.

The next shot kicked up chunks of masonry from the roof's edge, three feet to the right of the transmitter. I moved my aim a hair to the left, steadied myself, and let a shot go.

The transmitter sparked and the top portion fell over. I dropped the gun and ran to Kira. Even with the transmitter disabled, she still wasn't moving. Maybe I had been wrong. I felt like I was going to throw up. This time not from the wavelength. From what I was going to discover as I pressed my fingers to her throat.

Nothing.

I felt something rising from my gut, like an involuntary scream was about to explode out of me, but my throat tightened and nothing came out. Like watching my father and mother back when there was nothing I could do. To stop it, like I would do then, I tried to just hold it in. I clenched my throat, but I couldn't do it. My body convulsed and a half snort, half sob wrenched out of me, a snot bubble coming out my nose.

"Get up."

I turned and looked up at Reilly aiming a gun at my head. He jabbed it at me. "Get the fuck up. *Now.*"

CHAPTER THIRTY-ONE

"We got Bird Two," Frost said. "Hostages safe. One wounded but not serious. Bird One is in the air."

"Tracked?" Pruitt asked, pressing a hand to her shoulder wound.

"41.224440 - 74.070388, running due west."

They had them; as good as the new technology of these aircraft was, there's always a way to track. Pruitt hadn't been worried about that. They would have them no matter where they tried to fly.

And that's what was gnawing at her. They had gone to all this trouble. They had the technological wherewithal to do whatever *that* was with the transmitter. Her head was still aching. It felt like there was sandpaper rubbing against the back side of her eyes. Who knew how scrambled their brains might be right now if that transmitter hadn't shut off, Pruitt wondered. Speaking of which . . . *who destroyed the transmitter?* She could see from the piece dangling that someone had. She had heard gunshots too. Four to be exact. Someone not very experienced based on the broken window twenty feet off and the hole in the masonry.

But after it was disabled, it didn't take her guys long. She had to give them credit. Even with compromised equilibrium they'd cleared the auditorium and stormed the remaining copter. Three of Reilly's men had returned fire, but outgunned, they were quickly overtaken. A fourth managed to grab a hostage. Worth a shot, she thought, but never works out the way it does on TV. Sure, you could grab a hostage and keep at bay the four guys aiming guns at you. Just not the fifth guy standing ten feet behind you. Unbeknownst to you, he was going to pump a bullet into your skull before you could even make your first demand.

Another question shot around her frazzled brain: why wouldn't they split the hostages so each copter was bubbled? It's possible they hadn't anticipated their transmitter getting destroyed, so they would have assumed they had all kinds of time to ditch the copters somewhere and escape by other means.

"Disposal?" she asked.

"They've dismantled it and are searching the area for any other ordnance. Jackson has teams out searching for any remaining holdouts. We think there may be two or three armed still on the grounds somewhere."

As Frost was updating her, she scanned the crowd being loaded out on the far side of the gate. She could see the Dixon woman pleading, trying to get back inside.

The boy. It had to be him.

But if it was, then how did he overcome the attack on his nervous system? Pruitt could barely aim with the way her body had been responding; she was certain he wouldn't have been able to. Maybe he got a lucky shot. But with no vision and no equilibrium? Luck wasn't enough. It would have been impossible unless he had whatever the others had that stabilized their nervous systems.

So where is he?

❧

For the second time today I found myself headed to a graveyard.

They say things tend to go in threes. The way things were looking, I could see a third and final time in my very near future.

This time, though, I was still alive. And, thank God, so was Kira.

Unfortunately, walking behind us with a gun was Reilly. I'd been relieved when she had started to regain consciousness back outside the auditorium. But the relief was short-lived when Reilly had made me take her with us. She'd come to, but not having had the needle shot like I had, she was still pretty groggy.

It seemed kinda stupid to me for him to insist on taking us both. One hostage or two, what's the difference? Why slow yourself down with a hostage that needed to be more or less dragged along?

As we had made our way across the field in the direction of the cemetery, I thought back to how I had felt earlier, running across here with Kira. I'd thought it was over, that we'd be safe up there, and I had already started feeling that surge in my gut I used to get during fights when a move I had executed made the outcome feel inevitable. The hard work and uncertainty were over; now it was just a matter of closing out the match.

I had wanted to feel like that forever. That sense of completion. I'd never felt so sure of myself. And wouldn't that have been the time, if I was ever going to kiss a girl? It would be in the movies. But then again, pretty much everything that had happened today didn't work out the way I thought this type of shit would.

My current situation included.

By now Kira no longer needed to be propped up, but she still held onto my shoulder to keep her balance, and those eyes that were always looking with piercing interest, they now had a haze of confusion.

I stopped. "Just leave her here. You got a better chance getting out of here without dragging her along."

"Maybe it's sexism, but cops tread lighter with a damsel in

distress. I'm not giving up the leverage of a cute little girl for an annoying prick like you."

I could feel him press the gun barrel to my head.

"Keep moving or I'll relieve myself of the annoying prick."

I mumbled a satisfying, albeit highly pointless, "Fuck *you*." As I said it, I braced for what I knew was coming. And it did: the butt of the gun to my head. I fell forward, stunned but still conscious.

I turned and looked at Reilly aiming the gun in my direction. "Keep her moving."

"You're not stupid enough to draw attention with a gunshot." The words came out fuzzy sounding. At least to me they did.

He clicked off the safety. "The whole point of taking hostages is the other side has to know you've got 'em."

We stood in silence, two, maybe three seconds, and then he clicked the safety back on. "Come on. Keep moving."

That's when I had the sinking realization why he needed both of us.

Because one of us wasn't there as a hostage.

~

"Sir, we need everyone to stay on this side of the gate," Officer Witten said, putting his hand out in front of Weaver.

Weaver tried to maneuver his way around, but Witten grabbed his arm and said more forcefully this time, "The area isn't clear yet. *No one* goes in."

Weaver scanned the grounds. Until he was out of range and undetectable, he had no way of knowing whether the billion-five was in his accounts or whether Reilly had double-crossed him and moved it to his own. Weaver hadn't seen Reilly among the men the cops had killed or captured. It didn't surprise him that Reilly would have a back-up plan ready just for himself. The guy was too smart not to, Weaver knew. *The guy's also too smart to not try to screw me for a billion five.* One thing Weaver knew for sure: the longer the cops didn't come up with Reilly, the more likely Reilly had double-crossed him before he had the chance to do the same to him.

And it wouldn't just be the cash they had fleeced off these other parents, but his own. $183 million and change. Cash he had to put up so as to not look like he was in on it. And now that was likely gone too if the cops didn't get Reilly.

"Where's the ringleader? That guy on the radio who tried to threaten our kids?" Weaver asked.

"Sir, we are taking care of it," said Witten.

"That man was going to kill our children. I have the right to know where he is."

"Sir, we will let you know when we know."

Weaver couldn't leave it up to these guys. If they took Reilly alive, Weaver was still not out of it. Reilly would have the leverage on him.

Weaver walked back to his SUV. He pulled out a metallic sphere from a false-bottom panel under the floor mat. He depressed the buttons in a particular sequence and said, "Get me Larimee."

CHAPTER THIRTY-TWO

Reilly never planned to be here. He had laid out everything perfectly. The bomb to distract. The copters to mislead. The sound-wave transmitter to sow confusion and debilitate everyone. All of which would allow him to disappear in plain sight. They would have assumed he had died in the copter that he had placed the briefcase of explosives on, and they'd never bother looking further.

But now, it wasn't going to be so easy. With the transmitter off, and Pruitt's team functioning again, he wasn't going to be able to walk out the way he had planned. He needed another out, so he had made for the far side of the property in hopes he could find a way out undetected before anyone figured out he wasn't on the first copter. Unfortunately, for once his guys hadn't been completely incompetent and had indeed wired the detonators all along the wall like they were supposed to.

He had a contingency plan for that too, though. Reilly always did.

The only one who knew he was still alive was Weaver, and he had nearly as big an incentive for Reilly not to be taken as Reilly himself. Reilly was the only one who could link Weaver to this whole thing. Therefore Weaver wanted him to escape too. Or—

even better, Reilly presumed—dead. By now the copter would have blown, and Weaver would have to know Reilly had gone rogue. And if he knew that, Reilly figured, he also knew Reilly was planning on cutting him out. Weaver would soon be realizing he had no access to the accounts the cash had been funneled off. And thus, he needed to find Reilly as badly as anyone else.

So Reilly needed a way out. And the kid was about to provide it. *Kid knows it too,* Reilly sensed. *He looks scared this time.* Reilly had been surprised at the kid's balls before, but now it was different; the kid could sense Reilly's contingency plan, and there was genuine fear in his eyes.

"Let's go," Hastings said to his son a second time. The two, along with Mrs. Hastings, were in line for the buses taking the hostages and parents to the off-site holding area. Sean had stopped and the other families were passing around him. "*Sean.* Let's go. Now."

"No. I fucked up."

"Don't use that word. Get up here."

"I fucked up." Sean turned and headed back toward the command trailer. He felt sick. It had made sense in the moment: *a man makes his own opportunity.* He had needed to do anything he could to escape the situation. But removed from it, he realized what he had done. Or tried to.

By the trailer door there was a cluster of cops talking. Sean approached them.

"Whoever you still have who isn't jobbed up, get them out there looking," Pruitt said.

"Did they find him?" Sean asked.

Pruitt ignored him and continued, "Longer they're MIA, the more dangerous they get. Find the . . ."

"Cade. The one who was loose. Did they find him?"

"The bus," Jackson snapped at him. "We need everyone on the bus."

"Find the . . ."

"Is he . . . dead?" Sean interrupted Pruitt again. That sick feeling rose up from his stomach into his throat.

Jackson jabbed his finger toward the bus. "Now."

"Find the kids now. If they find them first, we're back to a hostage situation again. And cornered, they're way more likely to do something stupid."

"The two could be anywhere," Aldridge said.

"Well, no shit," Jackson said. "Start looking."

"I think I know . . ."

For the first time since he had come up to them, all four cops turned and looked at Sean.

"Head to the back." Reilly jabbed his gun toward the far side of the cemetery, at the shed backed up against the stone wall that ran around the entire campus. Hop up on the shed, and you could reach the top of the wall and pull yourself over. Run off into the woods and hide. You could, that is, if not for those silver grenade-shaped explosives wired the length of the wall.

About twenty feet from the shed, Kira stopped. I could tell she had just realized what was about to happen. Like me, though, she didn't know which one of us it was going to be.

"Move it." Reilly pressed the gun into Kira's side and pushed her toward the shed. She stumbled forward a couple steps and stopped again. Reilly jammed the gun harder into her ribs, and this time she complied.

As the two of us walked toward the shed, we looked at each other. I didn't know if it was the adrenaline running through her or the focus of knowing one of us was about to die, but the haziness was gone from those eyes. My favorite thing on this planet: those two orbs. Rather, those two orbs looking at me. Like I was it. The only thing she wanted to look at, the only person she wanted to listen to. I always felt she just did that with everyone. Right now, though, it was all me. She was looking at me so forcefully, so intently, like she was trying to convey something to me. I knew it was crazy, but somehow I believed I just might figure out what it was if I tried hard enough.

I wondered if she knew we were both dead either way. Even the one he didn't send over the wall to set off the bomb, making it safe for him to cross, even the one of us he kept as a hostage, that one would soon be expendable too. We were dealing with a psychopath, a man who had no qualms about blowing up thirty-some-odd people just to camouflage his escape. We had studied psychopathic behavior in Abnormal Psych class. This guy exhibited all the traits. The lack of remorse. The grandiose sense of self. The callousness. The lack of empathy for those thirty families.

Even now there was something funny to me at the idea that "*We* had studied." Kira was in the class; I merely observed from the crawl space above the room. That made *me* the abnormal one. The weird dude who loved watching Kira being so utterly locked in on something she loved. It had made me believe she really would fix all those broken minds when she got older.

"You over the wall."

"No," Kira said.

"Let's go. Up."

Now that he said it, it made sense why he'd dragged her along. With her equilibrium still off, she'd be too slow to take as hostage. Use her for fodder over the wall and then take me with him as the hostage.

"No. Those'll blow me up."

"It's been turned off. Let's go."

"Okay, you first then."

He looked at Kira and grinned. "I will happily shoot both of you right now."

"I'll go first."

He looked at me. I could see him considering my offer. Any faint hope I had that he actually might have turned them off disappeared when he said, "No, she goes first."

I thought about lunging for the gun, one last-ditch attempt, but Reilly was smart enough to keep a healthy distance that would give him time to react and blow a hole through me if I tried anything. I looked at Kira, her eyes boring into me. Whatever she was trying to convey, I wasn't getting it. And when she dropped to her knees, I still didn't get it. I thought it was just the tweaked equilibrium, but when she fell to her hands and knees and started barking, I finally got it.

Reilly certainly didn't. How could he? How could one's brain wrap itself around the reality of a seventeen-year-old girl suddenly dropping to all fours and barking loudly and madly like a lonely dog? The brain was not wired for such unexpected actions. That went for even Reilly, who probably prided himself on planning for the unexpected. But "the unexpected" included planning for contingencies he could imagine. Like someone pulling a hidden gun. Or there being a radio breakdown. Or the bomb not detonating. A girl barking on the ground in front of him? Anyone would need a second or two to recalibrate before reacting.

Anyone, that is, who hadn't read *Perception vs. Deception* by Reginald Barry, specifically the chapter covering the incident of a particular high school basketball team, where when inbounding the ball with seconds left in a tie game, a player started barking, completely mesmerizing the other team with this abnormal action. Something that should never occur in that context.

The moment she started barking, I knew I had a solid two seconds before Reilly's brain caught up to the situation. I took a running start and drove my shoulder into the arm holding the gun. Reilly and I hit the ground hard, the gun dislodging from his hand as he slammed up against the base of a large granite gravestone.

As soon as I had him to the ground, Kira hopped to her feet and ran toward the gun.

Reilly was way more agile than the two other men I'd jumped. As soon as I attempted an arm triangle choke, he slipped out of it and rolled over on top, pressing his own arm into my throat. I thrashed, trying to buck Reilly off. On my third attempt, Reilly fell back and toward the right. I added to his momentum and shoved his head toward the gravestone. "George Adams. 1810-1821." A student who probably died of pneumonia while at school, and had lain here for 200 quiet years, nothing much happening until two centuries later a fight to the death commenced six feet above. Had I been able to direct Reilly's head an inch or so to the right when I drove him backward, George Adams would have finished Reilly off for me, his head gashed by the corner of the stone. Instead, it was merely a glancing blow.

I saw Reilly take in Kira holding the gun toward us. Ignoring her, he grabbed for my leg, apparently confident she would never be able to pull the trigger. I felt the same way; she may have been training the gun in his direction, but like me, the odds that she had it in her to take a life were minuscule. With the arrows, she was thinking: injure. With a gun you couldn't help but think it was to kill. Anyone can blast away on *Grand Theft Auto* or *Call of Duty*. But video games aren't the gateway drug to murder; you gotta have it in you.

Reilly wrenched my leg as I tried to stand, yanking me back and forcefully twisting the leg at the knee. I screamed as one of my tendons ripped.

"Stop!" Kira yelled. "I've got the gun."

Unconcerned, Reilly pushed his forearm into the side of my knee, heightening the pain. He climbed on top of me and pressed his knees onto my arms and grabbed my throat with one hand. I thrashed about, but he squeezed tighter.

"I've got the gun . . ."

Reilly didn't even bother looking at her. He squeezed my

neck with his left hand and repeatedly punched me in the face with the other. I flailed with my free arm but couldn't muster more than what felt like a slow motion round hook that missed its target. I tried again, but this time my arm didn't move, like the signal from my brain had gotten lost on its way to my fist. I had been choked out before in wrestling, but this was different. As my vision darkened, and I started to fade out, I knew he wasn't planning on stopping when I passed out.

The last thing I heard was a muffled thumping sound. Then everything went dark.

CHAPTER THIRTY-THREE

The thing that surprised Kira the most wasn't that she had pulled the trigger; it was the fact Reilly had lurched backward. She had intentionally aimed way over his head, hoping the warning shot would be enough to stop him from killing Cade. But somehow she must have hit him. One panic replaced another. The new one stemming from the fact she had just killed another human being. It wasn't until the next shot rang out—the one that knocked Reilly off Cade—that Kira realized someone else had been shooting too. In the moment, Kira hadn't seen the woman in the black windbreaker, standing by the gate. But now as she stared at the woman with the handgun and the two cops trailing her, things retroactively made sense. The echo she'd thought she'd heard wasn't an echo after all, but rather a second shooter. And the bullet she thought she had sailed over his head, had. It wasn't her who killed the man bleeding out on the grass. It was the cop.

～

Pruitt put a hand to Cade's neck and felt for a pulse.

She couldn't get over the fact she was looking at the face of a seventeen-year-old boy. A motionless, bloodied mess with the bottom half of his right leg jutting out at a peculiar angle. A lifeless face. *The mother*. Pruitt was already dreading having to tell her.

They had done all this. He and the girl had somehow stopped all this. They'd been right about the bomb too. Not only right, but had done something about it.

Pruitt repositioned her fingers on his neck and pressed again. Had she gotten here just a few seconds earlier, maybe he'd still be alive, she thought. After the Hastings kid had told her about the crypt, she and Aldridge and Witten had sprinted up here. Got here in time to save the girl. But the boy . . . Reilly must have been . . .

Her train of thought screeched to a halt. Had she just felt something? Probably just wishful thinking, she thought as she pressed her fingers deeper. But then she felt it again. It was faint, but it was there.

CHAPTER THIRTY-FOUR

By the time I came to, I didn't know what the medic standing over me had done to me, but I did know this: he'd been pretty generous with the painkillers. Santa Claus generous. The hint being I didn't feel a thing in my knee, despite the fact it appeared to be *bent the wrong fucking way*.

I stared at my foot that was angling off on some new trajectory, and I laughed. No, I giggled. I don't think I'd ever "giggled" before, but it sounded like a giggle.

Yeah, they'd been *very* generous.

I tried to picture the diagram on the wall of Anatomy class so I could figure out which muscles and ligaments had been shredded in my knee. The gracilis. The vastus medialis. Anterior, lateral, posterior, all. I was at the gastrocnemius when I realized I wasn't alone with the medic. Somebody's hand was rubbing my head. Turning my eyes up in that direction, I saw my mother hovering over me, smiling at me as she stroked the back of my head like she did when I couldn't fall asleep as a kid. I looked over the side of the bed. But it wasn't a bed. It was apparently a rolling stretcher. It started to come back to me. The graveyard. Reilly. His death grip. Kira.

Kira.

"Hey, where's, is Kira where?" The words sounded right; I just couldn't get them out of my mouth in the right order.

"Right over there."

I turned in the direction my mother pointed. I could see a medic at the back of an ambulance, treating someone, but I couldn't see who. The couple standing next to the medic looked my way, and seeing me see them, they walked over.

"You're very brave. Thank you. Thank for saving our daughter."

"Who's your daughter? Hoosier . . . Whoooossssyer . . . Funny word."

"Kira."

"Uh-uh. She did. I mean, she saved *me*. She's a badass; she shot that dude."

"Actually that was Officer Pruitt."

"Well, she shot that other dude. She was amazing."

"What other person?"

"The one she speared like shiskabob. With an arrow. Two arrows. Shissshhhhkah-bob. That's another funny one. My name is Bob Shishka." I laughed. They didn't. No wonder people get hooked on these meds; everything's funny as shit.

I tried to match their serious tone. They seemed to want me to. "Thank you," I said trying to look Kira's mother in the eye, "for your daughter."

"Well, you're welcome," Mrs. Harris said with a smile.

Behind them, I saw the medic move away and Kira stand up. "Hey," I yelled over to her. "You're a good barker. You were like a world-class dog barker. Like Westminster Dog Show great."

I could see Mr. and Mrs. Harris eye me with puzzled looks. My mother too. Probably all of them figuring this seeming non sequitur had something to do with the painkillers. The medic gave them a "don't blame me" shrug.

"Thanks," Kira said.

"Did you listen to the song yet?"

"What song?"

"The one I told you about when we were . . ." Did I tell her? I'd been thinking about telling her. I was having a little trouble untangling my thoughts from my words. I wasn't 100 percent sure which was which. "'Sweet Things.' The song. . . maybe I wasn't telling you about it? I listen to it every day."

"By who?"

"Are we still friends?"

She laughed. "Yes, I think we're still friends."

"Even though I was thinking of choking you out?"

"We'll call it even," she said, reaching out and squeezing my hand.

"Even? What'd you do to me?"

"Nuth. Yet." She smiled. "But I'll think of something."

Outside, Pruitt watched her team load the gunmen into the transport vehicle and body-bag Reilly. She shook her head as she saw two members of the crew load up dozens of to-go boxes with all the extra takeout. She would swear some of these guys only did these jobs for the free food.

While she watched the final cleanup, Weaver and Taylor came toward her with purpose. *This should be good*, she thought.

"Any progress?" She turned around to see Weaver glaring at her. Next to him was Taylor.

"The bomb is out. All the students and teachers are accounted for. Ditto my crew," Pruitt answered, knowing she wasn't answering the question Weaver had in mind.

"What about the accounts? Have you located them?"

"No. And it's highly unlikely we will, given the encryption."

"Don't give me the highly unlikely bullshit. You claw that cash back or . . ."

"Or what? You garnish my wages? Might take you a while to get a billion dollars out of me one paycheck at a time."

"Do you have any idea how much money I just lost?"

Taylor grabbed his arm. "Bill, come on; calm down."

In fact, despite the angry tone, Weaver was quite calm. Weaver was only unleashing on Pruitt to add cover. Things had actually turned out even better than planned. From the start Larimee had monitored the transfers from New York, following the trail as Reilly attempted to reroute the payouts to his own accounts. Larimee had just confirmed every dollar of the $1.53 billion was accounted for.

Even though Reilly had tried to screw him, Weaver had to give him credit; his bidding idea had made Weaver about a billion and a half dollars. Well, $1.32 billion. Essentially, the $183 million he had needed to put up for cover had just moved from one offshore account to a new offshore account. But Taylor's money? And Hastings'? And all the others? That was all sitting in Weaver's accounts in Cyprus and Panama, and now that Pruitt had killed Reilly, he had no one he had to share it with. Not only that, seeing as none of Reilly's men knew who he was, there wasn't a single loose end to worry about.

Pruitt looked at the two men and said dryly, "But your kids are fine and that's the important thing, right?"

"Did you get to shoot anyone, dude?" Weav asked.

"No. But K did."

"You're both insane." Weav had joined us over by the ambulance. None of us were being allowed to leave until the entire place was swept or something. We'd all been here an hour or so apparently. The painkillers had started wearing off some, which was actually a good thing. I had been feeling like I was talking in Jello. If that makes any sense. Probably not. But it had an hour ago.

"It wasn't a gun," Kira said. "Just an arrow."

"Oh yeah, just an arrow," Weav laughed. "Into some dude. No, you're right; that's not insane."

"Alright, Mike, let's go." Weav's parents joined us. "They're letting everyone out," Weav's dad continued, his arm around Mrs. Weaver.

I'd have thought it was the painkillers, or something scrambled in my head after that brain-wobbling frequency earlier, and I'd have let the brief sensation go, had I not seen Kira's face. She had caught it too.

"Cade, get well, buddy." Mr. Weaver patted my shoulder. We had met a couple times over parents' weekends. The Weavers used to take a bunch of us out to dinner in town. "I want to see you and Mike next . . ."

I didn't hear the rest. I was looking at Kira. She was looking at me.

Fuck. I had forgotten all about the voice. The person on the other end of the phone line. I had thought it had sounded vaguely familiar, and now I knew why. But why would he have been the one on this side in on it? Why would he have let Reilly put Weav in danger of being one of the ten? There's no way he would have let his own son be in danger just to make a buck.

But that's the thing, I suddenly realized; *he never was in danger.* Weav couldn't have been safer. They'd never let him be the bottom one, and he was one of the first five to get out. The others were screwed, but he was going to be out on the other side before any bomb went off.

"It was you." I didn't say it; Kira beat me to it. "That was you," she said directly to Mr. Weaver.

"Me what?"

"That was your voice."

The Weavers and Kira's parents shared confused looks.

"You were the guy. That's the guy," she said to me, more emphatically now. "Right?"

"It's definitely him." I'm not great at reading faces, but Mr. Weaver was even worse at hiding what was on his. He looked like an animal backing into a corner.

"Hey! Hey!" Kira yelled toward the cops standing outside

the trailer. The Pruitt woman who had asked me all the questions when they got us back here started toward us.

"What is she talking about?" Mrs. Weaver said.

"I have no idea," Mr. Weaver said.

When Pruitt got over to us, Kira said again, "he's the guy. The one we heard on the phone. The guy who was out there. Out *here*."

"Oh, yeah, okay." Mr. Weaver laughed. "I think you've gotten a little carried away on this little adventure of yours."

"No. She's right. Check his leg. Or his ass. I bet he's got a needle prick like this," I said, indicating where I had plunged it into me.

"My own son was being held by these sociopaths," Mr. Weaver said angrily to Pruitt.

She shrugged. "So drop your drawers."

"What?"

"Let's see that ass."

He scoffed. "Come on, let's go." He grabbed Weav by the arm and led him and Mrs. Weaver away.

"Hold up," Agent Pruitt growled. And when I say growled, I mean it. That woman sounded like she was channeling a grizzly. Weaver stopped.

"If you think I'm taking my pants off because of some kids," Mr. Weaver said, glaring at her.

Even if she did get him to show them—and I don't know, can you even get a search warrant for someone's ass cheek?—I didn't think a needle prick in the glutes was the type of thing that was going to be enough to convict someone. And I was guessing the money they took was impossible to track. It was going to be our word against his.

"All you gotta do is listen to the recordings." Mr. Weaver's head spun toward Kira as she said this. "Cade left the computer on, recording whatever was said."

"Where?" Agent Pruitt asked.

"You are taking their word over mine?"

"Pretty much."

Mr. Weaver may well have been the mastermind behind all this, but his next move was one of desperation, not logic. The logical one would be to call Kira's bluff (not that he knew she had made up the bit about me recording anything). Whether it was the combination of knowing he had the scarlet needle prick on him and the possibility his voice was all over this thing, I don't know, but he lunged toward Kira. He wrapped his arm around her neck and backed away from Pruitt and the other officer, who both immediately pulled their weapons. I hadn't seen a gun, but Mr. Weaver's free hand wasn't visible behind Kira, so I couldn't be sure.

A desperate man. But how desperate? Enough to grab a hostage without a gun? And how did he think this was going to play out for him? Anytime I've seen a hostage situation in the movies, it makes at least some sense, but now this incredibly smart man, a guy who ran a Fortune 500 company that created some of the most advanced technology in the world, this theoretical "mastermind," very well, with no gun, had just taken a hostage. And the wrong one.

I was beginning to think the Reilly guy did all the heavy lifting.

Mr. Weaver did the whole, "Get back! Everyone back!" bit that you would expect from a man frantically trying to extricate himself from an impossible situation. You know how I said the "wrong one"? What I meant was Mrs. Harris or maybe even Weaver's own wife or kid would have been the right call. Or me, still laid out, immobile on the stretcher. But not the toughest girl I knew. Not a badass like Kira, who, if Mr. Weaver was only pretending to have a gun to her back, was no way not going to try to get her way out.

I should have been scared. I should have been worried this guy was in danger of hurting the girl I cared most about in the world. But I wasn't. In fact, I had a sense of happy anticipation. I know it sounds weird, and sure, there may have been a residual painkiller vibe adding to it, but it was like watching a movie scene unfold where I knew the hero was about to do something great.

I wasn't disappointed.

Kira bent her knees and drove herself up and backward. Being a good deal shorter than Mr. Weaver, the top of her head crushed into his chin, knocking him stumbling backward. His grip around her neck held, but the other hidden hand flailed to the side. It was empty. As soon as they realized this, Pruitt and the other guy raced forward. I coulda told them they needn't have. Kira reached for the hand around her neck, but rather than try to dislodge the grip, she grabbed one single finger, his left index finger, and yanked. Oftentimes it can be the small things that do you in, like a baseball player unable to pitch due to a blister or a runner with a tiny pebble in his shoe. In this case, a single finger rotated back at what looked about, oh 170, maybe even the full 180, degrees, was more than enough to cause Mr. Weaver to drop his arm from around her neck.

Before he could recover, Pruitt had him pinned to the ground.

CHAPTER THIRTY-FIVE

You know how you often sand off the rough edges on past memories, and only remember the good portions? The past always seems a little better to you? Well, it only took three days and I was already looking back on nearly getting killed in a sort of wistful way.

Not so much wistful for the crazy shit, but for the fact I got to spend the day with Kira. I'm a weirdo, right? Maybe, but having spent the last three days in the hospital, I couldn't help but miss it. It had been seventy-two hours now and I hadn't seen her. I didn't blame her; her parents had taken her home, and it's my own fault for not having a phone or else maybe I'd have gotten a text.

Actually it was my fault for even thinking we had any sort of moment. The reality had been, it was nothing more than some heightened experience. Not some grandiose action movie ending where they kissed or something. I was dreaming if I thought that was going to happen when I was running with her toward the graveyard. Or at the ambulance. Or here and her coming to look for me at the hospital. I'm sure even in those movies, three days later when everything blew over and they were back to their normal lives, it didn't work out for him either.

I was waiting for my mother to get back from the cafeteria with lunch, just starting to build up a good self-pity stew, when the door to my hospital room opened.

Rather than stewing in self-pity, I should have been doing something about the stewing in my own bed, shower-less for the past three days. Because standing there in the doorway was Kira. And I stunk.

"Hey."

"Hey."

"How's the . . ." Kira waved her hand over in my general direction. "I guess, most everything?"

"Not bad," I said.

"I was going to text you, but, well, you may not know this, but they have these things. Phones. They send messages." She smiled. "You may want to think about getting one."

"I was considering it."

"Did you know there are like five songs named 'Sweet Things'?"

"I didn't." I only listened to the one that made me think of her.

"I listened to them all because you hadn't said who."

"The Canadian one. Danny Michel," I said.

"Good, I'm glad." She looked like she was smiling as she plopped in the seat next to the bed.

"So . . ." Normally, I had a million things I wanted to ask her about, but all I currently had was "so." And then, "So, what're you doing here?" I didn't mean to, but the way I said it came out kind of accusatory.

"Nothing."

"Oh."

"You remember asking me if I wanted to get together and do nothing sometime?"

"Yeah. That sounded kinda stupid, didn't it?"

"I liked it." She leaned back in the chair and put her feet up on the side of the bed. "I'm here to do nothing."

I looked at her smiling at me. Garvey's Tragically Hip song about being thirty and yet to kiss a girl flitted across my brain again.

Crap. Here I was seventeen years old and still just like him.

I squeezed her toes and smiled back at her as we did nothing.

Well . . .

At least I was getting closer.

ABOUT THE AUTHOR

Find out more about Hector and Cade at:

LostOneStanding.com

facebook.com/LostOneStanding

twitter.com/LostOneStanding

instagram.com/lostonestanding

CPSIA information can be obtained
at www.ICGtesting.com
Printed in the USA
LVHW030537041220
673318LV00010B/1898

9 781734 692419